ROBYN CARR

A VIRGIN RIVER CHRISTMAS

A VIRGIN RIVER NOVEL

ISBN-13: 978-0-7783-2573-4
ISBN-10: 0-7783-2573-3

A VIRGIN RIVER CHRISTMAS

www.MIRABooks.com

Printed in U.S.A.

Dear Reader,

It was such an honor to be asked to create a Christmas story that would take place in Virgin River, especially because, in my mind, the miracle of Christmas is synonymous with that special town. Virgin River seems to be a place of kindness, friendship, love and miracles.

In this story you'll meet Ian and Marcie, two courageous people who have weathered too many storms in their young lives. Both of them need two things to help them get to a place of peace and happiness: namely, faith and love. Between them they have a lot of history but, at the same time, they're just getting to know one another. And what they find in their renewed relationship could bring them closer to the peace and serenity they both need so much.

The Virgin River novels are part of an ongoing series, and *A Virgin River Christmas* is a special addition to that series. While many of the well-known Virgin River characters are present in this book, you don't have to read the first three in the series to feel at home here. But for those of you who have started at the beginning, and have waited patiently for this next book, let me put you in the time frame. *A Virgin River Christmas* takes place just a few weeks before Christmas—right in the middle of *Whispering Rock,* the third book in the continuing series.

Christmas can mean many different things to each of us. For Marcie and Ian, I've tried to create a special time for two people who couldn't be more deserving.

It was a privilege to create this story. I hope you'll treasure it.

My best wishes to you and yours,

Robyn Carr

A Virgin River Christmas is dedicated to Kris and Edna Kitna, with deep gratitude for your help, your incomparable hospitality and your friendship.

Prologue

Marcie stood beside her lime-green Volkswagen, shivering in the November chill, the morning sun barely over the horizon. She was packed and ready, as excited as she was scared about this undertaking. In the backseat she had a small cooler with snacks and sodas. There was a case of bottled water in the trunk and a thermos of coffee on the passenger seat. She'd brought a sleeping bag just in case the motel bedding wasn't to her standards; the clothes she'd packed in her duffel were mostly jeans, sweatshirts, heavy socks and boots, all appropriate for tramping around small mountain towns. She was itching to hit the road, but her younger brother, Drew, and her older sister, Erin, were stretching out the goodbyes.

"You have the phone cards I gave you? In case you don't have good cell reception?" Erin asked.

"Got 'em."

"Sure you have enough money?"

"I'll be fine."

"Thanksgiving is in less than two weeks."

"It shouldn't take that long," Marcie said, because if she said anything else, there would be yet another showdown. "I figure I'm going to find Ian pretty quick. I think I have his location narrowed down."

"Rethink this, Marcie," Erin said, giving it one last try. "I know some of the best private detectives in the business—the law firm employs them all the time. We could locate Ian and have the things you want to give him delivered."

"We've been over this," Marcie said. "I want to see him, talk to him."

"We could find him first and then you could—"

"Tell her, Drew," Marcie implored.

Drew took a breath. "She's going to find him, talk to him, find out what's going on with him, spend some time with him, give him the baseball cards, show him the letter, and then she'll come home."

"But we could—"

Marcie put a hand on her older sister's arm and looked at her with determined green eyes. "Stop. I can't move on until I do this, and do it my way, not your way. We're done talking about it. I know you think it's dumb, but it's what I'm going to do." She leaned toward Erin and gave her a kiss on the cheek. Erin, so sleek, beautiful, accomplished and sophisticated—so nothing like Marcie—had been like a mother to her since she was a little girl. She had a hard time leaving off the mothering. "Don't worry—there's nothing to worry about. I'll be careful. I won't be gone long."

Then she kissed Drew's cheek and said, "Can't you get her some Xanax or something?" Drew was in med school and, no, he couldn't write prescriptions.

He laughed and wrapped his arms around her, hugging

her tight for a moment. "Just hurry up and get this over with. Erin's going to drive me nuts."

Marcie narrowed her eyes at Erin. "Go easy on him," she said. "This was my idea. I'll be back before you know it."

And then she got in the car, leaving them standing on the curb in front of the house as she pulled away. She made it all the way to the highway before she felt her eyes sting with tears. She knew she was worrying her siblings, but she had no choice.

Marcie's husband, Bobby, had died almost a year ago, just before Christmas, at the age of twenty-six. That came after more than three years in hospitals and then in a nursing home—hopelessly disabled and brain damaged, with injuries incurred as a marine serving in Iraq. Ian Buchanan was his sergeant and best friend, a marine Bobby said would do twenty. But Ian exited the Marine Corps shortly after Bobby was wounded and had been out of touch ever since.

Since she knew that Bobby would never recover, since she had grieved his loss for a long time before he actually died, Marcie would have expected to feel a sense of relief in his passing—at least for him. She thought she'd be more than ready to step into a new life, one that had been put on hold for years. At the tender age of twenty-seven, already a widow, there was still plenty of time for things like education, dating, travel—so many possibilities. But it had been just shy of a year, and she was stuck. Unable to move forward. Wondering, always wondering, why the man Bobby had loved like a brother had dropped out of sight and had never called or written. He'd estranged himself from his marine brothers and his father. Estranged himself from her, his best friend's wife.

So there were these baseball cards. If she stretched her imagination to the limit she couldn't come up with anything her lawyer sister would find more ridiculous than wanting to be sure Ian had Bobby's baseball cards. But since she'd met Bobby at the age of fourteen, she knew how obsessed he was with his collection. There wasn't a player or stat he didn't have memorized. It turned out that Ian was also a baseball nut and had his own collection; she knew from Bobby's letters that they had talked about trading.

In the deserts and towns of Iraq, while they hunted insurgents and worried about suicide bombers and sniper fire, Bobby and Ian had talked about trading baseball cards. It was surreal.

Then there was this letter that Bobby wrote to her from Iraq before he was wounded. It was all about Ian and how proud it would make him to be like Ian. He was a marine's marine—the guy who got into the mess with his men, led them with strength and courage, never let them down, hung with them through everything—whether they were up to their necks in a fight or crying over a dear-John letter. He was a funny guy, who made them all laugh, but he was a tough sergeant who also made them work hard, learn and follow every rule to the letter so they'd be safe. It was in that letter that Bobby had told her he hoped she'd support him if he decided to make it a career. Like Ian Buchanan had. If he could be half the man Ian was, he'd be damn proud; all the men saw him as a hero, someone on his way to being a legend. Marcie wasn't sure she could part with the letter, even though it was all about Ian. But he should know. Ian should know how Bobby felt about him.

In the year since Bobby had moved into a quiet and peaceful death, she had passed his birthday, their anniversary, every holiday, and still, it was as though there was this unfinished business. There was a big piece missing; something yet to be resolved.

Ian had saved Bobby's life. He didn't make it out whole, but still—Ian had braved death to carry Bobby to safety. And then he'd disappeared. It was like a hangnail; she couldn't leave it alone. Couldn't let it go.

Marcie didn't have much money; she'd had the same secretarial job for five years—a good job with good people, but with pay that couldn't support a family. She was lucky her boss gave her as much time as she wanted right after Bobby was wounded, because she'd traveled first to Germany, then to D.C. to be near him, and the expenses had been enormous, far more than his paycheck could bear. As a third-year enlisted marine, he'd earned less than fifteen hundred dollars a month. She'd pushed the credit cards to the max and took out loans, despite the willingness of Erin and Bobby's family to help her. In the end, his military life insurance hadn't gone too far to pay those bills, and the widow's death benefit wasn't much either.

The miracle was getting him home to Chico, which was probably entirely due to Erin's bulldogging. Many families of military men who were 100 percent disabled and in long-term care actually relocated to be near the patient, because the government wouldn't or couldn't send the patient home to them. But Erin managed to get them into CHAMPUS, a private nursing home in Chico paid for by the Civilian Health and Medical Program of the Uniformed Services. Most soldiers were not so fortunate. It was a complicated and strained system, now heavy with casualties. Erin had taken care of everything—using her exquisite lawyer's brain to get the best benefits and stipend possible from the Corps. Erin hadn't wanted Marcie to be stressed by benefit or money worries on top of everything else. Erin had done it all, even paid all the household bills. In addition to all that, she was somehow managing the cost of Drew's medical college.

So, for this excursion, she couldn't take a dime from her sister. Erin had already given so much. Drew did have some pocket change, but being a poor medical student, he didn't have much. It would have been far more practical to wait till spring—until she'd had a chance to put aside a little more—to head into the small towns and mountains of Northern California looking for Ian Buchanan, but there was something about the anniversary of Bobby's death and Christmas approaching that filled her with a fierce longing to get the matter settled once and for all. Wouldn't it be nice, she kept thinking, if the questions could be answered and the contact renewed before the holidays?

Marcie meant to find him. To give peace to the ghosts. And then they could all get on with their lives....

One

Marcie Sullivan drove into the small town, her sixth small mountain town of the day, and found herself face-to-face with a Christmas-tree trimming. The assembled staff didn't look big enough for the job—the tree was enormous.

She pulled up beside a large cabin with a wide porch, parked her Volkswagen and got out. There were three women at work on a Christmas fir that stood about thirty feet. One was about Marcie's age, with soft brown hair and she held an open box, perhaps containing ornaments. One woman was old, with springy white hair and black-framed glasses, who pointed upward, as if someone had put her in charge, and the third was a beautiful blonde at the top of a tall, A-frame ladder.

The tree stood between the cabin and an old boarded-up church with two tall steeples and one stained-glass window still intact—a church that must have once been a beautiful structure.

While Marcie watched the trimming, a man came out onto the cabin's porch, stopped, looked up and cursed, then took long strides to the base of the ladder. "Don't move. Don't breathe," he said in a low, commanding voice. He took the rungs every other one, climbing quickly until he reached the blonde. Then he slipped an arm around her, somewhere above what Marcie realized must be a little pregnant bulge and beneath her breasts and said, "Down. Slowly."

"Jack!" she scolded. "Leave me alone!"

"If I have to, I'll carry you down. Back down the ladder, slowly. Now."

"Oh for God's—"

"*Now,*" he said evenly, fiercely.

She began to descend, one rung at a time between his big, sturdy feet, while he held her safe against him. When they got to the bottom, she put her hands on her hips and glared up at him. "I knew exactly what I was doing!"

"Where is your brain? What if you fell from that height?"

"It's an excellent ladder! I wasn't going to fall!"

"You're psychic, too? You can argue all you want, I'm not letting you that high up a ladder in your condition," he said, his hands also on his hips. "I'll stand guard over you if I have to." Then he looked over his shoulder at the other two women.

"I told her I thought you wouldn't like that," the brown-haired one said with a helpless shrug.

He glared at the white-haired woman. "I don't get into domestic things. That's your problem, not mine," she said, pushing her big glasses up on her nose.

And Marcie became homesick. So homesick. It had only been a few weeks that she'd been driving around this area, but she missed all the family squabbles, the tiresome complications. She missed her girlfriends, her job. She longed for her bossy older sister's interference, her goofy younger brother and whatever current girlfriend was shadowing him. She missed her late husband's large, fun, passionate family.

She hadn't made it home for Thanksgiving—she'd been afraid to go for even a day or two, afraid she'd never pry herself out of Erin's grip a second time. Home was Chico, California, just a few hours away, but no one—not her brother and sister, not Bobby's family—thought what she was doing a good idea. So, she'd been calling, lying and saying she had tips about Ian and was close to finding him. Every time she called, at least every other day, she said she was getting closer when really, she wasn't. But she was *not* ready to quit.

But one problem was looming large—she was just about out of money. She'd been sleeping in her car lately rather than in motels, and it was getting uncomfortable as the temperatures dropped in the mountains. At any moment snow would be falling now that it was early December, or rain could turn to sleet and that little VeeDub could sail off the mountainside like a missile.

She'd just hate to go home with this mission incomplete. More than anything, she wanted to see it through. If she wasn't successful now, she'd only go home to earn a little money and then do it all again. She just couldn't give up on him. On herself.

They were all looking at her. She pushed her wildly curly, out of control, bright red hair over one shoulder nervously.

"I… Ah… I could go up there, if you want. I'm not afraid of heights or anything…"

"You don't have to go up the ladder," the pregnant blonde said, and her voice had softened considerably. She smiled sweetly.

"I'll go up the ladder," the man said. "Or I'll *get* someone to go up the goddamn ladder, but it's not you."

"Jack! Be polite!"

He cleared his throat. "Don't worry about the ladder," he said more calmly. "Anything we can do for you?"

"I... Ah..." She walked toward them. She pulled a picture out of the inside of her down vest and extended it toward the man. "I'm looking for someone. He dropped out of sight just over three years ago, but I know he's around here somewhere. He seems to be taking mail at Fortuna Post Office general delivery."

She passed the picture to the man. "Jesus," he said.

"You know him?" she asked hopefully.

"No," he said, shaking his head. "No, I don't, and that's strange. The guy's a marine," he said, studying the picture of a man in uniform. It was Ian's official Marine Corps portrait, a handsome man all clean shaven and trussed up in dress blues, hat and medals. "I can't believe there's a marine within fifty miles of here I don't at least know about."

"He might be keeping that fact to himself—he and the Marine Corps had a troubled relationship at the end. So I've heard..."

He looked back at her face and his expression was much more tender. "I'm Jack Sheridan," he said. "My wife, Mel. That's Paige," he said, nodding toward the younger woman. "And Hope McCrea, town busybody." He put out his hand to Marcie.

She placed hers in his. "Marcie Sullivan," she said.

"Why are you looking for this marine?" Jack asked.

"Long story," she said. "A friend of my late husband. I'm sure he doesn't look like this anymore—he had some injuries. There's a scar down his left cheek and on that same side, no eyebrow. And he probably has a beard. He did the last time he was seen, about three or four years ago."

"No shortage of beards around here," Jack said. "Lumber country—men get a little scruffy-looking sometimes."

"But he could've changed in other ways, too. Like—he's older. Thirty-five now—that picture was taken when he was twenty-eight."

"Friend of your husband's? From the Corps?" Jack confirmed.

"Yes," she said. "I'd like to find him. You know—because he's been out of touch for a long time."

Jack seemed to think while he studied the face in the picture. It was several silent moments before he said, "Come on into the bar. Have a bite, a beer maybe, or whatever you like. Tell me a little about him and why you want to find him. How's that?"

"The bar?" she said, looking around.

"It's a bar and grill," he said with a smile. "Food and drink. We can eat and talk."

"Oh," she said. Her stomach growled angrily. It was late in the day, about four o'clock, and she hadn't eaten yet, but she was saving her money for the gas tank and she figured she could forget about food a while longer. Maybe she'd get something real, real cheap to tide her over, like a loaf of day-old bread to go with that half a jar of peanut butter in the car.... Then, she'd find a safe spot to park and button down for the night. "A glass of water would be really welcome—I've been driving around for hours, showing his picture to anyone who will take a look. But I'm not hungry."

"Got lots of water," Jack said with a smile. He put a hand on her shoulder and started to direct her toward the porch of the bar, but then he stopped suddenly. His brows drew together in a frown. "Go ahead," he said to her. "I'm right behind you."

Marcie walked up on the porch and turned to see what he was doing. He was confiscating the ladder so his pregnant wife wouldn't climb it again, that's what he was doing. It was a jackknife kind of affair that could be a short or tall A-frame ladder, and he collapsed it, folded it up until he could lift it with one hand. It was about six feet long dismantled and he carried it right into the bar. Behind him, Marcie heard his wife yell, "You're a bossy pain in the ass! When did I ever indicate I'd take my orders from you?"

Jack didn't say anything back, but he grinned as though she'd just thrown him a kiss. "Hop up there," he said to Marcie, indicating the bar. "I'll be right back." And he carried the ladder through a door behind the bar.

She took a deep breath and thought, Oh hell—I'm not going to be able to survive the aromas! Her stomach made itself heard again and she put a hand against her belly, pushing. Something in the kitchen was sending out waves of delicious smells—something simmering, rich, hot and thick, like beefy, seasoned soup; fresh bread; something sweet and chocolate.

And when the man named Jack came back, he was carrying a tray with a steaming bowl on it. He put everything in front of her; chili, corn bread and honey butter, a small bowl of salad. "Gee, um, sorry," she said. "Really, I'm not hungry..."

He drew a cold draft and her mouth actually watered. Gratefully she didn't drool on the bar. She swallowed hard. She had about thirty bucks and didn't want to waste it on a fancy meal, not when she needed every cent for gas to hit all these little mountain towns.

"Fine, then you'll only eat what you want," he said. "Just have a taste. I showed the picture to Preacher, my cook. He hasn't seen the guy either. We'll check with Mike—he's the town cop and gets around all the back roads, just to know who's out there—maybe he'll have a tip or two. They're also marines."

"Where exactly am I?" she asked.

"Virgin River," he said. "Population six hundred twenty-seven at last count."

"Ah, that made the map."

"I should hope so—we're a screaming metropolis compared to a lot of small towns out here. Just try it," he said, nodding at the bowl.

Her hand trembled a little as she picked up the spoon and sampled some of the finest chili she'd ever eaten. It melted in her mouth, and she actually sighed.

"Made with venison," he said. "We got a nice buck a couple months ago and when that happens, we have some of the best chili, stew, burgers and sausage in the world, for months." He patted a big jar of jerky that rested on the bar. "Preacher makes some unbelievable venison jerky, too."

Her eyes watered—the food was so good. Despite all her promises to Erin and Drew, she hadn't been eating well or playing it carefully, scrimping on food and sleeping in the car. When Erin saw the way her jeans were hanging off her little frame, the shit was going to hit the fan.

"Want to tell me a little about our guy, between bites?" Jack asked.

Oh, what the hell, Marcie thought. She hadn't had a really good hot meal in days, and once she was out of money there would be no choice but to go home. She'd just have to spend a little of that money, maybe leave the mountains a day earlier than she wanted to. She had to eat, for God's sake! Couldn't hardly perform a manhunt without food!

She took a couple of quick bites to beat back the worst of her ravenous hunger, then a sip of that icy beer to wash it down. It was heaven, pure heaven. "His name's Ian Buchanan. We came from the same town, but didn't know each other growing up, even though Chico's small—only about fifty thousand. Ian's eight years older than we are. Were. My husband and I, we grew up together, went through high school together and got married real young, at nineteen. Bobby went into the Marine Corps right out of high school."

"So did I," Jack said. "Did twenty. What was your husband's name?"

"Bobby Sullivan. Robert Wilson Sullivan. Any chance…?"

"I don't recall a Bobby Sullivan or an Ian Buchanan. Got a picture of your husband?"

She reached into her vest pocket and pulled out a wallet, flipped it open and turned it to face Jack. There were several pictures in the clear plastic sleeves. She ate while Jack flipped through—the nineteen-year-olds' wedding picture, Bobby's official Marine Corps portrait—a fine-looking young man, a beautiful man. There were a couple of casual shots showing off his strong profile, powerful shoulders and arms, and then the last one—Bobby, almost unrecognizable, thin, gaunt, pale, eyes open but unfocused, in a raised hospital bed, Marcie sitting beside him, cradling his head against her shoulder, smiling.

Jack lifted his gaze from the pictures and looked at her solemnly. She put the spoon in the chili and patted her lips with the napkin. "He went over to Iraq in the first wave," she said. "He was twenty-two. Twenty-three when he was wounded. Spinal cord injury and brain damage. He spent over three years like that."

"Aw, kid," Jack said, his strong voice weak. "Must'a been awful hard…"

She blinked a few times, but her eyes didn't tear up. Yeah, there were times it was terrible, times it was heartbreaking, even times she resented the hell out of what the Marine Corps left her to deal with at her young age. There were also times she'd lie beside him in bed, pull him into her arms, press her lips against his cheek and just hold them there, remembering. "Yeah, sometimes," she answered. "We got by. There was a lot of support. My family and his family. I wasn't in it all alone." She swallowed. "He didn't seem to be in pain."

"When did he pass?" Jack asked.

"Almost a year ago, right before Christmas. Quietly. Very quietly."

"My condolences," Jack said.

"Thank you. He served with Ian. Ian was his sergeant. Bobby loved him. He wrote me about him all the time, called him the best sergeant in the Corps. They became good friends almost right away. Ian was the kind of leader who was right in it with his men. Bobby was so happy that Ian turned out to be from our hometown. They were going to be pals forever, long after they were out of the Corps."

"I went to Iraq right away, too. Went the first time, too. I was probably there at the same time. Fallujah."

"Hmm. That's where it happened."

Jack shook his head. "I'm so goddamn sorry." Jack slid the wallet back. "That why you're looking for Buchanan? To tell him?"

"He might already know—I wrote to him a lot. Care of general delivery in Fortuna. The letters didn't come back, so I assume he picked them up."

Jack's brow wrinkled curiously.

"I don't know what happened to Ian. Right after Bobby got hurt, while he was hospitalized in Germany and then in Washington, D.C., at Walter Reed, I wrote to Ian and he answered my letters. He wanted to know about Bobby's condition and how I was holding up. I looked forward to his letters—I could see what Bobby saw. I felt kind of close to Ian just from Bobby's letters, then when we started to correspond and I was getting to know him myself, he started to feel like my friend, too. I can't explain it—it was just letters. And they were mostly about Bobby. But I think I got close to him—"

"Lotta servicemen get really attached to pen pals," Jack said. "Especially when they're on isolated tours like that."

"Well, no indication Ian got close to me, but I did to him. Then he came back from Iraq, looked in on us once and got out of the Marines shortly after that. He drifted away and didn't come back to Chico. He had some trouble in the Corps after Iraq. I don't know the details, but his father thought he was a lifer, yet he got out at the first opportunity, right on the heels of having a real hard time." A huff of sad laughter escaped. "He never called or wrote again. He broke up with his girl, fell out with his father and went away. About a year later, I found out he was living in the woods like an old hermit."

"How do you know that he's out in the woods?"

"There's a VA outpatient clinic in Chico I got pretty cozy with because of Bobby. A few people there knew I wanted to get in touch with Ian. I'm sure they weren't supposed to tell me things, but vets—they help each other all they can. Turns out, Ian showed up at the clinic once—it must have been the nearest facility for him. He said he didn't have an address because he was out in the forest and the nearest big town was Fortuna, and he could get any VA forms or whatever at general delivery there. He hurt himself chopping wood and needed stitches, a tetanus shot and antibiotics. He was right there—where we were, where his father was—and he didn't even phone to say he was all right, or to ask how Bobby was doing. This just doesn't seem like the man my husband had described to me. The man I got to know."

Jack was quiet a moment, and Marcie took a few more bites of food. She spread butter on the corn bread and gobbled up half, giving lie to her "not hungry" state.

"I started sending letters to Fortuna after that, but he didn't respond. I think I wrote him more for myself than for him, and I pictured him reading them, but… I invited him to call me collect, but I never heard from him."

"And you're going after him?" Jack finally said.

"I'm going to find him," she affirmed. "I have to know if he's all right. I've thought about it a lot—for all I know, he might've come back from Iraq with some serious issues, maybe not as plain to the naked eye as Bobby's issues. I'd blame the Marine Corps for not helping him, if that was the case."

"Well, you're right—if he needed help, they should've helped. But try not to be too hard on the Corps. It gets complicated—you train a marine to be fearless, then expect him to ask for help? Doesn't add up. When I figure out how they should get around that, I'll write the state department."

"Just the same…"

"Could be he chose the lifestyle he wants. I came out of the Corps looking for a quiet place to hunt and fish and found Virgin River. I holed up for a while, too."

"Did you lose contact with your family?" she asked, lifting one tawny brow. "Refuse to answer mail?"

Jack had not only had constant contact with his family, but with his squad. And he appreciated it. "No. Point taken."

"I'm going to find him. Some things need to be sorted out. Finished. You know?"

"Listen, what if he's not all right?" Jack ventured, leaning both hands on the bar and looking at her closely. Intensely. "What if he's a little nuts or something? Even dangerous?"

"He still has a father who's getting older and isn't well. Things are unsettled with the two of them. Mr. Buchanan is a stubborn, crotchety old coot, but I bet underneath all that crust he wants his son back, no matter what he is. I would." She started on her salad.

"I get that," Jack said. "But what if he's dangerous to you?"

She let go a short laugh. "I guess it's possible, but I doubt it," she said. "I've been to the police department, sheriff's department and every gas station, hardware store and bar around—he doesn't have a record and no one knows him. If he was dangerous, he would probably have drawn some attention to himself, don't you think? He's probably just a sulky, troubled, screwed-up marine who thinks dropping out is better than dealing with his baggage. And he'd be wrong."

"You wanna think this through?" he asked. "Marines all screwed up by war have a lot of mysterious reasons for taking that route, dropping out like that. Could be he'd like to forget, and seeing you just makes things worse."

"Well, you've been to war, so you would know something about that—"

"*Boy howdy,* as my wife would say. I've carried around

my own crap, had a problem or two with PTSD. Luckily, I have strong support."

"He's only thirty-five, time enough to start over, patch things up with anyone he's alienated himself from, get beyond any trauma he has over what happened to Bobby. His father might've been a little pissed off back when they fought, but the old man still loves his son. I'd bet on that." She took a sip of her beer and said, quietly, "I might lose my money, but I'd bet."

"Then why doesn't his father try to find him?" Jack asked.

"Why didn't anyone? His ex-fiancée really hates him for ditching her, his father is seventy-one and sick. Widowed, bitter, stubborn. I gotta say, he's one mean, unforgiving old man. But even if there's no help for that, I can get to know Bobby's best friend again. We only wrote for a few months, but I thought I knew him. And he was sweet. This is going to sound silly—his handwriting was strong and nice, the things he wrote were kind and sensitive. I kind of feel like I lost a friend and..." She smiled at Jack. "Besides, no one's as determined as I am."

"And why is that? Why are you so determined?"

She looked down. "I can't move on until I know why the man my husband loved most, admired most, would disappear like that. Ignore us the way he did. Let himself be gobbled up by a forest and not have any contact with his family, his friends. Really—that's the insane part. I have to know why. I want to be sure he's okay. Then I'll let it go." She looked up. "Then maybe we can all move on."

Jack couldn't help but grin at her; she sure knew what she wanted. He watched her shovel the last of her salad into her mouth. "Chocolate cake?" he asked. "It'll bring you to your knees."

"No, thanks. This was good." Her wallet still sat on the bar. She drained the beer, then began leafing through the bills in her wallet. "What do I owe you?"

"You're kidding me, right? You're going out in the woods to find one of my brothers and you think I'd take your money? Hell, I'd offer to help, but you can see—I can't leave Melinda alone for one second. She's trouble. Nah, it's my pleasure to give you a little meal. Anytime you want, in fact. Check in here regular, fuel up your belly, let us know if you find anything…anyone. We'd all appreciate that. Bunch of us jarheads from Fallujah around here."

"Why are there marines here?"

"Sweetheart, there are marines everywhere." He grinned. "Once I opened the bar, a lot of my old squad started showing up to hunt or fish. A couple of them didn't have better options and moved here. Really, we try to look out for our kind. All for one," he added.

She closed the wallet and smiled at him, an affectionate, grateful smile. She was well-trained in taking whatever help was offered. "Then I'll have the cake," she said.

"And coffee?" he asked.

"Oh, God, yes, coffee," she said, almost sighing in appreciation. A cold beer, a hot cup of good coffee—two of her biggest weaknesses.

"Best coffee you'll ever taste," he said, filling a cup for her. When a thick slice of cake sat before her, he asked, "When you find him, what are your plans?"

"He was awful good to Bobby—I'd just like to thank him. Talk to him. Get to know him again, like I started to before. I have something of Bobby's to give him. I plan to ask him what happened, see if there's anything I can do for him now. Maybe once we get through all that, we'll both be happier. Obviously he hasn't moved on, and I need a little more closure. Wouldn't it be great if we could both get that? Aw, I don't know, Jack. Freedom? The freedom to put the past in the past?"

Jack's eyebrows rose. "And if he's not inclined to talk?"

She put a big forkful of velvety, rich chocolate cake into her mouth, scraping the icing off the fork with her teeth and lips. She let her eyes drop closed for a brief luxurious moment. Then she smiled at Jack Sheridan and said, "Then I'll be his worst nightmare until he comes around. I'm not giving up."

Before Marcie had finished her coffee, a good-looking Hispanic man came into the bar by way of the side door. He had a disgruntled look on his face and was carrying a catalog. "Your wife has me in search of the perfect tree topper," he said to Jack. "Whose idea was this again?"

"I think it was yours," Jack said. "And don't complain to me—there's no way to decorate that tree without a cherry picker. I'm going to have to rent one before I see Mel using ropes and pulleys to get to the top. Mike, meet Marcie—Marcie, say hello to Mike Valenzuela."

"How do you do," she said, sticking out a hand.

He took it, smiled and said, "Pleasure. *This* was *his* idea—the big tree. Trying to impress his wife. She requested a *large* tree—he had us out in the hills a full day till he found the biggest tree we could take down in one piece."

Just a little embarrassed, Jack interrupted Mike, "Marcie here is looking for a marine who dropped out after Iraq. Show him the picture, Marcie."

She pulled it out again and once again explained the possible changes in his appearance since the photo was taken.

"Don't know him," Mike said.

"But he might be so different…"

"Don't know the eyes," Mike said.

She let out a heavy sigh. "Any ideas where I might look?"

"Well," Mike began, scratching his chin. "I haven't seen him, but that doesn't mean he hasn't been seen. There are a lot of people out in the mountains who have been there for years and they aren't real sociable—maybe one of them has seen him."

"Can you tell me where to go?" she asked.

"I can give you a couple of markers," he said. "More important, I'd like to tell you a few places to steer clear of—there are some illegal growers out there who get real territorial. Real unfriendly. Sometimes their property is booby-trapped." He pulled a large napkin out from under the bar, brought his pen out of his shirt pocket and drew a line on the napkin. "Here's highway 36…" In ten minutes, he had drawn a rough map of a half-dozen cabins in the mountains where people lived—people who just might have seen Ian Buchanan. As well, he listed three locations she should avoid.

The cabins Mike X'd on the map were located down abandoned logging roads, sometimes gated, snuggled behind trees and shrubs, impossible to see from the highway. A lot of that mountain property had been homesteaded and logged. Once a property was logged, the owner had to wait another thirty to fifty years to log it again. It became an acreage full of oak, madrone, young fir and pine fifty to sixty feet tall—real pretty, but not mature enough for logging.

"I've been roaming around back in there, just checking it out, just to know who's out there. There are a couple of old men living alone out in the sticks and a couple of old widows. There's a man and woman combo or two, even a family of five. But so far, no single thirty-five-year-old male."

"Maybe he's not single anymore."

Mike shook his head. "Pretty sure there's no one in that age group; not with those eyes. Even with a beard."

"Believe him," Jack said. "He used to be a real cop, LAPD, before he was Andy of Mayberry where we have almost no crime."

"Nice," Marcie said. "No crime and a big tree. I take it you've never done a big tree like that before?"

They both laughed. "Twenty-seven feet," Jack said. "We thought we were so manly, finding us a big one like that, till we had it down and almost had to rent a flatbed truck to bring it back to town. We tied the limbs tight and dragged it behind a truck. And *that* wasn't the hard part. Standing it up took a day."

"Two days," Mike corrected. "We got up the next morning and it was lying in the street. Frickin' miracle it didn't fall on the bar and crush the roof."

She laughed at them. "Why now? You're trying to show off for your wife?"

"Nah. Now was the time. We just lost a comrade in Iraq and one of the local boys—a real special one—went into the Corps. We thought it would be good to erect a symbol, a monument to the men and women who serve. Next year, I think we look for a slightly smaller symbol. Cheaper and easier on the nerves. But I'll go over to Eureka and find a cherry picker for rent and get it done. Melinda and the other women have put a lot into making it a perfect tree."

"It's a pretty awesome tree," Marcie said, growing a

little melancholy. She really wanted to find Ian before Christmas. For some reason, that seem crucial.

As she was leaving, the sun was lowering and the bar was starting to fill with locals. It was already getting too dark to venture into the back woods to check out the few cabins Mike had told her about. It was time for her to find a place to park for the night, somewhere safe and not too far from a service station for her morning rituals of peeing, face washing, teeth brushing. She'd start again in the morning, though she wasn't feeling optimistic she'd find her guy. She'd been disappointed so many times. At this point in her search, crossing all the places off her list meant as much as striking pay dirt.

But before going to her car, she approached the tree, partially decorated to about twelve feet. She got up close and looked at some of the ornaments. Between red, white and blue balls and gold stars were patches—the kind you'd wear on a uniform—from various Marine and other military commands. She touched one reverently; 1st Battalion, 8th Marines; 2nd Battalion, 10th Marine Regiment; 1st Marine Special Operations Battalion, all laminated to protect them against the outdoor elements. Airborne Division, Sniper Squad, 41st Infantry Battalion. Her throat got tight; her eyes blurred.

This was exactly why she was determined to find Ian Buchanan—because these men never forgot, never walked away. There had to be powerful reasons for him to leave his military brothers, his Corps, his family, his town. You don't save a comrade's life and then ignore him. Ian Buchanan was given both the Bronze Star and Purple Heart for carrying Bobby through sniper fire to medical transport. He took two bullets and kept going. He was not a man who gave up. So why? Why give up now?

Two

Marcie's thirty bucks—$28.87, to be exact—lasted another thirty-six hours. Twenty-five of them went in the gas tank; she could hardly afford the gas even with the great mileage she got in her little green bug. Three dollars for a loaf of bread and two apples and she finished off the peanut butter. Then she went back to that little Virgin River bar and asked if she could use the phone to make a call to her sister—she'd almost exhausted the phone cards because she wasn't supposed to be gone this long, but there was a little time left on one. Erin, seven years older than Marcie, had taken charge of the family long ago, and she was growing extremely irritable by Marcie's time away.

The cook, a guy they all called Preacher, let her into the kitchen.

Marcie called Erin and, though it made her stomach clench, she asked for money. "Call it a loan," she said. She lied and said she was getting so close, that Ian had been seen.

"We had a deal, Marcie," Erin said. "You promised

you'd only be gone a couple of weeks and it's been a month. You didn't even come home for Thanksgiving."

"I couldn't. I explained about that. I had a tip—"

"It's time for you to come home now and think about another way to find him."

"No. I'm not stopping. I'm not giving up," Marcie said resolutely.

"Okay, but come back to Chico and we'll try it my way—we'll get a professional to find him for you—then you can go from there. Really, the only way I know to get you home and through with this madness is to say no. No money, Marcie, for your own good. The only money I'll wire you is enough to get home. Come home now. *Right now.* This is scaring me to death."

"No," she said. "I'm not done!"

Marcie then called her younger brother, Drew, who might not agree with what she was doing any more than Erin did, but he was a softer touch. He said, "Marcie, I can't. Erin's right, this has gone on too long. You have to give this up now. Come on, I can't stand to think about what you're doing. You're going after a friggin' lunatic, by yourself!"

"Please," she whimpered. "We don't know he's a lunatic—he could be perfectly normal. Or maybe just sad. Please, just a few more days. Please. I'm so close."

Drew let out a breath, defeated. "I'll wire you a hundred bucks, then you come back, you hear me? And don't you dare tell Erin what I did."

"I won't tell," she said, wiping at her cheeks, smiling into the phone. "Thank you, Drew. I love you so much."

"Yeah, well, I'm afraid I'm not showing you how much I care by doing this. I worry about you."

"Don't worry, Drew," she said with a sniff. "Can you just

put some cash in my checking account? I'll go to Fortuna and withdraw it from the branch there. I'll be there in less than an hour—and I'm running on fumes. Fortunately, I can coast downhill most of the way."

"Where was he seen?" Drew asked.

"Um… He was seen…um…out in a cabin off the highway a ways. I'll check out there later to see if it's really him," she said, and then her cheeks actually flushed. She said goodbye, disconnected and fanned her face, saying, "Whew." She looked up and found herself staring into the fierce eyes of the giant in the kitchen. She actually started.

"He hasn't been seen," Preacher said, his thick dark brows furrowing. "Has he?"

"Well, maybe he has. And I'm just about to find out."

"Sometimes a man just wants to be left alone for a while. You account for that?" Preacher asked. While he was talking, he pulled a plastic grocery sack out of a drawer, then turned to get something that looked like a wrapped sandwich out of the refrigerator and put it in the sack. Then a second one went in.

"It's been longer than a while," she said. "But I'll certainly give him a chance to tell me, if that's the case. If that's it, I'll have the opportunity to thank him for his friendship to my husband, then I'll go back to Chico and tell his father and anyone else who cares that he's just a man who wants to be left alone. But isn't there something 'off' about that? That he's been out of touch for years now?"

Preacher took a big bowl out of the refrigerator, flipped the lid and spooned potato salad into a smaller plastic container, then sealed it. "You're real insistent on this, then?"

She didn't want to admit that, for no accountable reason,

she'd been obsessed about Ian Buchanan's disappearance. She'd written him a couple dozen letters—at first for him, updating him on Bobby and whatever else was going on in her family, her life, giving information and reassurance. Then, it was more for herself—like keeping a journal. She didn't know exactly why, but he had been with her a long time. So she shrugged. "There are a few of us who want to know. Well, there's me. I want to know." Quietly she added, "Have to know."

Preacher added the container and a spoon to the bag. Then he got out a huge jar of pickles and picked out three big ones, putting them in a handy ziplock bag. "Well then, I guess you're not going to quit early."

"I guess not," she said.

He pushed the whole business toward her. "Don't let that potato salad sit and get warm. It's cold enough outside to keep it all day if you leave it in the trunk and not in a warm car. Just remember, old warm potato salad has a nasty reputation."

"What's this?"

"The car can coast," he said, lifting one of those menacing black brows. "You, on the other hand, can only run on fumes so long."

Her mouth dropped open a bit and she stared at him. She wondered if he'd done that because he'd seen the way her once-tight jeans hung off her fanny. "That's nice," she finally said. "I'll…ah…bring back the spoon."

"If you drop by, fine. If you don't, we have plenty of spoons."

"Thanks," she said, accepting the bag.

"Good luck," Preacher said. "I hope it goes the way you want."

"Me, too," she said with a sheepish smile.

Several hours later, as the day drew into afternoon, she was driving up her fifth or sixth unmarked dirt road, but she was a hundred bucks richer. Well, eighty bucks richer, the Volkswagen belching on a good, healthy half tank. She'd had half a ham and cheese sandwich, a pickle and some of the best potato salad she'd ever eaten, thinking *The guy's a genius with a boiled potato.*

The roads all backed into the trees and most were in godawful condition. Her little bug was bouncing and struggling, but hanging in there like the little champ she was. Marcie wished she could have found a way to get a Jeep or some other all-wheel-drive vehicle. If she could have waited longer to embark on this search, it might've been possible to have saved enough for a down payment, but she couldn't wait that long. She took what little she'd put aside for this exact purpose and planned her route. Despite what she'd told Erin and Drew about being away for a couple of weeks, she'd taken an unpaid leave of absence from her job until the first of the year. She had worked at the insurance company since Bobby went to Iraq—five years ago—and her boss had been understanding.

Erin had been completely against this wild notion that she had to find Ian from the very start. It took months of arguing to convince her there was some purpose for Marcie in this search. Then Erin had come up with a hundred better ideas that she'd offered to take care of herself—a people search, a private detective, anything but Marcie going after him alone. But there was a driving force in Marcie to see him, know him, talk to him, connect again, like she thought she had before.

Bobby's family wasn't much in favor of the idea either, but it didn't involve any ill will toward Ian—they barely knew about him. Bobby had written Marcie about Ian all the time, but in his short letters to his family he'd only mentioned him a few times. The Sullivans suggested that, if Ian hadn't been around while Bobby was in the nursing home, the bond was not as solid as Bobby thought. Then there was Ian's father—one of the nastiest and most negative old men Marcie had ever met. He told her she was wasting her time; he had no interest in finding his only son. "He left without a word and never got in touch. That's enough message for me."

Through perseverance, Marcie learned that the elder Buchanan had not experienced good health in the past few years. He'd had a mild stroke, was being treated for high blood pressure, prostate cancer, Parkinson's and, she suspected, a tish of dementia.

"Don't you miss him?" she asked. "Wonder what's become of him?"

"Not on your life," he said. "He's the one burned his bridges and run off."

But when he said that, there was wet in the folds under his old eyes and she thought: He can't give much more than this, but he would love to see his son once more, or at least know he was all right. Wouldn't he?

Ian's former fiancée, Shelly, was still angry about the way she'd been abandoned, even though she'd married someone else three years ago and was pregnant now with her first baby. She had not a kind or sympathetic word for the man who'd run through sniper fire, taken injuries to save a comrade, won both a Bronze Star and Purple Heart. She pretty much hated Ian for the way he'd dumped her and bolted. A thought came to Marcie—if Shelly was happy with her life now, why would Ian's obvious troubles cause her such prolonged hate? Couldn't she see how war would shift his thinking, cause his emotional confusion? After having a life-limited husband for so long—a hopeless invalid who couldn't even smile at her—giving a little patience and understanding to a man who'd been through a lot of trauma seemed a small thing.

But, Marcie had reminded herself, I don't know the weight of anyone else's burdens—only my own. She didn't judge. She didn't feel smart or strong enough to judge.

It was beyond important to Marcie to look at Ian's face and ask him how he could save her beautiful young husband's life and then never respond to her letters.

Maybe Ian couldn't give her answers that would make everything feel settled for her, and to that end, she thought it made sense for them to talk about it. Talk it through. They called it "closure" in the shrink club.

As she pulled up to a small, roughly hewn house, she caught sight of a man coming around the corner, his arms laden with firewood. He was clean shaven but stooped, his legs bowed with age, his head bald. He stopped walking when he saw her. She got out of her car, then went toward him. "Afternoon, sir," she said.

He put down the logs and the scowl on his face said he was suspicious of her.

"I wonder if you might be able to help me. I'm looking for someone." She pulled the photo out again. "This was taken about seven years ago, so he's obviously aged and I hear he's got a beard now, but the rumor is, he's living somewhere out in these hills. I'm trying to find him. Thirty-five years old, big man—I think he's over six feet."

The man took the photo in his bent, arthritic fingers. "You family?" he asked.

"More or less," she said. "He and my husband were good friends in the Marines. I should tell him, my husband passed."

"Ain't seen him. Ain't seen no one looks like that, anyway."

"But what if he was kind of gone to seed?" she said. "I mean, older, maybe heavier, bearded, maybe bald, maybe has a pot belly or is way too thin—who knows?"

"He grow weed?" the man asked, handing her back the picture.

"I don't know," she answered.

"Only folks I know around here about that age grow pot. And even if he's family, you might wanna cut him a wide berth. There's trouble around the growers sometimes."

"I heard that, yeah. Still—you know anybody like that I should just have a look at? Just to rule them out? I'll be real careful."

"There's a guy up on the ridge, kind of hard to find. Could be twenty, could be fifty, but he's got a beard and he's good-sized. You'd have to go back where you came, down 36 a mile or so and then up again. It's a dirt road, but halfway up the hill there's an iron gate. It ain't never been locked because you can't see the gate or the house from the main road. Only reason I know about it, is a guy I used to know lived up there in one room. Nice big room, though. He's been gone a couple years at least. Guy who lives there now was with him at the end."

"How will I know what road?"

He shrugged. "No markers. It goes right and about a half mile up, you'll either come to a gate or turn around and try the next road."

"You want to come with me maybe? Show me where? And I'll bring you back?"

"Nah," he said, shaking his head. "I got no business with him. He's odd. Talks to hisself, whistles and sings before the sun's up. And he thinks he's a bear."

"Huh?"

"Heard him roar like an animal when I was out near his place. You prob'ly ought to just let him be."

"Sure," she said, tucking her picture away. "Right. Thanks."

And off she went, encouraged about another whack job who almost fit the description. It was hardly the first time; she'd been to VA outreach, homeless shelters in Eureka, hospitals, the Gospel Mission. She'd followed bums down alleys and country roads, traipsed around the forest, met up with ranch hands and lumberjacks. But it was never him; no one had heard of Ian Buchanan. All she'd have to do was look into the eyes.

She'd *never* forget his eyes. They were brown, same shade as his brown hair, except they had a ton of amber in them. She'd seen them both soft and almost reverent, and then fierce and angry—all in the space of fifteen minutes—the one and only time he'd come to see Bobby. Ian was on leave and Marcie had brought Bobby home to Chico to care for him while they waited on a facility that could take him. She watched as Ian ran his huge hand over Bobby's brow and head, murmuring, "Aw, buddy… Aw, buddy…" Of course Bobby didn't respond; he had been unresponsive since the injury. Then, after a few moments of that, he turned almost-wild eyes on her and the gold in them flashed. "I shouldn't have let this happen to you. This is *wrong,* this is all *wrong.*"

Ian's visit had come five months after Bobby was wounded in Fallujah and it lasted less than half an hour. She always thought he'd be back, but that was it. She'd never seen him since.

If he'd read her letters, he would know that, soon after his one visit, they'd moved Bobby into a nursing home. Over time, she felt Bobby had had some recognition—there were times he'd turn his head, seem to look at her, even move his head closer as if nuzzling her, then close his eyes as though he knew she was there, as though he could smell her, feel her. She might've been the only one to think that way, but she believed that, somewhere inside that completely incapacitated body, he lived a little bit, knew he was with his wife and family, knew he was loved. Whether that was enough for a life, she didn't know. His family wanted the feeding tube pulled so that he'd die, but she couldn't do that. Ultimately, she took peace in the fact that it wasn't up to her, she wasn't in charge. Her job was to stay with him, do her best to comfort and love him, make sure he had everything he needed. She wasn't a real religious person and she rarely went to church. She prayed when she was afraid or in trouble, and forgot when things were going all right. But beneath it all, she believed God would take Bobby home when it was his time. And what would be, would be.

What had been, had been.

It was her fourth little dirt road that finally presented a gate, and she sighed in audible relief because her little bug was churning, burning oil, straining over the bumps and up the steep grades. The gate wasn't closed and she pressed on further, praying it wasn't going to be far. And who knew how far it actually was? She was only going ten miles an hour. By the time she got close enough to spot a small house with an old pickup parked outside, it was growing late in the afternoon. This time of year, dark would descend before long.

Marcie was tired enough that she never gave a thought to what she would do if this turned out to be him; it had not been him so many times. She pulled right up to the house and gave the horn a toot, the country way of announcing yourself. Mountain people didn't have doorbells. They could be inside or out in the yard or woods or somewhere down by the stream. The only way they knew there was a visitor is if someone hollered, shot off a gun or blasted the horn. Poor little VeeDub didn't have a blast, but a pathetic bleep.

She got out and looked around. The house, a cabin really, had to be more than fifty years old. It looked as though it might have once been painted orange, a long, long time ago. The land around it was cleared of trees and there was a large stack of logs under a tarp near the house, but no corral or livestock or barn. No porch; the windows were small and high. There was a small chimney, an outhouse and a storage shed that might've measured eight by ten. How does a person live out here like this, so far from humanity, so far from all conveniences?

She would go to the door in a minute, but she waited to see if the guy who lived here showed himself first. She should've been all spooled up, hopeful. But hell, she'd totally lied to Erin and Drew—no one had sighted Ian and she'd talked to dozens if not hundreds of people, in the towns, in the country, in the mountains. She was just plain tired and ready to eat the rest of that sandwich and more potato salad, hit a gas station bathroom and find a place to park for the night.

Then he came around the corner of his house with an

ax in his hand. He was scary-big, his shoulders were very broad and his beard was bushy and reached inches below his chin. He wore a dirty tan jacket that was frayed at the hem and sleeves; some of the plaid lining was torn and hanging out. His boots had worked hard; his pants were patched on the knees. At first glance, she thought, damn, not Ian. The beard was burnished red, though the hair on his head was brown—long and tied back into a ponytail—and he had both eyebrows, so it couldn't be him. "Hi," she said. "Sorry, don't mean to bother you, but…"

He took several long strides toward her, an angry scowl on his face. "What the hell are you doing here?"

She looked way up into those eyes and the amber came alive in them, on fire, glowing. Dear Jesus in heaven, it *was* him.

She took a step forward, stunned. "Ian?"

"I said, what the hell are you doing here?"

"I've been… I was… I'm looking for you. I'm—"

"I know who you are! Now you found me, so you can go away."

"Wait! Now I've found you, we should talk."

"I don't want to talk!"

"But wait—I want to tell you about Bobby. He's gone. He passed away. Almost a year ago now. I wrote you!"

He pinched his eyes closed and stood perfectly still for a long moment, his arms stiff at his sides and fists balled. Pain. It was pain and grief she saw.

"I wrote you—"

"Okay," he said more softly. "Message delivered."

"But Ian—"

"Go home," he said. "Get on with your life." Then he turned and walked into the little cabin and slammed the door.

For a moment, Marcie just stared at the cabin, at the closed door. Then she looked over the ridge to see the sun lowering. Then at her watch. It was only five o'clock and she was standing at the top of a hill, so the descending sun was giving them a little more daylight on this December afternoon. If she were down the mountain, the tall trees combined with sunset would have already plunged her into near darkness.

She didn't relish having unfinished business between them after dark, but after all she'd been through, she wasn't about to let him get away now. She took a few deep breaths, remembered that he was probably just troubled and not crazy, and stomped toward the house. She rapped on the door. Then she moved back a few steps to be safe.

The door jerked open and he glowered at her. "What do you want?"

"Hey! Why are you mad at me? I just want to talk to you."

"I don't want to talk," he said, pushing the door closed.

With inexplicable courage, she put her booted foot in its path. "Then maybe you can *listen.*"

"No!" he bellowed.

"You're not going to scare me!" she shouted at him.

Then he roared like a wild animal. He bared his teeth, his eyes lit like there were gold flames in them, and the sound that came out of him was otherworldly.

She jumped back, her eyes as wide as hubcaps. "Okay," she said, putting up her hands, palms toward him. "Maybe you do scare me. A little."

His eyes narrowed to angry slits, and he slammed the door again.

She yelled at the closed door. "But I've come too goddamn far and gone to too much goddamn trouble to be scared for long!" She kicked the closed door as hard as she could, then yelped and hopped around from the pain in her toes.

It obviously had no effect on him. Marcie stood for a moment, staring at the closed door. She took a second to decide what to do next. She wasn't likely to turn tail and run just because he roared—the big bully—but then again, she wouldn't confront him right away. Apparently he needed a little time to calm down—and to realize she wasn't giving up. So she decided her best course of action was to wait. And eat.

She went to the little bug and got the rest of Preacher's lunch out of her portable refrigerator—the trunk. Then she got into the backseat, pushing the front seats up as far as they'd go, and spread out her sleeping bag to sit on. It was like a little nest; she settled in. And she thought about his glower and his roar, as she slowly opened up the bag and took out the second half of her sandwich.

All right, she thought—it was *not* supposed to go like this. In every fantasy she'd had about finding him, there had been many possibilities. He could be glad to see her, embracing her in welcome. Or he could be withdrawn. He could even be a raving lunatic, on another planet, totally out of touch with this world. But never had she imagined he would take one look at her, cringe in obvious despair at the news of Bobby's death and cruelly, heartlessly, meanly, scream at her to go away.

Her mouth was a little dry for eating and she tried some of the water out of her thermos—bottled water had become too expensive. She kept an eye on the front door of the cabin. She could feel the heat on her cheeks, furious that he'd do that to her after she'd looked so hard for him. All she wanted in the world was to make sure he was all right.

The asshole. And then she felt her eyes cloud with tears for the very same reasons. His reaction really hurt her. What had she ever done to him? It made her absolutely enraged and broke her heart at the same time. How could he do that? Roar at her and slam the door like that? Without even hearing her? All he had to do was invite her in, tell her he was just fine, explain he wanted to be alone, accept the baseball cards and…

She just let the tears roll soundlessly down her cheeks for a moment. It had been a while since she'd cried. She realized then that her hopes for how this would turn out had been too idealized—exactly the reason Erin had wanted to hire a professional to handle this. Ian Buchanan had gone away, because he didn't want anything to do with anyone from his former life, not because he needed help. Especially her help.

With a hiccup of emotion, Marcie admitted to herself—*she* might need *his* help. This business of moving on, it might have to do with Ian helping her understand his relationship with Bobby and with her, and how everything had changed. Ian's growling and slamming the door in her face wasn't going to get her where she needed to go. She was going to have to sit it out until he understood—she wasn't done with him yet. And this whole business was going to get complicated, since there were good odds he *was* actually nuts.

She tried to gnaw at her sandwich, even though she now had no appetite. The sun sank slowly, and she ended up wrapping it up and putting it back in the grocery sack, unfinished. The thing was—if you didn't eat that much, you didn't feel like eating that much.

The sun dipped below the horizon, the lights in the

cabin shone, and a thin curl of smoke rose from the little chimney. She leaned back against the sleeping bag, physically comfortable even if she was an emotional wreck. But the decision had been made—she was sitting right here until she figured out what to do.

On a more practical matter, she really hoped she wouldn't have to pee in the night. She'd been choosing her sleeping spots carefully, so that if nature called in the dark of night, she wouldn't have to venture far from the little bug.

She'd never been any kind of camper, never had been good at relieving a full bladder on a whim. Never had quite figured out that squat; it seemed like she'd always wet her right foot. But after a little over a month of searching the hills and sleeping in her car in various parking lots, quiet residential streets, rest stops and country roads, she had it figured out. She could squat, whizz, get the job done, jump back in the car and lock the doors in just over a minute. There were showers available at the YWCA and at workout rooms in community colleges where they didn't check ID's too closely. She'd indulged in motels the first week out and then quickly realized her money would go further if she slept in her car. And with no hints of Ian's whereabouts, she needed to make her money last.

Then she remembered—that was an outhouse out there, wasn't it? Wow, how hilarious to think she'd be glad to see an outhouse! Life had gotten real interesting.

Drew and *especially* Erin would absolutely die if they found out she'd been sleeping in the bug. She shook her head. *I'm as nuts as he is, for sure.* And then she noticed snow flurries against the window of the bug. Very pretty, light, fluffy snowflakes in the waning light with a narrow streak of sunlight in the west through the clouds—the flakes glittered as they fell. The view over the ridge was amazing—there was a rainbow shining through the snow drifting down onto the tall pines—it was magnificent. She just couldn't be upset in this place. Not with Ian, in any case. Maybe he had forgotten they were friends.

He probably wanted her to think he was crazy, roaring like that, but she wanted to believe that, underneath the bluster, he would still be all the things Bobby said he was, all the things he'd been in their early letters, before Ian got out of the Marines—strong, compassionate, gentle, loyal. Brave. He'd been so courageous to do what he had done.

With the snow lightly falling, and the sun causing the rainbow to fade into dusk, she relaxed and closed her eyes for just a second. To think.

Three

Ian tried to keep himself from looking out the window; he'd be damned if he'd open the door. The silence in the mountains was such that if she'd turned the ignition to start the car, he could have heard the click. So he refreshed the fire in the woodstove, fired up the propane cookstove and heated large pans of water for a bath.

He'd made it a year in this cabin without a tub, shower or electricity, but he had made a few adjustments; he bought a generator and wired up a couple of lights inside. He found an old clawfoot tub in a salvage yard that he'd repaired and patched, enabling him to wash out of something larger than the kitchen sink.

It was always a shallow bath—a couple of pans of cold water hand pumped into a pot in the sink from the spring-fed well under the house, and a couple of large pans of boiling water didn't make for a nice long soak. In the winter, he got in, got clean and got out real quick. He would probably never have plumbing other than the pump; he worried about money and he wasn't skilled enough to do the plumbing himself. He hadn't had a real honest-to-God shower in years. But he was a guy—he didn't exactly primp. This was all he really needed. It got him good and clean.

After a quick scrub and some clean clothes, he warmed some stew on the stove, leaving it right in the can with the paper ripped off the outside. He wanted to see where she was, what she was doing, but he wouldn't let himself. He'd ignore her, refuse to talk to her, and she'd go away. Soon, he hoped.

After all this time, Ian had managed not to dwell on everything that came before the mountains, but one look at that fiery red mane and her flashing green eyes brought everything rushing back. The first time he'd seen that beautiful little face had been in a photo that Bobby carried with him.

That kid was something else. Ian had been twenty-eight and Bobby twenty with a couple of years in the Marines when they first met. Bobby already had himself some stripes. Ian was just getting a new command and he took to the kid immediately—he was funny and fearless. Big, like Ian—about six feet of hard body—and no attitude. At first, Ian just worked him to death, but found himself responding right away to Bobby's incredible endurance and commitment. It didn't take long before Ian was mentoring him; teaching him and building him into one of the best of the best. Also, he was having a beer with him now and then and talking about home, about things that were not military—sports, music, cars and hunting. And then they went to Iraq together.

They got out pictures of their girls and read the letters they got to each other, sometimes leaving out the more personal parts, sometimes not. Bobby had married his girl, but Ian had been engaged less than a year when they went to Iraq in the same unit.

Ian had Shelly back then. While he was gone, she was planning a wedding that would take place when he got back. Bobby and Marcie were hoping to start a family. Their women were beautiful—Marcie was small and fragile-looking with that great mass of curly red hair and a completely impish smile. Shelly was a tall, thin, sophisticated-looking blonde with long straight hair. Ian remembered that Marcie had sent Bobby a pair of her panties that he proudly showed to the guys, but *no* one was allowed to touch. Shelly sent Ian a lock of hair, but he'd have rather had panties. Marcie sent Bobby a picture of herself in her underwear on Bobby's motorcycle; Shelly sent a picture of herself posed in front of a Christmas tree, wearing slacks and a turtleneck sweater. Their girls also sent them cookies, books, cards, socks and tapes, anything they could think of. When the flak jackets ran low and soldiers started buying their own, Marcie and Shelly sent their men armor as well.

He didn't want to think about this. Couldn't she understand that? He didn't want to be haunted by it. He absolutely couldn't talk about it. He sat at his small table, head in his hands, but the memories assaulted him nonetheless.

There was no such thing as a routine mission in Fallujah. Ian's squad hadn't seen much action, but that day they hung tight against buildings while they did their door-to-door search for insurgents. The street was nearly deserted; a couple of women stood in doorways, watching them warily. Then it hit fast and hard. There were a couple of sudden explosions—a car bomb and grenade—and then a breakout of sniper fire. Ian saw one of his marines fly through the air, catapulted by the explosion. The second the noise subsided a little, Ian saw that it was Bobby who was down. He quickly assessed the rest of his squad; they'd taken cover and were returning fire. Bobby, however, got a double whammy—he'd been thrown probably twenty feet by the force of the explosion and by the time Ian got to him, there'd been a couple of gunshot wounds as well—head and torso.

Bobby looked up at him and said in a hoarse whisper, "Take cover, Sarge."

And Ian had replied, "Fuck off. I'm getting you outta here." Ian scooped him up, and right that second, he knew how bad it was going to turn out. He knew that fast. Bobby was limp as a hundred and eighty pound bag of sand. Carrying him over his shoulder, Ian got him behind the wall of a decimated building, called for a medic, an EMT who could administer battlefield first-aid. Ian put his hand over Bobby's head wound in an attempt to stanch the bleeding and waited for help.

The medic who traveled with their squad finally came and opened up Bobby's BDUs, the desert camouflage battle dress. He rolled him carefully. "It's through and through," he said of the torso wound, applying a compress to stop the bleeding. "We won't know how much damage till we get a closer look. His vitals are hanging in there."

"He's gonna make it," Ian said, though Bobby was out cold.

"We're not going anywhere fast," the medic said, getting out his gauze and tape to close up the head wound. "We can't get a chopper in this close. We'll have to carry the wounded or use litters."

"Just keep him going till we get transport," Ian demanded. But the medic was called to another wounded marine and Ian knew it was down to him to do everything

he could to keep Bobby alive, to get him to that helicopter. Bobby was unconscious and barely breathing.

It wasn't that long, but it seemed a lifetime, before the medic's radio alerted them to a helicopter a few blocks away in a safe zone. Ian knew in his gut that Bobby wasn't getting out of this okay, but he refused to think about it. "You're going to be okay, buddy," he kept saying. "You stay with me, I'll get you outta here."

The minute sniper fire seemed to have abated, Ian hefted Bobby into his arms and began to run down the dusty, bullet-riddled streets of Fallujah toward the chopper and the paramedics who had better equipment than what was available in the field. He took sniper fire in the thigh, but it was muscle not bone, and he ran through the pain. He took another one across the face, but he still couldn't feel the pain. He felt the fire on his cheek. Then he saw the corner of the building on the other side of which would be medical transport.

He got Bobby to the chopper, where the rescue crew took over. He tried to go back to his squad, when one of the medics snagged his sleeve and said, "Hold up there, Sarge. Let's have a look."

Ian looked down. He was covered with blood. He couldn't tell his from Bobby's. Right then, his leg throbbed and his face burned; his vision blurred from blood running into his eye.

"Whoa, Sarge—you're not going anywhere. We gotta look at—"

"Take care of him, *" Ian said sternly. "I'll be fine."*

"Everyone's getting taken care of, Sarge," the medic said, taking the scissors to his pants, cutting them up to his thigh to expose a bleeding hole.

"Oh," Ian said. "Damn." And he swayed a little.

He sat while the medic attended to his face wounds—a cut across his eyebrow and a flesh wound that ran down the length of his check. While this was going on, while they were waiting for a couple more wounded marines, Ian watched as they worked on Bobby.

One of the medics said, "No casualties today."

Little did they know…

The chopper finally lifted off and headed for the nearest camp hospital. There was a full surgical setup in tents and hastily erected buildings. That's where Ian was separated from Bobby. Ian was taken into a treatment area while Bobby went straight to surgery. Some young doctor had shaved off Ian's eyebrow to get a nice, clean stitch on the laceration; the nurse informed him it might never grow back. By the time Ian had a bandage and some crutches, Bobby had been stabilized and airlifted to Germany.

Ian stayed in Iraq. His injuries left some ugly scars but his recovery was relatively short. While Ian was behind the action for two months, he wrote letters to Bobby's wife, letters telling her he was sure Bobby would be fine. Marcie went immediately to Germany and wrote back to Ian. Then she followed Bobby to Washington D.C.—to the Walter Reed Medical Center, and they wrote some more.

While Ian went back into action, Bobby went from Germany to Walter Reed to a VA hospital in Texas, then home to his wife. Ian kept up the correspondence—he heard from Marcie all the time and answered her every letter. She said things like, "He's still pretty much unresponsive, but they're working with him in physical therapy," and "He's not on a respirator or anything," and,

"I swear, Ian, he smiled at me today." She said there was some paralysis and they feared brain damage, not from the bullet wound but from brain swelling. "Feared," she had written. And "some paralysis."

It was a few months later when she wrote to Ian again, "We have to face it—he's not going to recover. He's paralyzed from the neck down and he's conscious but unresponsive." The news hit Ian in the gut like a torpedo. He reread the previous letters; there wasn't a hint of doom, yet the facts were there. A combination of his denial and her hope had kept the inevitable bad news at bay.

And then Marcie wrote, "I'm so relieved to have him home."

Ian was given medals for saving Bobby's life. Every day he asked himself why he should get medals for that, for saving a man to live in a dead body.

Since Ian had the basic information about his friend, he thought he was prepared for the visit he would pay when he was next stateside on leave. Marcie was so excited to see him, to throw her arms around him and thank *him. He wasn't sure what he had expected, but it sure as hell hadn't been what he'd seen. Just from earlier photos, he could tell Marcie had become thinner and more pale, even more fragile-looking. She was so tiny, so frail.*

And Bobby? The man he'd seen did not resemble his friend. This man was a wasted, emaciated version of Bobby—his musculature gone, staring off at nothing, being fed through a tube, not responding to his young wife or his best friend. Bobby was gone, completely gone, yet his heart pumped and his lungs spontaneously filled with air. It was a travesty. And Ian had accepted medals for that?

* * *

Ian opened his eyes and they felt gritty. Sandy. He'd been literally transported to the past, a thing he'd been running from for years. He'd never been entirely sure if what happened next was due to the whole Iraq experience, or to the events that changed Bobby's life so irrevocably. Whatever it was, it came to an ugly end when he got back from Iraq, a mess, his head all screwed up. He'd visited Bobby for probably less than fifteen minutes and it devastated him to see what he'd done—saving Bobby to live a life like that. He called off his wedding, tearing Shelly to shreds. He reported back for duty, not the same stalwart man, but a wreck who was impossibly short tempered. There was a phone call from Marcie's sister saying it would be nice if Ian could at least be in touch with her—she was up against so much with Bobby, which added guilt to his growing list of demons.

Ian suddenly couldn't stay out of trouble. Rather than being an example, he was a problem. He ended up spending a couple of nights in jail for stupid, random fights, and his father told him he was never so goddamned ashamed of him in his life. Ian's response to that was to screw up enough so the Corps suggested it was time for him to exit and see if he'd be better as a civilian. He couldn't face any of it. He had let Bobby down, disgraced his father, shattered and abandoned his woman. And he hadn't been there for Marcie, who deserved better from him. He just wandered off, trying to figure out his head, but the task proved to be impossible.

He didn't want to see Marcie now. He didn't want to relive all that. There was no way he could apologize enough, no way to undo what he'd done. She should go away, let him figure out how to coexist alone with his monsters, someplace where he wouldn't do any harm. He'd found some contentment here; there was nothing to be gained by going over the details again. God knew, he'd been over the details too many times, often without meaning to.

He had such horrible guilt. If Bobby was condemned to wasted life, why should he just pick up where he left off and thrive? Couldn't, he couldn't. But he could avoid hearing all the details of the traumatic last few years.

He looked at his watch. It was ten o'clock and he had to pee. He'd been in some flashback for more than a couple of hours. He seriously considered using the small pot he kept for emergencies, but it was time to see if she'd gone while he was in that other world.

He put on his jacket to take a trip out back, hoping beyond hope that when he opened the door, that little Volkswagen would be gone.

But damn, it was right there—covered with a thin layer of snow. It made him furious and he let out a loud, scary roar. But there was no response from within the car. He banged on the window. "Hey! You! Get outta here! Just go home!" Still, there was nothing from inside. He put his big hands on the top of the little car and began to rock it, shake it. When it settled, there was no movement, no sound.

Shit, he thought. It's freezing. She wouldn't fall asleep in there while the temperature dropped and the little car was covered with snow? No one would be that stupid. He pulled open the passenger door. She was gone.

"Goddamn it!" he cursed, turning around in a circle. "Goddamn you, Marcie! Where the hell are you?"

The night was silent. The snow drifted lazily to the

ground. Then he heard the vague squeak of hinges and he looked across the dark. The outhouse door was open, drifting in the gentle breeze.

Dread colder than the winter sky filled him, and he ran to the little hut. She was slumped in the open doorway, her upper body inside and her legs covered with snow. Holy Jesus, she'd been like that long enough to have a dusting of snow on her legs.

He didn't even think—he lifted her into his arms quickly and put his lips against her forehead to judge her body temperature. She was cold as ice. He ran to the cabin with her in his arms, conscious of the fact that she wasn't stiff, wasn't frozen solid, and he did something he hadn't done in so long—he prayed. *Oh God, I didn't mean to roar like that—I just thought it best for both of us if she went away! Please, let her be okay! I'll do anything...anything...* When he got her inside, he put her on the couch, then rushed to put a couple more logs into the woodstove.

Then he hurried back to her and checked for a pulse. She was still okay, though hypothermic enough to induce unconsciousness. He knew what he had to do and started getting her out of her cold, wet clothes. First the quilted vest, then the boots and jeans. At least they'd been thick denim jeans and solid leather boots; it might've saved her from frostbite. She flopped weakly as he pulled her sweater over her head. Then he threw off his own jacket, ripped off his shirt, tore off his boots and shed his pants. He covered her small body with his and warmed her, skin to skin, holding himself up so as not to crush her with his weight.

He turned her face so that it lay gently against his shoulder. After minutes passed, he could feel the chill leaving her body. His arms trembled from holding his nearly two hundred pounds off her, keeping flesh on flesh, and the strangest image came back to him. *Drop and give me twenty! And twenty! And twenty!* God, how many push-ups had he given, then demanded....

He warmed her for an hour, while at the same time, the woodstove heated up the cabin. Her breath was soft and even on his shoulder; her body still and warm to the touch. He stayed over her a bit longer than necessary. Somewhat reluctant, he pushed himself off her, then wrapped her in a soft old quilt that lay at the foot of the couch.

Dressed again, he fed the woodstove and put a kettle of water on the cookstove.

Inside his one-room house was a couch, a table and two chairs, the clawfoot tub, the woodstove and a Coleman cookstove that ran on propane gas on the counter by the sink. There was a thick, rolled pallet he slept on and a stack of dry wood beside the woodstove. He had a few cupboards and a sink with a pump. There were two large trunks and a small metal box in which he kept his possessions and few valuables. Leaning in the corners were fishing gear and two rifles of the caliber to hunt game on the land that had become his. He had a stack of six books from the library; every two weeks he went to the public library using the card that had belonged to old Raleigh, the man who had lived here before him and died here, leaving a letter saying Ian could have the property.

He checked Marcie again. She was all right, sleeping soundly. So he took his trip to the outhouse and he made it real fast.

Ordinarily he'd be asleep long before now, there being little else to do. But instead, he sat in a chair at the table and opened the book he was currently reading. When the kettle whistled, he turned off the flame and checked on her. She was warmer and breathing regularly, so he read a while longer. Then he recharged the kettle, checked her again and found her the same.

That hair… It was everywhere on the couch pillow, thick and springy. If he didn't have so much beard of his own, he could have enjoyed the feel of it against his face. He bunched some of it up in his hand and it was soft and thick. He couldn't help but think of that girl, all of twenty-three and already a wife of four years, tending to a man who was nothing but flesh and bone. God, what kind of life must that have been?

Several more times, he reheated the water for hot tea, read, checked her. And then he heard a snuffling on the couch. A dry cough. He looked at his watch—a ten-dollar thing that had run for four years—and saw it was almost four o'clock. He went and knelt beside the couch. "You gonna wake up?"

She lazily opened her eyes and jolted awake, scooting up on her elbows. "What? What?"

"Easy. It's okay. Sort of."

She blinked a few times and then her eyes were wide. "Where am I?"

"I brought you inside. I had to. You were on your way to freezing to death. You must not have a brain in your head."

She squinted at him, pursing her lips. "Oh—I have a brain. I'm just not real experienced in mountain life." She struggled to sit up. "Gee, if I'd known you got your eyebrow back and grew your beard in red, I might've found you sooner. I'll get out of your hair, which I notice, you have plenty of."

"You're not going anywhere," he said, putting a big

hand against her sternum, holding her down. "You're stuck—and so am I."

"No problem," she said. "I sleep in the car every night. I have a good sleeping bag..."

"Did you hear me? You were passed out on your way back from the john, covered with snow and damn near frozen to death. You wanted to see me, you're going to get your wish."

Her eyes widened suddenly. "I'm...ah...naked under here?"

"You're not naked. You have underwear. I had to get your wet clothes off you. That or just let you die. It wasn't an easy decision," he lied.

"You undressed me and wrapped me in this quilt?" she asked.

"Pretty much," he said. *And felt your small, soft body against mine for an hour, the first female body that's been against mine in five years.* Until tonight, he hadn't thought he missed that feeling. "What happened out there? How'd you end up in the doorway of the john like that?"

"I don't have the first idea. I was so glad there was an outhouse for once and I wouldn't have to squat behind a bush. I was going to make it quick, but I was so tired I could hardly move, and that's the last thing I remember till I woke up." She coughed. "I didn't think I was so tired I'd fall asleep on the way."

"You didn't fall asleep," he said. "You lost consciousness. Hypothermia. Like I said—half frozen."

"Hmm. Well, I have to pee now," she said. "And I'm feeling really, really hot in here."

So, she'd been half-frozen before she made the trek out of her VW. He stared at her for a minute, then went over by the stove where he had her wet clothes draped over one of his two chairs to dry out. He felt them, then he went to one of the two trunks, opened it and pulled out a flannel shirt of his own. He took it to her and said, "Here, just put this on." Next he reached behind the woodstove and picked up a navy blue porcelain pot with white dots that was probably fifty years old if it was a day. When he turned back to her, she was sitting up and buttoning the flannel shirt. "Use this."

"For what?"

"To pee in."

"I don't think so," she said. "Maybe, if you'll give me my jeans and boots, I'll just step outside…" Then she coughed again, several times.

"No, you can't do that. And you better not get sick. I don't have time to deal with a sick person."

"I'm not sick, just a little dry in the throat. I could use a drink of water, but not until I take a trip out to the—"

"Let's be clear," Ian said gruffly. "I'm not letting you back outside. Not for a few more hours at least." The kettle whistled. He shut off the propane stove and shrugged into his jacket. "*I'll* step outside. You do your thing. Then you'll have a cup of tea and go back to sleep."

She just stared up at him with eyes that were dull green and very wide. She wiggled a little in discomfort. "Do you have any…tissue?"

He sighed deeply, letting his eyes fall closed impatiently. After handing her the pot, he went to one of his cupboards and pulled out a new roll of toilet tissue. Then he went out the door, hoping it wouldn't take her very long to do her business. He shivered out there for five minutes and then he tentatively knocked on his own front door. He was answered by a round of hard coughing and he didn't wait for further invitation.

She was leaning back on the couch looking flushed, her skinny bare legs sticking out from beneath the huge shirt, holding the pan possessively on her lap. She looked up at him and said, "What should I do with this?"

"I'll take care of it," he said. She didn't move. "Let me have it now." Reluctantly, she gave it up. "I'll be right back." And again he left her, this time to pour the contents down the outhouse hole. And as he was returning he thought, she's sick. No question about it. She's been sleeping in her damn car—who knew for how long?—and got weakened. She must have had a bug in her that was ready to strike, and that bad chill just added to her troubles.

He said nothing as he came in the cabin. He put the pot back behind the stove for her use if she needed it. He washed his hands, made her a cup of tea, and while it steeped, he poured a cup of water and brought her three aspirins.

"Huh?" she said. "What's this?"

"I think you have a fever. Might be from damn near freezing to death, might be from something else. First we try aspirin."

"Yeah," she said, taking them in her small hand. "Thanks."

While Marcie took the aspirin with water, he fixed up the tea. They traded, water cup for mug of tea. He stayed across the room at his table while she sipped the tea. When she was almost done, he said, "Okay, here's the deal. I have to work this morning. I'll be gone till noon or so—depends how long it takes. When I get back, you're going to be here. After we're sure you're not sick, then you'll go. But not till I tell you it's time to go. I want you to sleep. Rest. Use the pot, don't go outside. I don't want to stretch this out. And I don't want to have to go looking for you to make sure you're all right. You understand?"

She smiled, though weakly. "Aw, Ian, you care."

He snarled at her, baring his teeth like an animal.

She laughed a little, which turned into a cough. "You get a lot of mileage out of that? The roars and growls, like you're about to tear a person to pieces with your teeth?"

He looked away.

"Must keep people back pretty good. Your old neighbor said you were crazy. You howl at the moon and everything?"

"How about you don't press your luck," he said as meanly as he could. "You need more tea?"

"If it's all the same to you, I think I'll nap. I don't want to be any trouble, but I'm awful tired."

He went to her and took the cup out of her hand. "If you didn't want to be any trouble, why didn't you just leave me the hell alone?"

"Gee, I just had this wild urge to find an old friend..." She lay back on the couch, pulling that soft quilt around her. "What kind of work do you do?"

"I sell firewood out of the back of my truck." He went to his metal box, which was nailed to the floor from the inside so it couldn't be stolen if someone happened by his cabin, which was unlikely. He unlocked it and took out a roll of bills he kept in there and put it in his pocket, then relocked it. "First snowfall of winter—should be a good day. Maybe I'll get back early, but no matter what, I want you here until I say you go. You get that?"

"Listen, if I'm here, it's because it's where I want to be, and you better get *that*. I'm the one who came looking for you, so don't get the idea you're going to bully me around and scare me. If I wasn't so damn tired, I might leave—just to piss you off. But I get the idea you *like* being pissed off."

He stood and got into his jacket, pulled gloves out of the pockets. "I guess we understand each other as well as we can."

"Wait—it's not even light!"

"I start before light. I have to load the truck."

And he was gone.

Marcie reclined on the couch and closed her eyes. At first she heard the heavy thumping of logs being stacked in the back of the truck. Then she heard some soft whistling while she dozed off. Very pretty whistling with a distinct melody. She wasn't sure what woke her, but when she opened her eyes the cabin was dimly lit with the first rays of dawn and she heard…*singing.* A beautiful male baritone. She couldn't hear the words, but it was him and it took her breath away.

And she knew something. If you're angry and in pain, you can't sing. Can't.

Four

Snow didn't fall all the way into the valley, down near the ocean towns of Eureka and Arcata. But up here it was overcast, damp and chilly, and more snow was forecast. Ian had his truck parked along the road leading to a busy thoroughfare just before seven o'clock. At that juncture, he caught people on their way to work and, after four years, he was selling to the same customers over and over. Since he didn't have a phone and no one knew where he lived, they watched for him to show up. Five cars right in a row pulled up and he made deals for as many half cords of wood. He took addresses in his little notebook and promised to deliver the wood in the next couple of days. Two of them he'd done business with in the past and accepted their checks, but the other three would have their wives give him the cash upon delivery.

The sixth customer was the police chief. He bought a cord from Ian every winter and must trust him by now because he paid cash in advance of delivery; other customers liked to see the wood before they shelled out the money for the delivery. "Got a good supply this winter, buddy?" the chief asked, pulling off his bills.

"Yes, sir. We'll get you through. I'll take this load right over."

"Will you stack it up in the shed out back and put a little on the porch by the mudroom door for me?"

"You betcha. As usual," Ian said, taking the money.

"You take care now," the chief said. "Listen… There was this woman looking for a guy about your size, age… Aw, never mind…"

Ian smiled inwardly. *No, chief, couldn't be me,* he thought. "I'll get that wood over this morning."

"Thanks, buddy."

Twenty minutes later, a truck pulled up and Ian took his last order for wood, then was on his way to deliver his load to the chief. He made a stop for gas and a few supplies—broth cubes, half a roaster, an onion, some celery, a bag of frozen mixed vegetables, noodles, couple of small orange juices plus some fresh apples and oranges, coffee, bread, peanut butter and honey. He was back at the cabin before noon.

The room had chilled down because the stove hadn't been fed, but she'd kicked off her covers and her little rump was sticking out—lavender and lace. Her face was glowing pink. He put down his groceries and fed the stove. Then he took her juice and more aspirin, waking her. He pulled the quilt over her and made her sit up.

"When are you leaving?" she asked him groggily.

"I'm back. Here, you have to take aspirin. You have a fever. Where are you sick, Marcie? Head, stomach, throat, chest? Where?"

"Ugh. I don't know," she said, struggling awake. "I think I'm just tired and achy. I'll be fine."

"Juice and aspirin," he said, lifting her. "Come on now. You got a bug."

"Ugh," she said again, lifting up. "I'm sorry. I'll be better in a little while. It's probably just a little cold or something." She took the aspirin—four this time—and washed it down with orange juice.

"I have to go out again, Marcie. There's more juice on the table. You need that blue pot closer to the couch while I'm gone?"

"No," she said, settling back against the couch. "I don't like that pot."

"I'm going to go see if I can get you some medicine. There's an old doc in Virgin River—he might have some stuff on hand for cold and flu. It'll take me almost a half hour to get there, the same coming back."

"Virgin River," she said dreamily, eyes closed. "Ian, they have the most beautiful Christmas tree… You should see it…"

"Yeah, right. I'll be an hour or so. The fire should more than last, but will you try to keep the blanket on? Till I get back?"

"I'm just too warm for it…"

"You won't be in a half hour, when that aspirin kicks in and drops your temperature. Can you just do this for me?"

Her eyes fluttered open. "I bet you're really pissed at me right now, huh? I just wanted to find you, not make so much trouble for you."

He brushed that wild red hair off her brow where a couple of curly red tendrils stuck to the dampness on her face. "I'm not pissed anymore, Marcie," he said softly. "When you're all over this flu, I'll give you what for. How's that?"

"Whatever. You can howl at me with that big, mean animal roar if you want to. I have a feeling you like doing that."

He grinned in spite of himself. "I do," he said. "I do like it." Then he stood and said, "Stay covered and I'll get back as soon as I can."

When Ian pulled into town, the first thing he saw was the tree. Somehow he thought she might've been hallucinating from the fever, which had scared the hell out of him. But there it was—biggest damn thing he'd ever seen. The bottom third was decorated with red-white-and-blue balls, gold stars and some other stuff; the top part was still bare. He actually slowed the truck for a moment, taking it in. But what was that patriotic color scheme about? Did they do this every winter? Did they have some town kids in the war?

He shook it off; he had to get something for Marcie. The old doc used to come out to his place when old Raleigh was at the end and real sick, years ago now. Ian had to use Raleigh's ancient truck to fetch the doctor; Raleigh had never even considered a phone. And neither had Ian.

When he walked into the doc's house, he saw a young blonde at the desk. "Hi, there," she said. She stood up and he noted the pregnant tummy.

"Hey. Doc around?"

"Sure. I'll get him for you. I've been here less than two years—does he know you?"

"Sort of, yeah."

She smiled over her shoulder and went to Doc's office. Momentarily, the old man was limping toward him, glasses perched on his nose, wild white eyebrows spiking. "Afternoon," Doc said.

"Hey, Doc," Ian said, putting out a hand. "Any chance you have anything on hand for a flu bug?"

"Sorry, son—I can't remember the name. The face I know. You're…?"

"Buchanan. Ian Buchanan from out on Clint Mountain. The old Raleigh place. I was the one taking care of him at the end."

"Right," he said. "That's right. What's your complaint?"

"It's not me, Doc. I've got a visitor who showed up yesterday and she took sick in the night. Fever, chills, aches, sore throat… I'm giving her aspirin and juice. I didn't want to bring her out in this cold—the heater in the truck isn't too good. But if you have any medicine—"

"I'm chock full of medicine, boy—but I usually like to make my own diagnosis."

"It's way out there— You remember."

"Yeah, yeah, can't hardly forget that old coot. No problem—I get around. Let me stock up a bag and I'll follow you back. Most roads out that way are a goddamn mystery."

Ian felt the roll of bills in his pocket shrink. He was ahead for the winter, but if he ended up needing a lot of diesel fuel and propane through the cold months, he wouldn't stay that way for long. Then in the spring, the tax bill would come on the property. Summers were easy; they weren't hot summers but he didn't need to heat food or water, daylight lasted a lot longer and so did his fuel. He conserved cash for possible truck repairs and things like that. He worked for a moving company on and off in the summer and was paid cash under the table. That gave him time for a garden, fishing and cutting down trees for the winter firewood. He'd get by fine if no major crisis came along—like a serious illness.

Really, the cost didn't matter. No matter what she needed, even if it was the hospital, he'd find a way. He couldn't let her be sick. In less than twenty-four hours, all he really wanted was to see her smile like she had in that old picture Bobby had shown him.

He was barely conscious that the woman in the office had made a phone call and shrugged into her coat.

When Doc returned with his bag, he frowned at her. It was more like a glower. "Where do you think you're going?"

"With you. Jack has David and this is a woman. You'll end up wanting me there."

"You're pregnant and don't need to be around flu."

She laughed and her face lit up so pretty. "Like I haven't been drenched in flu since the cold and rain hit. Gimme a break. Let's go." And she headed out the door.

"Damn pigheaded woman," Doc muttered. "She'd never take an order from me, but you'd think a little friendly advice would be welcome—" Ian held the door open for him. "Women are nothing but a pain in the— Why I never married. Not quite true, no one would have me." He stopped and navigated the stairs down the porch with his cane.

"Um, Doc—you wanna lock up?" Ian asked.

"Nah. I locked up the drugs and Jack and Preacher are across the street. They smell trouble and they're armed to the teeth. It's a dead fool that bothers my place."

"Hmm," Ian said. They had it all worked out in this little town. Made him wonder just what that felt like. He hadn't had things all worked out in a long, long time.

There was a shiny Hummer sitting beside his old truck and the pregnant blonde was at the wheel, waiting. They must do a brisk business these days to afford a ride like that. The roll of bills in his pocket shrank again.

* * *

Ian opened the door for Doc Mullins and Mel and once again, Marcie slept so soundly she didn't realize he was back. "I'll just check the stove for wood and then wait outside," he said.

Mel pulled a chair from the table and put it by the couch, giving it a tap so Doc would take a seat. Then she gently jostled Marcie's shoulder and called out to her, talking over Doc's shoulder. "Marcie, can you wake up? Come on, open your eyes."

When Marcie's eyes came open, Mel smiled. "Hi there. Not feeling so good, huh? You remember me—Mel Sheridan from Virgin River. I'm the one who was dragged off a ladder in the middle of town by a brute."

"Yes," Marcie said. "Sure." And she came awake with a dry cough, turning her head aside.

"This is Doc Mullins. I work with him. He's a family practitioner. I'm a nurse practitioner and midwife. Ian came for us. His diagnosis is flu. What's yours?"

"Ugh. It's probably just a bad cold."

"But your nose ain't running," Doc said. "Sit up for me, girl. I have to hear your chest." While Doc slid the cold stethoscope under the flannel shirt to listen to her lungs, she treated him to a deep, brittle cough. When she recovered, she took a few deep breaths for him, then sat patiently while he looked in her ears and throat, taking her temperature and palpating her glands.

Mel said, "So, you found your man."

"I did," Marcie said. "Your husband told you?"

"Uh-huh. I don't tell patient business without permission, but Jack's an open book unless he has specific instructions to keep a secret. How'd Ian take to being found?"

"Thoroughly pissed him off. You should hear him—he can roar like a Siberian tiger. It's kind of amazing. Scared the liver out of me at first."

"And now?" Mel asked.

She looked up at Mel. "He saved my life. He said I almost froze to death and he brought me in and warmed me up. He went for you…"

"He said he didn't want to bring you to town because the heater in his truck isn't working very well. But I have a good heater and we have a couple of beds at the clinic—"

"Can't I just stay here?" she asked.

"Are you sure?"

"I came all this way… I've been looking for him…"

"You can come to town with us until you feel better, then decide what to do. You can come back if you have unfinished business here. If you need a little backup, there's my husband and me."

"No," she said, shaking her head. "I'd rather see this through, then I'll go home." And what she didn't say was that she was a little afraid he might disappear again.

"But do you feel safe with him? It's pretty rugged out here. Your tiger doesn't have a lot of creature comforts."

"I don't think Ian has much, being out here like this. But it's enough, isn't it? It's warm, there's food, he made me tea, bought me orange juice. He gave me aspirin…"

"I don't know him, Marcie," Mel said. "And from what I hear, you don't know him either. He's a recluse—does he even have any friends?"

"I don't know," she shrugged. "He has me."

"Do I take that to mean he's not roaring at you anymore?" Mel asked.

"I hope so. I think he's all calmed down."

"I don't want to leave you in a bad place. That would be irresponsible of me."

Marcie smiled a little. "When he was loading his truck with firewood to sell, he was singing. You should have heard him. He has the most beautiful voice. I knew when I heard that voice that he's ferocious on the outside, but on the inside he's a tender soul. And I think he's proving I'm right, in spite of himself."

"Of course, it's your decision," Mel said. "But there's help if you need it."

"Flu," Doc said shortly. "Boy's good—he should practice medicine. You'll be all right after a couple of days of feeling like crap. I'm going to give you an antibiotic injection, although it will only treat any bacterial infection you might've picked up as a result of a viral flu. You'll have to ride it out, but you're young and healthy and seem to have a decent nurse. Ian took good care of the old man who lived here before him. He's up to the job."

"That may be," Mel said. "But before I leave, I'm going to make sure he wants to do that. I'm going to have to ask him, Marcie. If he doesn't want to take care of you through this illness, he shouldn't have to—not when there's an alternative. If his means are slim and he's not inclined—"

"All right," she said. "But when you ask him, will you please tell him I have eighty dollars I can give him? For anything I eat or drink?"

Mel smiled. "I'll be sure to tell him that."

"And can I ask a favor?"

"Sure. Ask away."

"Any chance you have an older sister?"

"I certainly do."

"Well, so do I—Erin Elizabeth. Our mother died when

I was only four and our dad when I was fifteen. Erin's seven years older and took complete responsibility for my younger brother and me. She's a good person, if a little on the bossy side. She was adamantly opposed to me looking for Ian by myself. In the end there wasn't much she could do to stop me—I *am* an adult, though she might argue that. Our compromise was that I check in every couple of days and, believe me, she's more than ready for me to call off the hunt. Erin doesn't mean to be, but she's controlling. Sometimes a little hard to take…"

"Well, I have an older sister who can fill that bill. And heavens, you *saw* Jack!"

Marcie smiled. "I saw. Yes, I suppose you can relate. I need someone to call Erin, tell her that I found Ian, that I'm safe and sound and staying with him for a little while. If you could just explain he has no phone, so I'll call her the next time I'm in town, it might give her a little peace of mind."

"Is that the extent of your family?" Mel asked.

"Yes," she said. "Me and Erin and our brother, Drew. But I also have my late husband's family and there are a million of them. Just because he's gone now, they won't ever give me up. I'm far from alone, believe me. If I write down the number, will you call for me?"

"Provided Ian goes along with your idea, I'll be glad to," Mel said.

"We don't have to tell her I got sick. Do we?"

"Oh, Marcie, I don't like stretching the truth," Mel said.

"Well—you don't tell patient business. And you do think I'll be just fine, don't you?"

Mel made a face and shook her head. "Is this the way you've been getting around your sister?"

"You have to think fast around Erin. She's brilliant."

"Bottoms up," Doc said, tapping the air bubbles out of a syringe. "I'll give you some decongestant and cough medicine and beyond that, it's just rest, juice, water, light meals—broth would be good for a day or so. Listen to your body and rest when you're tired. A lot of sleep and fluids almost always kicks this sucker fast. No wood chopping or washing clothes in the creek. You'll come around pretty quick, I bet."

"But I can use the outdoor rather than the chamber pot, even though it's cold?"

"Of course. Cold doesn't make you sick, it makes you cold. Bundle up anyway, and make it quick."

"You probably don't have to recommend that… Have you ever felt the seat of an outhouse in December?" she asked.

"Girl, I had to get trained in how to flush when I was a young man," Doc said. "Gets you down to business real quick, now, doesn't it?"

"Marcie, if you need us, send Ian. I'll come and get you—no questions asked," Mel said.

"Thank you, that's sweet."

"Good luck."

Ian was pacing in front of the Hummer when Mel and Doc came out of the cabin. Mel paused to speak with Ian, as she had said she would. She took note of how ragged he was, how unkempt. His clothes were old and worn, his beard overgrown, but then most hardworking ranchers, farmers and loggers wouldn't be wearing their best duds on a workday. She was used to seeing this type of wardrobe out here, and it didn't always imply poverty. He didn't smell bad, she found herself thinking. She had spied the tub in the room; he kept himself and his cabin clean and he certainly wasn't thin. He was plenty well-nourished, a big man.

Doc made fast tracks to the Humvee and placed himself behind the wheel. She made a face.

"He sure can move when he wants to be the driver, despite all that arthritis," she said. "Mr. Buchanan, you were absolutely right—Marcie has the flu. She's going to need to rest, drink plenty of fluids and she probably won't feel well for at least a couple of days—maybe closer to a week, depending on how quickly she bounces back after some rest and medicine. Now, I offered to take her back to town and put her up at Doc's, but she'd rather stay here. The question is—are you willing? It's not as though you have to do that much for her—Doc cleared her for use of the outdoor facilities as long as she dresses warm. She doesn't need much attention, but it's *your* home."

"She wants to stay?" he asked, eyebrows arched. "Here?"

"She said that, yes. She also said to tell you she has eighty dollars for her food."

"Lord," he said, shaking his head. "If she wants to stay, she can stay. I can't see why she'd want to. It's not like I'm good company."

"I think she's very grateful for how well you've tended her so far. Maybe there are other reasons, but she didn't share them. But just so we're clear—I can come and get her anytime and we have a couple of hospital beds at the clinic. It's your decision. If it becomes a burden, you can let me know."

"I'll do my best. I bought some broth. Juice. A half chicken for soup that should go at least twice."

"Good idea. I swear by chicken soup. I guess you're on top of this. Is there anything else I can do for you?"

"Did you give her medicine?"

"Doc gave her a shot of antibiotic that probably won't perform any miracles, it being a viral flu. And he left her some pills and cough medicine. It's really tincture of time. The flu will do what it will do—sometimes it's a quick cure, sometimes it hangs on. Luckily, she's young and healthy. Try not to catch it, will you?"

He pulled a roll of bills out of his pocket and Mel, who had worked with Doc in these mountains for a while now, suspected that would be the whole of his fiduciary world. Most rural people way out here didn't deal with credit cards or checks; for many it was a cash existence. That wad of money would have to cover everything in his life, from fuel to food, for quite a while. "What do I owe you?" he asked.

"Well, let's see. I'm thinking ten for the shot and another ten for the pills and cough medicine."

"And for the house call?"

"Five for gas?" she said, by way of a question.

"And that's it?" he asked. "You cutting me some kind of break here? She give you money or something?"

Mel smiled. "No money from the patient. We're not exactly trading on the exchange yet. This isn't big business, it's just country medicine—clean and simple. It's important to break even whenever we can—helps us out in the long run."

"What would you charge me if I lived in a big house and drove a hot car?" he asked.

"We'd bill the insurance and take them for a ride," she answered easily. Then she grinned at him.

He laughed in spite of himself. Old Doc didn't have himself a pretty young nurse or Hummer when Raleigh was sick and dying, but he always said, "You're eighty-eight and sick as a damn dog—I'm not taking all your money and leaving you nothing for a burial." Ian pulled off three tens and gave them to her. "You eating all right at your house? I'm not shorting you?"

"I'm covered—I very cleverly married the guy in town who owns the bar and grill. I'm eating way better than I should. And by that belly on Doc, he's living well enough, too. But thanks. It's appreciated. I'll put the extra toward someone in trouble, I promise."

"That's good," he said. "I got a lot to make up for."

She put out her hand. "I bet not as much as you think." He shook the small hand and she hurried to the car and was gone.

When Ian finally came back inside, he didn't say a word. He fed the fire again, took off his jacket and went to what passed for his kitchen. He rolled up his sleeves and scrubbed his hands with soap and cold water. Next he pumped a pan full of water and set it on his little propane stove, unwrapped a half a chicken and plopped it in the water. He cut up an onion and some celery and put it in the pot. Then he put his jacket back on and went outside where she could hear the thumping that went along with loading wood into the truck. Whistling came eventually, but there didn't seem to be any singing today. She hoped she hadn't driven the music out of him.

The singing was a complete surprise. Bobby never mentioned it and it certainly hadn't come up in their few exchanged letters. But then would a big tough marine serenade his troops? Would he tell a soldier's wife that he loved to sing and had an angel's voice?

Her joints ached and she was feeling warm again, so she rolled over and let herself go back to sleep. She was vaguely aware that Ian was in and out of the cabin. She drifted. Now and then, she could hear the wood chopping, whistling, thunking of firewood into the truck bed.

She had no idea how long she'd slept, when she roused to the most pleasant smell. She rolled over to find the room dim, just the glow from the woodstove and a naked lightbulb hanging over the kitchen table. The sun had set and the big pot was steaming on the little stove. He was sitting at the table under that single light, looking down. She noticed that the things from her car—her sleeping bag, duffel, backpack and purse—were stacked at the end of the sofa. And he had changed clothes; he wore gray sweatpants and a navy blue T-shirt and socks. His former pants, shirt and jacket were draped over his trunk, near a stack of books piled on the floor.

She rose on her elbows. "What are you doing?" she asked him.

He flipped a book closed and looked up. "Just reading. You about ready for a little trip to the, ah, ladies' room?"

She sat up and flipped her legs over the edge of the couch. "As a matter of fact," she said, standing. That flannel shirt of his came nearly to her knees. She wobbled a little and it brought him instantly to his feet. She sat back down quickly. "Would you mind…handing me my jeans and boots?"

"Sure," he said, pulling them off the chair and carrying them to her. The minute they were in hand, he went about the business of pulling on his own boots and jacket, his back toward her. "You need any help?" he asked, not facing her.

"I'm okay," she said. First the jeans came up, then she sat again and pulled on her boots without socks. "Do I have a jacket around here somewhere?"

He fetched the down vest from the same chair back and held it for her.

"I'll just be a minute—"

But he wasn't having it. He swept her up in his arms and carried her to the door. "I don't think you're all that strong. Probably just being asleep for so long and all. But I don't want to have to lift you up off the ground or anything. Let's not take any chances."

They were halfway across the yard to the outhouse when she said, "You let me stay."

"It's what you said you wanted, according to the nurse. Even if I can't figure out why."

"You like me," she said, petting his thick, red beard. She put her head against his shoulder, arms about his neck. "Try to deny it." And then she coughed, most unattractively.

He turned his face away from her germs and grunted. Stopping in front of the outhouse door, he set her gently on her feet. She entered and, a moment later, was out again. "I'll walk, I think. If you don't mind."

"Don't fall. It's tougher to pick you up from the ground than from a standing position. Grab my arm if you need to." Their feet crunched on the frozen ground as they headed back to the cabin. "Sorry I don't have an indoor for you. Especially with you being sick."

"Actually, it's a luxury. I was hitting the gas stations for one last bathroom visit before bedding down in the car for the night. Usually I could make it till morning, but if I couldn't, I had to make do. That usually meant a quick squat behind a bush on a deserted road. And it's been real cold lately."

As he looked down at her, his eyes were both warm and curious. "You don't look as tough as that."

"I don't know how tough I am—look at me, sick as a pup. But I bet I can match you for stubborn."

A sound came out of him.

"Holy shit, Ian—was that a laugh?"

"A cough," he lied. "You probably got me sick."

Five

Back inside the little cabin, Marcie took her place on the couch while Ian went to his little propane stove and gave the pot a stir. "Can you eat a bit of soup?" he asked.

"I think so. It sure smells wonderful."

"It's not much. Just boiled down chicken…some vegetables," he said simply. She watched as he ladled some into a large mug, plopped a spoon in it and put a slice of buttered bread on a saucer. Then he loaded that onto a flat board and brought it to her. "I don't have things like a lot of different dishes—just what I need. Be careful, it's hot."

She balanced the board on her knees. "You sure can do a lot with a little bit, can't you?"

He grunted an affirmative reply and went back to the pot, ladling some into a mug for himself. Then he sat at the table with his meal.

She took a couple of spoons of chicken soup. It was either delicious or she was ravenous. Then she walked over to the table with her board-tray. She put it down opposite him, then dragged the other chair the short distance to sit with him. He just lifted his eyebrows and watched her. "It's very good, Ian. You suppose we could eat together?"

He just shrugged. "If that's what you want."

"We could actually talk," she suggested.

He put his spoon in his mug and leaned back in his chair. "Look, let me put this as simply as I can—I've spent the last few years trying to put all that business about Iraq out of my mind. Sometimes it would show up unannounced, give me headaches and cause dreams that weren't so nice. I don't want to talk about it. I don't want to answer a lot of questions about it."

She swallowed. "Perfectly understandable," she finally said, her voice soft.

"If that's what you came here for, you wasted your time," he informed her.

She lifted a spoonful of soup to her lips, looking into the mug. "I didn't waste my time."

"What did your family say about this thing you did? Looking for me like this?"

She gave a little shrug. "My sister didn't like it much…"

"Didn't like it? Much?"

Marcie took a breath. "She said it was foolish and reckless. That I had no idea what I was getting into. That I didn't know you."

"Well, she's right about that," he said.

"Technically," Marcie agreed. "I couldn't be sure what you would be like now, but I couldn't believe you'd changed that much. And see—I was right. You turned out to be a nice guy."

He snorted.

"We could talk about other things." She touched the

book that sat on the table, gave it a close look. "Like what you're reading. You go to the library?"

"It's free," he said dismissively. "I use the old library card that was left behind by the man who lived here before. No one questions that, though I'm sure they know. But I'm regular and never late, so it doesn't matter to anyone."

"That's something you could tell me about. The man who lived here before. Dr. Mullins said you took care of him."

Ian took a couple more bites. "After a while. First he took care of me, in a way."

She waited, but nothing came.

"In what way?" she asked.

He lifted his mug and drained it of soup, putting it back on the table. "I was camping on his land and he spotted me. He was old—older than dirt. Didn't have hardly a tooth left in his head, skinny as a pole. He'd been out here, alone, long over fifty years with no wife, no family, and he found me asleep in my sleeping bag under about four inches of snow. And he kicked me."

"He *kicked* you?" she repeated, appalled.

"Kicked me, and I jumped a foot. And he said, 'So, you're not dead yet. Good thing, because you'd just be food for the wildlife if you were—I sure as hell can't bury you. Ground's too hard and I'm too old.' That was our introduction. After a little glaring back and forth, he said that if I wanted, I could sleep indoors and eat from his cupboard if I'd keep the stove fed and help out when he needed it. I wasn't thinking real clear back then and didn't have a lot of options. I hadn't even thought about winter at five thousand feet. I froze my ass off for a couple more nights before knocking on his door and all he said was, ''Bout time. I figured you were dead.' It was a pretty simple arrangement. We hardly talked."

"Ever?" she asked.

"After a month or two conversation picked up, but not a lot. He'd been alone so long, he didn't much care to talk, kind of like me." He added a brief glare. But then he went on. "So I chopped wood, caught fish sometimes and used his rifle to shoot a bird or rabbit now and then. I kept the snow off his roof and the shed and the outhouse roof and drove the truck for him when he went for errands, like to pick up his social security check and to buy food. We ran out of firewood pretty quick and I had to chop more. I wasn't even sure how much of this land was his, but it's all trees and you can't see a neighbor. First tree I cut down damn near hit the house. He talked then—I thought he'd never shut the hell up. Then a few months later, we went for supplies and to the post office and he took me to the library and told me to pick out a book if I felt like it. He checked out picture books and sometimes children's books—small words and big print. I never asked but I don't think he got much school. When the weather warmed, he told me where he wanted the garden, made me re-dig the outhouse and showed me the tools in the shed. He said if I chopped enough wood in spring and summer and cured it, I could sell firewood out of the back of the truck if I wanted to. I got right on it, having no other way to earn money. That's just about the whole story."

"Must have been a little miserable—living with someone like that," she said.

"I've had experience with mean old men," Ian said unemotionally.

She finished her mug of soup and he shot to his feet to refill both their mugs. "Just half," she said, nibbling on the bread.

"Listen, eat as much as you'll hold. I think you lost a little flesh…"

"Yeah, maybe," she said. "But I lose weight real easy. I know I get skinny and looking kind of malnourished if I don't watch it."

"And you haven't been watching it," he said.

"Well, I was saving money for gas," she said softly.

"Did you just say you were saving money for gas? Looking for me?"

She looked up. "Have you noticed the price of gas lately?"

"Holy God," he said, shaking his head. "While you're here—you eat. There's bread, peanut butter, juice, fruit, jelly—"

"So, he got sick, didn't he?" she went on, interrupting him. "So I bet that was just the beginning of the story, you living here for chores."

"It just kind of happened," he said with a shrug. "I can't say we ever did get chummy—but I owed him for the roof over my head and brought in more than my share of food. When he got sick, I went for the doctor. It was a lesson—when people out here get sick, they don't go for tests and such, not if they're in their late eighties for sure. The old doc told Raleigh…that was his name, Raleigh… Doc Mullins said he could take him to Valley Hospital and medicare would take care of him and Raleigh said he'd shoot himself in the head first. It was settled that fast. Doc left some medicine and came back a few times. Then after about six months of that, Raleigh died in his sleep, and I went and got the doctor. He showed me that Raleigh had dictated him a note while he was sick that said, 'The man, Ian Buchanan, can have the house, truck, land and any money left, minus what's needed for burial. No tombstone.' He signed it, in his way, and Doc Mullins witnessed. I didn't think it would hold up. There was just about enough cash in that tin box to bury him real simple like he wanted. When I asked the old doc what I was supposed to do about the cabin and land and truck, he said, don't borrow trouble."

She laughed outright. "Now what does that mean?"

"I took it to mean I should just carry on and not pursue the matter, but in fact old Doc Mullins has a friend who's a lawyer or judge or something and he had done the transfer of title on the deed, so old Raleigh died penniless in my care and there was no probate. Slick as snot," he said. Then he looked up and said, "Sorry." He cleared his throat. "I looked at the truck title and when I saw he'd signed it over—or Doc had—I got the plates in my name so I wouldn't end up in jail. I keep up my driver's license and that's the total extent of my official paperwork. When the taxes come due on this property, I pay them with a money order."

"Ian," she said, momentarily surprised. "Do you own a mountain?"

"A mountain full of nothing. Logging's prohibited up here. I have what I've always had—a cabin and some trees. And taxes. I manage, but it costs more than it yields most of the time. It still seems temporary. It could always just go away the first time I don't make the taxes."

"And if the day ever comes you can't stay here anymore? Because it's not permanent enough?"

He shrugged. "I guess I'll have to think of something."

She was quiet while she finished her soup. Then she said, "When he was sick, was he very sick? Did you have to care for him a lot?"

"I'd have to say, he was very sick. He didn't get out of bed much for a long time. There used to be a small bed in here—a bunk bed, just the bottom, with a mattress so thin it was almost no mattress at all. He had some of those old-age problems. He couldn't feed himself. Et cetera. When he passed, I burned the whole thing."

"And you slept on the couch until I came?"

"I've never slept on that couch—it's too short and it sags under me. I unroll a pallet by the stove—it's exactly the way I want it. I could buy a used bed, if that's what I wanted."

"But it was hard work, Ian—caring for someone you barely knew. He must have been grateful—he left you all this."

He roared with totally facetious laughter. He wiped his hairy mouth on his sleeve and said, "All this? Mother of God, I don't even have something you can flush!"

"Is it because you can't?" she asked him.

"When I showed up at his door, there was no Coleman stove—he lit the place with lanterns. Washed out of a bucket, when he washed. I added the generator, strung some lights, bought the tub, the stove. Some of the furniture was older than him and I brought in a new couch and chair. Well, they're used, but better than what was here. The only thing I really miss is a shower—but I'd have no idea how to plumb a house."

She let him finish laughing and when he was done, she said, "You know, that first night? When you snarled at me and tried to scare me? Well—you scared me pretty good—"

"Couldn't scare any brains into you, though," he interrupted.

"Well, that's more my problem than yours. When I get my mind made up about something, it's hard to move me in any direction. But when I went to my car to eat the packed lunch I had, while the sun was setting and the snow started to fall, I thought I'd never in my life seen a more beautiful place. There was a rainbow in the snow! And I wasn't afraid, because it was just pristine and glorious. You can have all the extras in the world in the city, but this is something you just can't buy."

He was quiet for a minute. Then he said, "You know what Bobby said about you? He said you were a real pistol."

She watched his eyes. "That's almost talking about it," she said.

"Then pretend I didn't say anything. You should be in bed."

"When was the last time you slept?" she asked him.

"I should pull out my pallet, and you should be asleep again," he said. "Besides, this is more talking than I'm used to and I think I'm worn out."

"All right," she said. She stood from her chair and looked down at the book. "Thomas Jefferson?" she asked. "Did you ever read John Adams?"

He nodded.

"Me too. I loved that book. What I loved was Abigail—she was amazing. Old John left her with a farm, children, very little money in a country in revolution and she did it all. She was my idol. If I could be anyone, I'd be Abigail Adams."

"Because she did it all?" he asked.

"Because she was glad to do it all and never complained, that's how committed she was to what John was doing. I know—as a woman, a feminist, I'm not supposed to admire a woman who'd do all that for a man, but she was doing it for herself. As if that was the contribution she could make to the founding of America. And they wrote each other letters—not just romantic, loving letters, but letters asking each other for advice. They were first good friends, two people who respected each other's brains, and then obviously lovers, since they had a slew of kids. True partners, long before true partners were fashionable. And she—"

"I like biographies," he said, cutting her off as though he'd heard enough about Abigail. "Don't ask me why, I couldn't tell you."

She went to her couch and pulled off her boots. "Maybe you like figuring out why peoples' lives turn out the way they do. It's always a mystery, isn't it?"

He pumped some water into the sink and cleaned up the mugs and spoons. Then he covered the pot of soup, not responding.

"Hey—you don't have a refrigerator..."

"I have a shed," he said. "It'll keep some food cold enough for another day. Can't keep eggs or milk—they'll freeze. But if the soup freezes, we'll thaw it and cook it again."

"A shed for a refrigerator," she said, lying back on the sofa. "Is the truck loaded for morning?"

He nodded. "If I'm gone when you wake up, you think you'll be okay to walk out back on your own? Because there's always the blue pot..."

"If I'm shaky, I'll take advantage of the blue pot—but really, I'm feeling very much better. Just a little tired."

"Besides bread, peanut butter, honey and juice in here, there's also lots of stuff in cans you can open. Beans and soup," he said. "I'll probably be back and forth some tomorrow, loading and delivering." Then he headed out the door with his big pot of chicken soup.

"Thank you, Ian. For taking such good care of me. I know I'm a terrible imposition."

He didn't say anything, but he did stop in the doorway for a moment before going out.

She settled back on the couch. It wasn't much, this little

cabin. It was less than not much—it was stark and only the most absolutely necessary things were supplied. But considering she'd finally found him, it was extremely comfortable for her. If it was her cabin, she'd have soup bowls and plates, better furniture, an indoor biffy. She remembered Mel's words, "I have to ask him, in case his means are slim…" Really, there was no telling about that. Oh, he seemed to have very little money, but who knew how much of this mountain had been left to him and whether it was worth anything? It could be it was a little patch of worthless land. Or maybe it was vast and he had no idea the value. He didn't seem real focused on that.

She loved that he knew how to get by like this—and that he'd be willing to let her stay when she was so dependent. And there was also the fact she represented the very thing he was determined to forget, the past he was running from.

When he came back, he fed the fire, rolled out his pallet, turned off the light and laid down. After several minutes of quiet darkness, she heard his voice. "Sorry if I scared you. I don't roar that often."

A slow smile spread on her lips and she snuggled in under the old quilt, more content than she'd been in a while.

In the morning when she woke, Ian and the truck were gone. She pulled on her jeans and boots and headed for the loo. Halfway there, she heard a cry and looked up to see the soaring beauty of an American Eagle.

Over the next couple of days, Marcie got lots of sleep. Not only was she fighting off that flu, but there was absolutely nothing to do. Ian would come home in early afternoon and be busy with his chores, his work. He'd always bring a little food with him and simmer something for evening, like kidney beans and a ham shank or canned tomatoes thickened with paste for a kind of red sauce to pour over noodles.

He'd split some logs, reload his truck for the next day, work outside, then come in and wash up at the sink. She'd wake from a long nap to find he'd changed into indoor clothes—sweats, socks and a T-shirt.

One afternoon she rolled over on the couch, opened her eyes and saw him naked as he stood at the sink. She blinked a couple of times, taking in his lean, muscular back complete with ponytail that hung down right between his shoulder blades, his long legs and tight butt before she realized he was bathing. He was rubbing a soapy cloth under one arm, then around his neck. With a shriek of embarrassment, she rolled over and faced the back of the couch. He never said a word, but she heard his deep chuckle; it rumbled in her mind for hours. And when they sat at the table together for dinner, her face was as red as the tomato sauce on her noodles. That she should be surprised to catch him washing more than his hands was silly—after all, he smelled good; he kept himself clean. He had to do it sometime and some*where.* It wasn't as though he could excuse himself and go to the powder room. She managed to wash her face and brush her teeth while he was away, but he had no other choice—she was a fixture on his lumpy couch.

It might've been nice if he'd awakened her to say, "I'm getting naked to wash now, so if you don't want to be embarrassed, close your eyes." But then, no—Ian wouldn't do that. It was his cabin. And he was a man. It had always intrigued her the way men could stalk around naked, proud as lions, completely unconcerned about being seen, judged.

They ate at the table together in the evening, talked a little bit, but not so much. When dinner was over he'd say, "I usually turn in right after dinner; the day starts real early for me."

And although she'd have slept away most of the day, she found that, after a while of lying on the couch in the warm, dark cabin, she'd nod off again and not wake until he was gone the next morning.

Their dinner conversations were a wonderful diversion for her, and sometimes she could get him to talk about things she'd been wondering about for too long, but there was always a line she didn't dare cross. When she started to tell him about Bobby's large and devoted family, he pinched his eyes closed briefly, just enough of a message to say that he couldn't go there. The whole Fallujah event that left Bobby physically disabled and Ian emotionally crippled was off-limits.

"I visited your father," she bravely told him over dinner. Ian's brown eyes lifted and the amber in them sparkled. "He's very sick," Marcie said.

Ian just looked down at his plate and shoveled more hamburger gravy and boiled potatoes into his mouth.

"He's not particularly friendly," she courageously pointed out.

Ian chuckled and it was an unmistakably sardonic tone. "He isn't now, is he?"

"I assumed it's because of age, illness—"

"Don't assume. He's never been easy."

"I thought maybe because he's unwell—"

Ian's eyes snapped up, angry. "My father and I have never been close. Mostly because of that unfriendly nature."

She took a couple of bites that were hard to swallow. "I thought you'd want to know."

He took a breath and she could tell it took effort to keep his voice even. "Listen, he's not worried about me, all right? It's not keeping him up nights wondering where I am. What I'm doing with myself."

"But if he's just not well—"

"Marcie. My mom died when I was twenty. I checked in regularly to see if the old man was all right, but the fact is, he didn't write or call for seven years. *Seven.*"

She swallowed hard. "But you called him?"

"Yeah," he said, looking back to his plate, scooping up some food. "Yeah."

"That must have hurt."

There was a long moment of silence. "Maybe when I was younger," was all he said.

"What an old fool," she muttered, digging back into her own plate, angrily. "The idiot." She took a couple more bites, small ones. "I'm sorry I brought it up."

After a moment, Ian said, "You didn't know."

"Well, all I can say is, *his loss.* That's all."

Again, there was quiet. Ian scraped the last of his food off his plate. Then he rose and began to rinse the dishes in the sink. Finally the words came that ended the talk for the evening. "Time for bed."

Marcie was on her fourth day at Ian's. Her cough was still hanging on but she was feeling very much better—enough so that the boredom was getting to her. She rose after Ian was gone, ate bread and honey, walked out back to the facilities, drank the lukewarm coffee Ian had left sitting on the woodstove, and tried reading some of his library book. She had no idea what time it was when she walked out back again.

The air was clear and crisp, the sky blue, the ground covered with a couple of inches of packed snow. She hadn't even bothered to pull on her jeans, though she *had* put on her jacket. Her legs were bare between her calf-high boots and thigh-long flannel shirt. She might have wandered around a bit, but the woods were so dense beyond his lot, she was a little afraid of getting lost. A trip to the john was about all she dared.

She was near the outhouse door when she heard a noise and the hair on the back of her neck crinkled up. She turned to see an animal standing right between two big trees at the tree line. As she stared, wide-eyed, the animal crouched and hissed, baring its fangs. It was some sort of big cat. It looked like a small jungle cat—a tawny and unspotted animal. She'd never seen anything like it except in a zoo; it was as big as a good-sized golden retriever. She glanced at the cabin, at the outhouse. And then the cat darted across the yard.

In two long strides Marcie dashed into the outhouse, slamming the door. She sat down on the seat just to get her wits. There was a bang on the door as if the beast had hurled himself at it, then came a scratching and a snarling. Oh shit, she thought—he's out there, after me! Waiting for me!

Well, it was cold, but it was probably better to freeze to death than to be mauled by some mysterious wild cat. So she stood up, lowered the seat—which was just an old Home Depot toilet seat, and tried to get comfortable, though the cold seeped through that flannel shirt pretty quickly, freezing her buns. Stupid not to even put her jeans on for this trek, but then she hadn't been expecting company. She glanced at her wrist—of course she hadn't even been wearing her watch.

The fact was, she'd been living in one of Ian's flannel

shirts for four days, sleeping in it, eating in it, wandering out to the loo in it, with only her boots in addition. She ran a hand over her head; it felt as though her naturally curly, bright copper hair was standing on end, big as a house. She'd managed a little teeth brushing and panty changing, but other than that, nothing. She must look like a vagrant. A homeless person hiding out in Ian's outhouse.

She glanced at her naked wrist again and shivered. She started counting in her head to mark the passing of the minutes. How long does a small lion wait for his prey? He had a coat, so they weren't matched opponents. She started thinking; if she opened the door and he was nowhere to be seen, could she make the mad dash for the cabin? But first, she should do what she came to do, so she wouldn't have to use the little blue pot.

Task finished, she sat a few minutes longer, very quietly. Then she sheepishly opened the outhouse door, cursing the squeaking hinges as she stuck her head out. She saw nothing, so she took a careful step outside. She heard a hiss and snarl and saw the cat lurking around the shed, twenty feet away. She retreated, slamming the door. "Shit," she said aloud. "Shit, shit, shit!"

So she brought up her feet so that her heels rested on the seat and pulled the huge flannel shirt over her knees, hugging them. There was nothing in the outhouse with which to defend herself. In fact, there was also no reading material—not even a truck or sports magazine. Leave it to Ian—bare to the bone. No extras. He didn't even keep a book in the house unless it came from the library. After a little while, she began to shake with cold. It didn't help that she began coughing, even though she tried to control it, stop it, muffle it; the big cat could probably hear her and know his prey was still alive, trapped.

So be it. She would freeze to death. She didn't remember anything from the last time she nearly froze to death. Remembering nothing implied it was painless.

Then she heard the sound of Ian's truck come up the road. There was no mistaking that engine; it was rough and growly. She sprang to her feet, because suddenly her only thought was that Ian could be attacked by the feline beast that waited for her. She pressed her ear against the rough wooden door. She heard nothing until the screech of Ian's truck door opening. She flung the door to the outhouse open and yelled, "Ian! Look out! There's a—"

She was cut off by the snarl and lunge of the cat at the door. She ducked in quickly with a scream, inexplicably happy that the cat had come after her and not gone after an unprepared Ian.

So, she thought, *here we are. I'm trapped in the john and he's trapped in either the truck or the cabin. And it's colder than hell. Great. And to think I was wishing for a microwave.*

But only seconds seemed to have passed before there was a huge blast that caused her to sit up straight and catch her breath. Then the outhouse door opened sharply, and Ian stood there with a startled look on his face and a big gun in his hand. "How long have you been in here?" he asked.

"I have no idea," she said. "I think maybe d-d-days."

He got a sheepish look on his face. "You about done in here?" he asked.

She burst into laughter, which brought another coughing spasm, then laughter again. "Yes, Ian," she finally said. "I've widdled and wiped. Can I please go home now?"

"Home? Marcie—that car of yours—"

"The cabin, Ian." She laughed. "Jesus, do you have no sense of humor?"

"That wasn't so funny. I can't imagine what he was doing around here. I don't keep food out or small livestock..."

"He was hanging around the shed. You think maybe he likes chicken soup?"

"I've never had a problem like that before. That's bold, getting out where people can see him, challenge him—"

"What the hell *was* that?"

"Puma," he said. "Mountain lion."

"I *knew* that was a lion." She stopped suddenly. "You didn't hurt him, did you?"

"Marcie, he wanted to *eat* you! Are you worried about his soul or something?"

"I just wanted him to go away," she said. "I didn't want him to go dead."

"I just scared him off. Listen," he said, walking her quickly to the cabin, "if it had been down to you or him, could you have shot him?"

"No," she said.

"No?" he asked.

"Well, I've never fired a gun, so I don't like my chances. If I'd had a big gun like that in my hands I could've probably shot you or the cabin or shot the crap out of that outhouse..." She burst into laughter at her pun. "But he was way smaller. You have a frying pan, right? A big iron one, right?"

"What for?"

"So, in future, I can get to the bathroom with some protection. I was once a very good hitter in softball."

He stopped walking and looked down at her. "Jesus, there's always the blue pot."

"Yeah, but there are some things a lady will risk her life to keep private."

He smiled. He actually smiled. "Is that so?"

Six

The very next day when Ian came home, he caught Marcie standing at the sink in his flannel shirt and calf-high boots. No pants. Panties maybe; he tried not to think about that. She was rubbing her face with a washcloth, and her hair was so bushy it looked like a clown's wig. He put the sack on the table. "Feeling better?" he asked.

"I must be," she said. "I'd kill for clean hair."

"You want to wash your hair?"

"It was tempting, but I didn't know if a cold, wet head was the best idea. The water out of this pump is freezing."

He chuckled. "I can't believe you've been here for days and haven't figured out much. Not like you to not pay attention to details, is it? So. Good day for bath day," he said.

"Have you had a bath since I've been here?" she asked.

"I admit, I've been putting that off, making do with a pot of hot soapy water at the sink, but not just because you're here. Have you noticed, it's a little cold?"

"I saw the tub of course, but I couldn't imagine how..."

He just shook his head. "You're right, you're not used

to roughing it. Here's how it's going to work—I'll put a big pot of water on the woodstove, feed it real good so we get the room nice and warm. I'll get another one going on the Coleman stove—that goes a lot faster—and we'll fill the sink with hot water for your hair and while we're taking care of that, get a second one going on the Coleman. By the time your hair is clean, we'll have two pots of near-boiling water for the tub. I'll add some cold from the pump and you take a little dip. Can't screw around—I can't get the tub full. If I just keep heating and adding water, by the time I get a boiling pot, the one in the tub has already turned cold. So it's a shallow bath, but it's warm and gets the job done."

"Wow," she said. "That's sure generous, that you'd do all that for me..."

"For us, Marcie. I'll get a bath after you. And tomorrow I'll stop at the coin laundry and wash up the dirty clothes. I'll take any of yours you'd like me to. Just because you haven't been feeling too good..."

She shifted from foot to foot, chewing on her lower lip.

"What's the matter? You don't want a bath?"

"I'd die for a bath," she said. "It's just that.... I couldn't help but notice, there doesn't seem to be a separate room with a door that closes... And I also noticed that doesn't seem to bother you too much."

The corners of his lips lifted. "I'll load the truck with tomorrow's wood while you have your bath," he finally said.

She thought about this for a second. "And I could sit in my car during your bath?" she suggested.

"I don't think so—your car is almost an igloo now. Just a little white mound. Not to mention mountain lions."

"Well, what am I supposed to do?"

"Well, you can take a nap, read a little of my book, or close your eyes. Or you could stare—get the thrill of your life."

She put her hands on her hips. "You really wouldn't care, would you?"

"Not really. A bath is a serious business when it's that much trouble. And it's pretty quick in winter." He started to chuckle.

"What's so funny?" she asked, a little irritated.

"I was just thinking. It's cold enough in here, you might not see that much."

Her cheeks went hot, so she pretended not to understand. "But in summer, you can lay in the tub all afternoon?"

"In summer, I wash in the creek." He grinned at her. "Why don't you comb the snarls out of your hair? You look like a wild banshee."

She stared at him a minute, then said, "Don't flirt with me. It won't do you any good." Then she coughed for him, a long string of deep croaks that reminded them both she had had a good, solid flu. Also, it covered what happened to be amused laughter from him.

While he pumped water into a big pot, he said, "Take your medicine. That sounds just god-awful. And I, for sure, don't want it."

It took a good thirty minutes to get the sink full of warm water. She was rolling up the sleeves of the overlong shirt, turning under the collar to keep it from getting wet, and grabbed the shampoo out of her duffel. He held out his hand. "What?" she said.

"Put your head in the sink," he said. "I'll do it."

"Why?"

"Because it'll be hard for you to know if the soap's out. It'll be faster and easier if I just do it for you."

She picked up the towel he'd laid out on the short counter, pressed it against her face and bent at the waist, dipping her head in the warm water. She could feel him use a cup to wet her hair, then begin to gently lather it. Those big calloused hands were slow and gentle, his fingertips kneading her scalp in a fabulous massage. She enjoyed it with her eyes closed, trying not to moan in pleasure. Finally she said, "You aren't going to offer to shave my legs for me, too, are you?"

His hands suddenly stopped moving. There was a stillness and a silence for such a drawn out moment, she wondered if she had somehow offended him. "Marcie," he finally said. "Why in the *world* would you shave your legs?"

"They're *hairy!*"

"So *what?* Who's gonna care?"

She thought about this for a second. She was on the top of a mountain in the middle of nowhere with a man who looked like Grizzly Adams in a place that didn't even have indoor plumbing. Why *would* she shave her legs? And armpits? Finally, in a little voice, she said, "I would."

He just let his breath out in a long sigh. Then he began rinsing her hair.

While she was towel drying her hair, he pulled a clean shirt from his trunk and handed it to her. This time it was an old soft denim one with fraying around the cuffs and collar and mismatched buttons. "You better wear this," he said. "That plaid flannel is about ready to walk to the laundry and throw itself in." When he turned away, she pulled it out and surreptitiously sniffed it herself.

"Smart-ass," she muttered under her breath.

Once the tub was poured and he'd refilled the big pots for his own bath, setting them to heat, he left her. She could hear the whistling and thumping of logs while she did, indeed, shave her legs. And armpits. The whistling wasn't just meaningless tweeting—he was gifted. The melody was clear, twirls and whorls and everything. She longed for the singing, but today, he just whistled.

When he came back inside, she was wearing the fresh shirt. She puzzled over the mismatched buttons, then realized he must replace buttons as he lost them, keeping even his oldest clothes as functional as possible for as long as he could. A very peculiar man. He lived in such a rustic, gone-to-the-devil lifestyle—his hair and beard gone mad—yet he seemed to take such jealous care of old, worn clothing.

To her surprise, he aped her routine exactly, leaning into the sink to suds his hair and beard while a second and third pot of water cooked, except he accomplished it bare-chested. She tried to read his library book while he did this, but she found herself continually peeking around the covers to get a good view of that broad expanse of back, that firm male butt. He kept the fitness of his body pretty-much concealed under his clothing, but really, he had the body of a god. Small wonder he'd be built so powerful, with the work he did. He chopped down trees and split logs all the time, loaded at least a cord of wood a day into his truck, then unloaded it when he delivered it—he was cut like a wrestler on steroids.

When she'd caught sight of him before, she'd whirled away too quickly to appreciate his physique. Given the fact that his hair and beard were so thick and full, she was expecting a gorilla with hair on his back. But, no—there was just a hairy chest that was broad and hard, biceps like small melons, back wide and muscled, waist narrow. He had tattoos on each upper arm—an eagle on the right, a banner that said USMC on the left.

He slicked back the hair on his head, retied it, and combed through his beard with an old brush while his bath water heated. She finally understood the reason for all the big pots stacked beside the kitchen cabinet—not for cooking big meals since there was but one resident, but for heating water.

He obviously trimmed his ponytail and beard occasionally. She just wondered, did he ever trim it enough to make a real difference, or did he let it go crazy and sometimes lop off an inch or two from the bottom? His hair and beard were both plentiful and thick with lots of curls, the hair on his head light brown and on his chin, reddish-brown. With those brown eyebrows, which were healthy, if he frowned, he looked beastly.

Maybe this was all just part of his hiding. Tucked away in the mountains, incognito behind that uncanny red beard and thick brown hair.

She plopped herself on the sofa with his book on her raised knees. When he dumped the water into the tub and began to unbuckle his belt, she sank into the sofa and put the book right over her face, blinding her against an accidental glance at more of him. She heard him chuckle lightly right before he said, "I'll tell you when I'm done." She heard the splashing and swishing of the water, and not ten minutes later he said, "I'm done." But she gave him an extra couple of minutes. He was just contrary enough to trick her.

When he gathered up the dirty clothes and stuffed them into a laundry bag, she turned over a couple of pair of jeans, four pair of socks, two sweatshirts and some sweatpants. She kept her undergarments to herself. When he left the next morning, she placed a big pot of water on top of the wood-burning stove and, when it was finally just a bit more than warm, she washed out her own underwear in the sink and draped her panties and bras along the rim of the tub to dry in front of the stove. When driven to the outhouse by sheer urgent need, she carried the big iron skillet. If that beast showed up again, teeth bared, she'd knock him into the middle of next week. She might not be a hunter, but she'd been a damn fine softball player in her day. Then, tired and coughing, she took her medicine and napped.

He came in carrying a long, rectangular cardboard box inside of which were neatly folded clothes. He put it down on one of his trunks and lifted a pair of panties off the rim of the tub. "I hope you're starting to feel better," he said. "I don't think I'm up to a lot of this. Old Raleigh is probably spinning in his grave…"

And she bolted off the couch, snatched up her dainties and tucked them into her duffel even though they weren't entirely dry.

That night's dinner was boiled potatoes, a few fresh, soft-cooked eggs and some thick chunks of ham. And then they talked a little as they ate: about his day, his customers and routine, but afterward, before she could sneak up on the subjects that brought her here, he said it was time for quiet so that he could read a little and sleep. She granted this without argument—he'd lived alone for a long time and it didn't mean he was unkind or cruel.

She began to relish the small things—his occasional subdued laughter. No one could call it an actual laugh, but he did cave into amusement if she shot him a smart-ass comment. He smiled at her from time to time—behind that bushy red-brown beard he had beautiful, healthy teeth.

But she was getting lonely. She wondered if she could wait out his silence.

One afternoon, she witnessed a most remarkable thing. He had been whistling while piling his wood in the truck and had finally started to sing, quietly at first and then louder, that incredible voice just making her heart flutter. Suddenly all sound stopped; no more logs, no more singing. And yet the door didn't open. At first, she thought he'd made a pass by the outhouse, but time stretched out. Finally, she stepped out the front door and quietly looked around the side of the cabin. She saw Ian out by the shed. He was standing in front of a very large buck with a huge, beautiful rack that must span over three feet. His hand was out and the buck seemed to be eating out of it; Ian was talking softly to the deer, stroking its jaw with the other hand.

She was frozen in the moment, silently watching as Ian and the deer, like best friends, spent this quiet, companionable time together. There was a kindness in this man that calmed the most skittish of wildlife. Would she ever be in touch with that side of his nature, she wondered? Did he only roar at people who frightened him?

She had frightened him with the past when she arrived. She'd been very careful not to do that again. A little time, a little more trust, and she would sneak up on those old issues carefully. The last thing she wanted was to hurt him. She knew that he was a good person.

How could a father have turned a cold shoulder to this man? she asked herself. *How?*

The deer took a couple of steps back, turned, and pranced back into the trees. Ian turned back to his work and caught sight of her standing there. He walked over to her.

"You saw my buddy, Buck," he said. "I keep an apple in my pocket when I work outside. Sometimes he shows up. If the apple starts to get soft before he comes, I eat it."

"How do you do that?" Marcie asked, entranced.

"It's not a trick. I found him when he was young. He was nicked by a hunter's bullet, separated from his mother, all spooked and confused and bleeding. So I kind of caught him. The old man, Raleigh, he said his eyes weren't any good anymore and he couldn't do anything, but I could do something about that wound, take care of him, give him a couple of apples and let him go. Which is what I did. I closed him in the shed, fed and watered him, gave him apples and when he was fine, I turned him loose. That's all."

"And he comes back?"

"Not regularly. I'm just happy he hasn't told his friends."

Marcie put her hand against her chest, touched. "Ian, that's incredible."

"Don't get sloppy, Marcie. If I had a freezer, I might shoot him."

"You *wouldn't!*"

He smiled at her. "I like venison. Don't you?"

She thought about that chili Jack had given her, how it melted in her mouth. But she said, "Not that much!" And she whirled and went into the house, his amused laughter at her back.

Midmorning, Marcie heard an engine and knew it wasn't Ian; the motor was too smooth. She opened the cabin door and saw the nurse, Mel, get out of a big Hummer with her bag in hand. "Well, hello," Mel said. "You must be feeling better."

"Much, thanks," Marcie said. "Alone this time?"

Mel came up to the door. "I thought I'd just drop by, see how you're doing."

Marcie laughed at her. "You don't just stop in here. I

remember how hard this place was to find. Come in. I'm afraid I can't fix tea and cookies."

"Marcie—I talked with your sister. I thought maybe I should tell you about it."

"Oh, God. Was she mean as a badger about this? Did she totally freak out?"

Mel chuckled a little. "Totally? No. But she has some strong opinions where this visit is concerned. I'll tell you how it went."

Marcie threw her arm toward the table with the two chairs and Mel took one. She got right to the point. "I think I did what you asked. I told her you had found Ian Buchanan, you were visiting with him, planned to stay a while and would call her when you were in town next. I honestly don't think I got out much more than that. She wanted to know why, if you found him and talked to him, you're not on your way home."

"Oh, holy cow. No—holy sister." Marcie put her head in her hand. "Well, because I got sick, but I wouldn't want her to know that. She might come up here with an ambulance. She can move mountains when she wants to. Mobilizing the National Guard wouldn't be impossible for Erin."

"I kind of got that impression."

"But this flu turns out to be a blessing. Because Ian's very slow to get close, and he's awful used to not having anyone to talk to. Just being here for a few days has gotten him used to me a little. We've nibbled around the edges of our individual lives without talking about things like the war, my late husband Bobby, what drove him to leave the Marines, his hometown, all that. But I'm getting closer. Because he's stuck with me, we've been getting acquainted. Reacquainted really—we were in touch right after Bobby was hurt—briefly. So, I'm trying to build trust and friendship. One of these days he's going to really talk to me."

"And?"

Marcie shrugged. "Mel, I don't know why I had to do this—come here like this. It was just something I couldn't live without doing. When I understand the man who saved my husband's life—"

"Wait a minute," Mel said. "He saved your husband's life?"

"Uh-huh," Marcie said. "Didn't I tell Jack that?"

"I guess not. At least Jack never mentioned it."

"Well, he did. He risked his life to save Bobby and was injured himself in the process. It's not Ian's fault Bobby lived with terrible disabilities. I appreciate that he did everything he could. I don't know if you can understand this, but despite the fact that Bobby might have lived too long in a dysfunctional body, with no concept of what was happening around him, I got to—" Marcie glanced away, swallowed back tears and said, so softly, "I was with him a little longer. I'm very grateful for the time I had with him. Unfair as that might seem to Bobby."

Mel took a deep breath. Jack was her second husband; she'd been widowed when she lost her first husband to a violent crime. She wasn't even tempted to explain the details at the moment. Instead she put her hand on Marcie's arm and said, "I understand completely."

"There are other things. The way Bobby felt about Ian—how much he admired him, for one thing. Bobby thought Ian was the greatest man ever, he wanted to be like him. And this great man—he ran away from everything and everybody. It doesn't add up. And then there's something so silly—baseball cards. They both collected baseball cards ever since they were boys and while they were sitting in the desert on the lookout for bombs and snipers, they talked about those stupid baseball cards. There are things I want to know. You see?"

Mel smiled. "I see," she said quietly.

"I tried to explain all this to Erin, but she doesn't get it. I think it's because I'm her first concern. All she thinks about is keeping me safe and from getting hurt any more than I've been over the last few years. I know Ian might never open up to me—I have to be prepared for that. He's been very blunt—he doesn't want to talk about any of it. Whatever happened left a very big hole in his heart."

"Okay," Mel said, leaning her elbows on the table. "I don't have a lot of experience with this sort of thing, but I do have a little. I have myself a marine who's been to war way too much and he has a shaky, vulnerable side. I don't know all the triggers. I wouldn't want you at risk when you finally decide to confront these things—"

"He's not going to snap," Marcie said. "In fact, I don't think he even realizes it, but he is *not* a tortured man. Maybe he was a few years ago, and maybe those memories are still disturbing, but now he's just a man who lives in the mountains…in a simplified life…and he lives alone. It's less complicated than it seems. At least, that's my opinion."

"I know. He sings," Mel said with a smile.

"It's not just that. He talks to me about other things. About the old man who gave him the cabin, about the deer that comes visiting. He washed my hair for me. He heated water so I could take a bath. He goes to the library and he reads every day—he doesn't read books about how to build bombs or make poisons—he has a big stack of biographies. He's intelligent. Has a sense of humor he doesn't really want me to see—I'm sure he thinks I'll get the misguided impression he's enjoying me."

"Still—"

"No, he's not on a hair-trigger," Marcie said, shaking her head. "For some reason he thinks being alone is better for him… Eventually I'll figure that out."

"Marcie, I think your sister has run out of time on this. She suggested she should come up here and get you."

Marcie stiffened. "Did you tell her not to?"

"I told her I saw you myself and that you were fine. But I lied when I said that, you weren't fine. You had a fever, a cough, and—"

"And I was being taken care of! I'm fine! My legs are even shaved!" Mel straightened up with a questioning look on her face. "It was a joke—I wanted to shave my legs and he wondered why that would matter out here, in the woods. But they're shaved, damn it!"

Mel smiled. "You're comfortable?" she asked.

"Hell, there's no refrigerator or indoor plumbing," Marcie said. "Ian's gone from before six in the morning till early afternoon and then he reloads his truck, so I don't see him until dinnertime. He always cooks something and we talk during dinner, which is early, and then he likes it quiet so he can just read his book and go to sleep, like he's always done. I'm lonesome and I want to watch *Medium*, and *Men in Trees*. I want my favorite CD's and DVD's—I used to watch *Love Actually* once a month. Comfortable? I'm getting by—better than when I was looking for him and sleeping in my car, but—"

"You were sleeping in your car?" Mel asked, aghast.

"Well, I was running low on money. And I hadn't found him. We shouldn't tell Erin about that…"

"That's not exactly medical business," Mel warned.

"I bet it is, somehow. I bet it helped get me sick!"

Mel just smiled. She reached down and picked up her bag. "Can I take your temperature, look in your throat, hear your chest?"

"Yeah, sure… I can't seem to shake the cough, but I feel pretty good."

Mel got busy. While she was giving Marcie a once-over, she said, "I think you should tell Ian you have to make a phone call. Talk to your sister yourself."

"I can drive. I'll just go into—"

"You have snow tires or chains?"

"Well—no, but—"

"Ohhhh, Marcie. That little VW of yours would slip right off the mountain real easy. We've had snow up here since you arrived, and a bit lower, some rain. You just don't have the weight or traction. Until we dry up a little, get a lift into town in something heavy—like that big, old truck of Ian's. Or, you can tell me when you'd like a trip to town and I'll come and get you—but, believe me, it's a crazy notion to drive that VW into town. It could be disastrous. Besides, it appears to be buried…"

"Okay, sure. Maybe I'll talk to him about that in the next day or two…"

"You're definitely on the mend, my girl. I don't think you're contagious. We'll keep an eye on the cough, and you take that expectorant Doc gave you. But your chest sounds good and I'm afraid it's not that unusual for the cough to hang on. Your throat is still a little irritated and your lungs want to clean themselves of drainage."

"Listen—was there a bill? For coming out here? For medicine?"

"Taken care of," Mel said, packing up her stuff.

"Ian?"

"Yes, as a matter of fact. I think it might've been a case of pride. Why don't you come to town for a few hours—it'll help you from going stir crazy. The bar's open from early morning till nine or ten at night. People are in and out all day. You can use the phone there or the one at the clinic."

"Ah. Not a bad idea. Mel? The tree? The Christmas tree in town? Is it done now?"

"Almost done. There's a little left to do. It's awful big, you know. It's beautiful," she said, beaming. "And don't tell Jack, but I got a ride in a cherry picker while he was away, running errands. It was so cool."

Marcie waited until dinner to broach the subject of going into town. She wanted to time it perfectly—not too early in their meal, but not at the last spoonful when he could get up with his empty plate and turn his back on her. Halfway through dinner she asked, "Is Virgin River out of your way when you go to sell wood?"

He looked up from his plate, meeting her eyes quizzically, lifting his good eyebrow. "Why?"

"If it wouldn't be too much trouble, I'd like a ride into town. I should call my sister. I had that nurse, Mel, call her and tell her I was here with you and there was no phone, and that I'd call her myself when I got to town. I should do that, so she doesn't worry."

"This would be the sister who thinks you're reckless and crazy?" he asked.

She smiled at him. "The same."

He leaned against the back of his chair, leaving his spoon to rest on his plate of stew over rice. "If you're feeling better, you should think about going home. You found me, you told me what you wanted to tell me."

She chewed her lip for a minute. Then she lifted her bright green eyes to his face. "Ian, I need your help here. I'm not saying this so you feel sorry for me—it's not necessary. But I was losing Bobby for a long time and I really thought that by the time he passed, I'd be ready for the next stage in my life. For three years I wondered what I'd do when he was gone. I thought about the possibilities—school, travel, maybe dating. Have my mornings and evenings free for… For whatever. But it's not working for me. He's been gone a year and I'm totally stuck. I don't want to do any of the things I considered. I can't seem to move on, and it's not just grief. It's like there's unfinished business. Being here with you—it's the right thing—"

"You're still here because you were *sick!*" he said in a very annoyed tone.

"Yeah, well, I haven't been too sick to appreciate getting to know you again. It's like getting reacquainted. It feels like it's helping."

"Reacquainted? What are you talking about?"

She looked down. "I knew you. Not like Bobby did—but in his letters he talked about you, and then we had a few letters, you and me. I felt like we knew each other. Like we were friends. You're the link—"

The palms of his hands came down on the tabletop hard enough to make her jump. "But I don't want to go over all that!"

"I *know!*" she shouted back at him. "Jesus, have I asked you to do that? You can be so damned obstinate sometimes! How the hell did you get by all this time without having anyone to fight with, huh? I know you have *issues*—but do you suppose you could think of someone besides yourself for five seconds? We talk and it's helping me put some stuff in perspective. If you want me to go, I'll go. But if you'll just let me stay a little while, till I feel— Shit." She ran a hand through her wild, fiery tresses. "Till I don't know when! Till I feel this part of my unfinished business is finished. I'll be glad to buy the food or help with chores or whatever—I just can't drive into town to call my sister because the bug doesn't have chains or snow tires." She took a breath. She swallowed. "That's all I have to say."

One corner of his mouth lifted. "Are you *sure* that's all you have to say?"

She leaned back and eyed him warily. "For now."

The other corner of his mouth lifted slightly. "You're one stubborn little broad, aren't you?"

"Told you," she said, lifting her chin. And she thought, *It's probably what got me through the worst of it.*

"You don't have to buy food or do chores. I just can't figure out how a grumpy old guy like me helps you with anything."

"Well," she said, a little mollified and somewhat confused, "it's because of the way—"

"Tomorrow I deliver wood. I'll go early with a load, come back empty and reload. I can take you to town then. It'll take me a couple hours to deliver that load, then I'll pick you up in town. You'll be okay in town for that long? Where will you go?"

"I'll sit in Jack's bar and drink coffee."

"Take your medicine first. That cough gets scary."

She smiled very happily. "Thank you, Ian." And that's when she knew. He might fight it, but he needed to go over the details of the past as much as she did. The more he acted out against it, the more obvious it became—he had a lot to get off his chest. They'd get to that in time. Then she'd show him Bobby's letter, give him the silly baseball cards and go home feeling lighter. Better.

Seven

Ian pulled into Virgin River and stopped in front of the tree. *My God, what a tree,* he thought. Decorated for the troops, obviously. And while it looked as if the trimming was complete, the cherry picker still stood behind it.

"Look for me in two and a half hours," he said to Marcie. "I don't want to have to try to find you."

She glanced at her watch. "I'll be waiting," she said. "Thank you."

He just nodded. But he watched her walk up the steps to the porch of the bar and then pulled slowly out of town.

It was very hard for him to admit it to himself, but having her around had brought him a strange comfort, and he had no idea why. Looking out for her made him feel better somehow. Making sure she was fed and protected against danger—that seemed to work for him, too. It was a lot of trouble, actually. If she hadn't been around, he wouldn't go to as much bother with meals. Three out of four nights he'd just open a can of something, but because she'd been sick and needed a hot meal he'd put his best foot forward. Plus, she needed to put on another few pounds. He had spent a lot of time wondering if searching for him, sleeping in her car and probably skipping meals had made her thin and weak.

Knowing she was going to be there when he got home, pestering and bothering him, made him hurry a little bit through his work, his chores. He couldn't figure out why—he was damn sure not going to go over all that old business about the war, about Bobby. Just thinking about that stuff put a boulder in his gut and made his head ache. And yet, he had a ridiculous fear that this phone call to her sister would result in her saying, "I have to go home now."

But there was no use worrying about it—she's going to leave soon no matter what the sister says. It's not as though she'd camp out in his cabin through the holidays—she had people at home. Never mind her grousing about her sister, at least she had a sister who loved her, cared about her. And what had she said when she asked for a ride to town? *Just a little while longer...*

It was the first relationship he'd had in about four years. Old Raleigh didn't count—that had been pure servitude. If the man hadn't left him part of a mountain, Ian would never have suspected Raleigh was even slightly grateful for the caretaking in the last months. Ian saw people regularly—he worked for the moving company when the weather was good, had his firewood route, went places like the library, had a meal out now and then. People were nice to him, and he was cordial in return. But he never got close; there had been no relationships. No one poked at him like she did, making him smile in spite of himself.

That business with the puma—her opening the outhouse

door and yelling at him like that—he knew what that was about. She was afraid he'd get hurt by the cat and risked her own skin to warn him. Been a long damn time since he felt anyone really cared about him at all.

Maybe that was it, he thought. Marcie thinks she cares, and it's because I was important to Bobby. If we'd just met somehow, it wouldn't be like this.

But that didn't matter to him right now. He liked the feeling, alien though it was. He'd be back for her in two and a half hours and while he was delivering a half a cord to some dentist in Fortuna he'd watch the time so he wouldn't be late getting back to pick her up. And with every split log he stacked, he'd be hoping her family wouldn't find a way to get her home right away.

It was just nine-thirty in the morning when Marcie walked into the bar, and there was no one around. She heard voices in the kitchen. She was going to have to go back there to use the phone anyway, but as she pushed the swinging door slowly open, she knocked on it a couple of times before she entered.

"Yeah, c'mon back," someone said. That response was accompanied by a woman's laughter.

There were four people gathered around the work island. Two couples. There was the cook, Preacher, and Paige, the woman who'd been helping to decorate the tree that first day. And then there was the local cop, Mike, and a very beautiful woman about thirty years old with light brown hair that went all the way to her waist. Mike was wearing an apron that was covered in red and green icing. "Hey," he said, grinning at her. "Marcie. Did you find your marine?"

"Wow," she said, astonished. "Mel really *doesn't* say anything." She shook her head. "I found him almost a week ago."

They all just exchanged knowing glances. Each one chuckled. Apparently they all knew Mel quite well. "Do you know everyone here?" Mike asked.

"Preacher, Paige, you…"

He put his arm around the beautiful woman and she leaned into him. "This is Brie, Jack's sister." He nuzzled her neck. "My girl."

"How do you do?" Marcie said, suddenly envious of all the love in the world.

Brie nodded and smiled. "Pleasure," she said.

"So. How is he? Your guy?" Mike asked.

"He's good," she said. "He's been living out on the top of a mountain for almost four years now. It's pretty rustic—but I've never seen anything so beautiful."

"And he was glad to see you?" Mike asked.

"Oh, yes," she lied. "Pretty much. As long as we don't have to talk about his experiences in Iraq, we're good company for each other." She shrugged. "He's letting me stay a little while. Well," she said, looking down. "I caught a bad…cold. And he was stuck with me. So I'm taking advantage of him." She looked up and smiled. "He's being very patient about it. Listen, I need to make a collect call. I promised to check in with my sister every couple of days and Ian doesn't have a phone."

"Help yourself," Preacher said. "Dial direct—we have one of those deals with the phone company—unlimited long distance for a monthly rate."

"Really?"

"Jack has four sisters and a father. Paige has girlfriends," he said with a shrug. "We make a lot of calls. Yours is free as long as it's in the U.S. Just go for it."

Paige stepped around the worktable. "Marcie, if you could use a little privacy, you're welcome to call from our apartment."

"You wouldn't mind?" Marcie returned.

"Not at all," she said. "Come with me. I'll show you where."

Marcie started to follow Paige, then turned back toward the group. "You're making Christmas cookies?" she asked.

"Paige and Brie were," Mike said. "They're having some kind of women's thing here today. I'm just doing this so they have someone to make fun of. I'm much better with a taco. And I can make some mean carne asada."

"Fortunately we have our cookies done," Brie said with a laugh. "Mike can eat his own mess. He's pathetic. Who ever heard of a person who can't even frost a Christmas tree cookie."

"Rules," Preacher said. "The men can't help with this because they all know I'm the best cookie wrangler in the business."

"Come on, Marcie," Paige said, pulling on her hand. "The phone's right in here."

Marcie let herself be led into a small efficiency apartment—a bedroom and living area right behind the kitchen. Paige pointed to a cordless phone on a side table between a leather sofa and chair. "Help yourself," she said.

"Thank you. You live here?"

"Uh-huh. This was Jack's place before he married Mel and moved out to her cabin. Then I married John and…"

"John?" Marcie asked.

"Oh, everyone calls him Preacher, but his name is

John. John Middleton. And I'm Paige Middleton," she said, beaming proudly. "Now make your call, and then we'll have some coffee and cookies. We'll send some home with you."

Then Paige pulled the door closed, leaving Marcie alone.

This was amazing, Marcie thought. She'd never been around people like this before. They were generous and sweet to a fault. Didn't they worry that she'd rifle through their closets and drawers? They didn't know her at all, knew virtually nothing about her, and yet they were all about helping her, accommodating her.

She sighed deeply. Ian should be around people like this a little more. He was turning into an old curmudgeon before his time. She lifted the phone and called Erin's office.

Erin's secretary answered, but explained that Erin was in court. Marcie actually let out a relieved breath. "That's okay, Barb. Will you tell her I called, that I'm fine and enjoying my visit very much and will try her again in a couple of days? I'd sure appreciate that."

"And everything is working out for you?" Barb asked.

"Absolutely. Perfect. But I'm staying with a friend out in the mountains and there's no phone. I can only call when I come into town. So, it'll be another couple of days before I can try her again. But tell her it's just beautiful here and I'm having a good time."

And then, given the no-charge situation, she called Drew's cell phone. He picked up on the third ring. "Drew," she said in a breath. "Drew, I found him!"

"This is the rumor," he said, chuckling. "You okay, Marce?"

"I'm very okay," she said, but then unexpectedly she coughed. And coughed again. "Sorry," she apologized. "I do have a cough—but I saw the town doctor and have some cough medicine. Nothing to worry about."

"Doesn't exactly sound great, Marcie. Are you sleeping in a heated house?"

"Of course." She laughed. "And he made me chicken soup and everything. Are you in class? Can I tell you about him without you freaking out?"

"I stepped out of class—the guy's just reading the syllabus anyway. Why would you worry about me freaking out? What's wrong with him?"

"Nothing. He's a good person. Kind and tenderhearted, but a little grumpy if the conversation gets too close to the war. So…we stay away from that for now. But, Drew, he's something else! No wonder I couldn't find him—he has a ponytail and a huge, bushy beard that grew in red. Not as red as me, but his hair is brown and his beard is more red than brown. He's been up here all alone for a long time now—since he got out of the Marines. He has a couple of jobs, hunts and fishes, chops wood. I'm getting to know him and I like him."

And then the thought came suddenly: *I do. I really like him.*

"So," Drew said slowly. "You're out of town, isolated, staying with this guy who has no phone, this guy who gets a little grumpy if—"

"We're having a good time together and there's nothing weird about him, unless you count an awful lot of hair. But around here, that's not so unusual. And in this town there are a lot of marines. They kind of all look out for me in a way, checking to be sure everything is okay." That was a white lie—*Mel* did the checking, but clearly all the men were interested and cared. "And everything is fine."

Drew took a breath. "And you're coming home?"

"Soon," she said. "I haven't had a chance to tell him some things I want to tell him—you know, about the letter, the baseball cards. And I want to know…" She wanted to know why he ran off like that, leaving everything he loved behind. "I want to know some things."

Drew's voice became fatherly. "And if he doesn't want to tell you the things you want to know? You'll thank him politely and come home?"

She should've answered more quickly. It took her two long seconds before she said, "Of course, Drew. He's a good person. I don't want to hurt him. I'd just like it if he told me some things about my husband, about his situation. But if he won't, I'll leave him alone."

"Erin's going nuts," Drew said. "She's on the verge of frantic. If she weren't so controlled all the time, she'd be biting her nails and tearing at her hair."

"I tried to call her. Tell her that—I tried to call her, but she's in court so I called you." She smiled to herself—great family negotiating! She hadn't really called Drew because Erin was in court, but because talking to Drew would feel good. "You can tell her everything—and that I'll call again in a couple of days. Okay?"

"Something about this isn't really—"

"Everything is better than I imagined," she broke in. "I'll be back in touch and, in the meantime, try to get Erin on some medication. Really, I hate carrying around the burden of her worry. I want to get done what I want to get done. It's why I came up here."

Drew sighed. "I know," he said. "I understand, even if I don't love it."

She laughed softly. "Go back to class. I'll talk to you again soon."

"Love you, pet," he said.

"Love you, baby brother." And she hung up the phone.

She sat quietly for a moment, relaxed in the soft tan leather of the chair. They didn't really understand what this had to do with her, but God they loved her enough to care what was happening, to be a little afraid she was making a mistake in putting herself in this strange man's care. Erin's love could be sometimes overbearing, based as it had so often been with concern, but balanced with Drew's boyish good humor she knew how lucky she was to have them. Without their love, she would be so empty inside.

They had no idea how much she missed them, how much she wished she could be home with them just sailing through the holidays as though nothing was missing. And this Christmas, it wasn't just that Bobby was missing; she'd already had her first Christmas without Bobby. *Ian* was missing, too—and she had to put all that together.

The bar was full of women, at least twenty of them, when Marcie stepped through the kitchen door. They had baskets, boxes, tins and large platters covered in plastic wrap laid out on the tables. They held mugs of coffee and tea and chattered happily. Marcie stood in the doorway looking into the room. This would be the *women's thing* that had been spoken of; this would preclude her sitting in the bar until Ian could return for her. She'd have to find something to do.

"There you are," Paige said. "You must have had a nice chat with your sister."

"Um, I couldn't reach my sister so I called my brother," Marcie said.

"You have a brother, too? Oh—you're so lucky. Are you close with them?"

She willed herself not to get teary. "Very," she said, giving a nod.

"How wonderful." Paige reached for her hand. "Come and meet some of the women," she said, pulling her along into the room. "This is their Christmas cookie exchange. Some of these women are world-class bakers—but don't tell John. He thinks no one can outbake him, but believe me, they're incredible."

"Maybe I shouldn't intrude…."

"Don't be silly—you're completely welcome. Unless… I mean, if you have somewhere to go…"

All she could do was shake her head. "It's just that… Of course I have no cookies."

Paige just laughed. "Neither does Mel. Mel can barely boil water. I made my cookies in the bar's kitchen, and so did Brie, but Mel just said 'Oh, the hell with it—there's no use pretending.'"

Right at that moment, from across the room, Mel spotted Paige and Marcie and came right over. "Oh good, you came to town! This has to beat sitting out at the cabin by yourself. And what a great morning to be here—you can meet some of the neighbors. And don't hesitate to sample. How about some coffee?"

"That would be so great," Marcie said. "It's just that I feel like I might be a party crasher."

"Not in this town," Mel said with a laugh. "People are always happy to meet someone new. Otherwise it's the same old faces."

Paige pressed a cup of fresh, steaming coffee into Marcie's hand and then Mel pulled her into the room full of women. Marcie made the acquaintance of many—Connie, who ran the town store, Joy who managed the library, Hope McCrea, whom she recognized from the tree-trimming, Lilly Anderson and her daughters and daughters-in-law. Lilly wore a knitted stocking cap pulled tight over her head and Marcie couldn't help but notice dark circles under her eyes, yet her smile was so warm and full of life. When Mel pulled Marcie away she whispered, "Chemo. She's lost her hair."

"Oh, how sad."

"She's fighting hard—don't be sad."

"Did you just tell a medical secret?" Marcie asked.

Mel shook her head. "Lilly likes me to explain for her when I can."

And then there were more women—ranchers' wives, a woman who, along with her husband, owned a vineyard, a couple of women from a neighboring town. Of course they asked Marcie what had brought her to Virgin River. She tossed it out there, pure and simple. "Well, my husband was critically wounded in Iraq, he was a marine, and he died last year. I heard his best friend from the Corps lived around here and I came to find him. Deliver the news. Get to know him."

"And did you?"

"I did," she said with a smile. "He lives in a cabin on a mountaintop. He dropped me off in town today while he delivers firewood to some of his customers and will pick me up in another hour. He's been... He is... I like this place," she finally said. "I love your tree!"

"Mel, Paige and Brie came up with the idea. Even though these local marines are out of the action now, they still feel close to the men and women who serve," someone said.

"We'll fix you up a sample plate to take back to him," someone else offered.

"Oh, you shouldn't..."

"But he'd like that, wouldn't he?" Mel asked her. "Because it would make the women feel good. Visit a while—I'll supervise." And that fast, Mel was gone, leaving Marcie on her own.

She only suffered a second of discomfort before there was someone beside her, chatting with her. They asked her about her hometown, her late husband, her job and family. It had been in her mind to ask the questions to keep them talking, but it didn't work that way—she was the newcomer, and they were curious.

A large plastic plate covered in plastic was pressed into her hands—a collection from all the other plates in the room—Santas and trees and ornaments; lemon bars, chocolate crispies, brownies; thin slices of specialty breads, lots of assorted treats.

And then the room fell silent as a young woman entered the bar. She was tall with long reddish-gold hair; she carried a box of cookies and she was very pregnant. Her smile was shy and she looked down in the silence. Stepping into the room behind her was a very tall man. He was also shy, Marcie thought, noting the man seemed a little uncomfortable.

But in just a moment the awkward silence seemed to pass and the women in the room surrounded her, embracing her, kissing her cheeks. Mel had an arm around her and held her hand, bringing her into the room. Once she'd greeted everyone, she went about the business of offering her cookies and putting together a sampling of the others to take home to her family.

"That's Vanessa," a voice said.

Marcie turned and looked into Brie's eyes.

"Her husband was killed in Iraq a couple of weeks ago.

Her baby is due soon—another six weeks or so, I guess. She's staying with her father and brother just out of town."

Marcie swallowed. "And the man with her?"

"Paul Haggerty, her late husband's best friend since childhood. He's stayed on since the funeral because Vanessa asked him to. Wherever you see Vanessa, Paul will not be far away. He's completely devoted to her through this difficult time."

"That's...so good of him," Marcie said weakly. She felt a pang of longing.

"Paul's one of Jack, Mike and Preacher's oldest friends. These guys—they really hang tight. And they're always close at hand for the family."

"He looks very sad," Marcie observed.

"There's no question about that," Brie said. "I'm sure his pain is equal to hers. He was best friends with Matt since about the eighth grade." Then she took a breath. "Thank God that baby's coming. What a blessing. Would you like to meet her?"

"Let her be with her friends," Marcie said quickly. "It can't have been easy for her to come out like this so soon after..."

"Okay. Then excuse me," Brie said. "I need to go give her a squeeze. I'll be back."

"Sure," Marcie said. "Please, take your time."

But the women in the room were consumed with Vanessa while Paul stood patiently near the door, never far away. After about twenty minutes, Vanessa returned to Paul with her collection of cookies and he slipped an arm around her waist as they exited the bar.

Leaving her own cookies on the bar, Marcie followed them out. They were just at the bottom of the porch steps when Marcie cleared her throat and said, softly, "Excuse me...Vanessa?"

They both turned and Marcie forced herself to step forward. "I'm…ah…so sorry for your loss."

"Thank you," she said, smiling sweetly though her eyes were sad. Paul never let go of her. "I don't know you, do I?"

"No. I'm just visiting. I'm also the widow of a marine," she managed. "Happened about a year ago."

"Oh!" Vanessa said, suddenly her emotions shifting from her own loss to Marcie's. "I'm so sorry!"

"Thank you. My husband was critically wounded in Iraq four years ago and died last year. And when I heard… Vanessa, I remember when the grief was so fresh and painful. I wish I could say something that would help you now."

She smiled so kindly, Marcie thought. Then Vanessa's hand came out and touched Marcie's red curls. "I think you just did. It was nice of you to say anything at all. I know you didn't have to."

"But I sure did have to," Marcie said, feeling the sting of tears in her own eyes. "I remember so plainly how hard it is at first. I'm so glad for you, that you have good friends to help, that you have a baby coming."

"No children?" Vanessa asked.

Marcie just shook her head. And then she heard the rough motor of Ian's old truck pulling into town. She resisted the urge to look at her watch.

Vanessa opened her arms to Marcie and Marcie stepped into the embrace. Vanessa held her and Marcie felt her tears run. There were so many reasons—the woman had lost her young husband, she was pregnant, the husband's best friend was there for her, and then—

Marcie laughed through tears. "I felt the baby kick," she said.

"It's a boy," Vanessa said. "And he's very active, thank God."

Marcie pulled back and wiped her eyes. "There's my ride," she said. "Godspeed."

"Thank you. What was your name?"

"Marcie Sullivan. I'm just here for a visit. I'll be going home to Chico soon, to have the holidays with my brother and sister, with my husband's family."

"Well, enjoy your visit. And Merry Christmas. Thank you for your kindness."

And then she watched as Paul helped Vanessa into the passenger seat of a big SUV.

Marcie held up a finger to Ian, indicating he should give her a minute. She ran back into the bar, gathered up her cookies and said a few quick goodbyes. Then she clambered into Ian's truck. He was driving out of town before he asked, "Mission accomplished?"

"My sister was tied up, so I talked to my younger brother. He'll pass on the word that everything is fine. And my timing was great—I stumbled into a Christmas cookie exchange. They insisted on making up a plate of samples to take home."

"Mmph," he answered. "I guess you made friends."

"A few. Very nice people in this town—you should give them a chance sometime."

"That woman?" he asked. "One of your new friends?"

"The one I was hugging?" Marcie asked, for clarification.

"She was the only one I saw besides you," he answered.

"Vanessa. I didn't get the last name. She lost her husband in Iraq a couple of weeks ago. I didn't know her, but I gave my condolences anyway."

"The man wasn't her husband?"

"The man was..." *Her late husband's best friend,* she wanted to say. Instead, she said, "Just a good friend, as I understood it."

Eight

One day tended to run into the next when you didn't get up and go to work, or have a TV set that kept you oriented with the news and regular shows. Marcie never knew if it was Tuesday or Saturday, but it didn't matter. Ian seemed to work seven days a week. Even though she felt completely over her flu—except for the cough that haunted her—she still tended to sleep late in the morning. The cabin stayed dark longer, given the shorter number of daylight hours, and Ian crept out silently. Sometimes she would hear the engine of his truck—an engine that could be grumpy as he was—and she'd just roll over and go back to sleep for a while. When she finally roused, Ian would be gone and she'd putter around, eat something, put a couple of logs in the stove, read one of his library books, which, frankly, often bored the enamel off her teeth. If she wanted to read a biography, it would more likely be of some remarkable woman.

But on this morning, the day after the Christmas cookie exchange, she rolled over to find Ian standing by the table, looking very different. He had on a navy-blue denim jacket rather than his old worn work jacket. He wore khakis and boots that weren't beat to hell. The shirt beneath the jacket was white. "I'm going to be out for a while. You'll be okay? You're feeling all right?"

"I'm good. Feeling back to normal. Are you going to sell firewood? Isn't it late for you?"

"Something else this morning. But I'll be back early."

"Ian, where are you going?" she asked, sitting up.

He glanced away for just a second and then, coming closer to the couch, he said, "I'm going to church. I do that once in a while. I'll be back—"

"You belong to a *church?*" she asked, straightening in surprise.

"No. No, no. I just drop in sometimes. Different ones. It doesn't matter which one, not really."

She was at full attention. "What denomination are you?" she asked.

"None. Really. I wasn't even raised in a church—we weren't religious. It's just a little thing I do. Not regularly. I'll be back in—"

"Please, can I go with you?" she asked.

"Marcie," he groaned, drawing it out almost painfully. "Let's not do that…"

But she jumped off the couch, nearly knocking him over as she grabbed up a pair of jeans from the top of her duffel. "I don't have any really nice clothes… Just jeans and boots, but last time I went to church, it was pretty casual. Not many people dress up anymore."

"You should stay home—"

"I won't be any trouble at all."

"Listen, can I be straight with you here?"

She pulled up her jeans quickly, not even thinking he might have caught a flash of her panties in the process until he turned away. "That would be fun—you being straight with me for once." She ripped his shirt over her head and dug around in her duffel for her best sweater.

Without looking at her, he said, "I go in real quiet, late, sit in the back. I'm not unfriendly. I say hello and God bless and move on. People don't remember me—I don't show up at the same church even twice a year. I don't want to belong to a church or anything—I just want to hear the music sometimes. I'm not a joiner—"

"Yeah, you're a loner. I know this..."

"I like the solitude, I do—but I see people all the time. I just live alone—and I don't belong to a church or a union or anything. That's all. I go to listen. Maybe there's something in it. I'm open to inspiration."

"Fine. That's fine. I'll say hello and God bless," she said, pulling her sweater over her head. She looked down at herself—all wrinkled. He turned around to find her completely changed. She sat on the sofa and pulled her boots over black socks. From the look on his face, if she took much more time in dressing, he'd be gone without her.

"No. No, it won't work. You're the kind of person people will want to talk to. You like making friends, getting connected and I don't. I'll just stay home and—"

She ran to the sink, pumped a little water to wet her hands. She ran them over her wild curls to calm them a bit. "Take me, too, Ian. I won't even sit with you. I'll pretend I don't know you. You can act like I'm some poorly dressed homeless person who just happens to be there the same time as you."

"Aw, Marcie—I wish I hadn't even told you the truth.

How about I bring you a book from the library? You tell me what you want."

"You're going to the *library?* Oh God, please please please can you take me with you? Ian, I've hardly been anywhere since I found your cabin! I don't have to talk to people. Really! But for God's sake, don't make me read another biography or whatever you pick out for me. I won't sit with you at the church and I'll be quiet at the library! God, I just want to go out and do something around people—I spent a month looking for you and talked to people all day till I hated talking to them! Now if I could just be in the world for a while… I promise—I won't make you uncomfortable. If I do one thing wrong, you can growl and roar at me all you want." And then she coughed.

"You're still sick. Listen to you."

She caught her breath. "It's because you got me worked up. Really, I'm all right. Mel said I was fine. She checked me over, said I'm not contagious and that it's not uncommon to have that cough a while. Please. Please. *Please!*"

"Goddamn it," he muttered.

She smiled at him. "Nice language for someone on his way to church."

Ian didn't talk the entire way into Fortuna. He stared stonily ahead and Marcie decided that since she had begged her way along, she'd better stay quiet and do exactly as she'd promised. When they pulled up to a Presbyterian church, she walked ahead of him into the building, took a program and found a seat in a pew in the back. Not surprisingly, Ian sat across the aisle from her in his own pew, acting as if he didn't know her.

Well, he wanted to be alone. And so this way he could

be. She wasn't about to let his peculiarities work her up. So she just listened to the scriptures, the choir. The sermon.

It was mid December, time to start examining the story of the birth of Christ. She usually didn't go to church at Christmas until it was closer to the actual day and she always enjoyed the story—the stable, the birth, the shepherds and wise men…

"One of the things that interests me year-round—as a Christian, as a theologian, as a human being—is that star," the minister said. "There's a lot of conjecture as to whether it was an actual astronomical event or something divinely created to announce the birth of Christ. You'll expect me to tell you that it is my belief, from scripture, that it was the latter. What's more important to me is not whether it was nature in motion, or a Godly miracle, but what it means to us today. It's a symbol of Christianity that reigns second only to the cross. It is a gift of light, of guidance, of leadership, of passage and understanding and illumination.

"Have you ever been driven to do something, but lacked direction? Have you ever been one of those people who didn't pray too often but were in sudden, desperate need of help and found yourself on your knees? The star is faith. A belief that a power greater than ourselves will, given the opportunity, lead us to our destination. The star is meaning, purpose, promise that we'll be given divine illumination. That our way will be filled with the light of understanding and keep us from stumbling. That is the miracle of the star.

"As we enter a season of loving, healing, forgiving…a season of *promise*…so many of us will look to the heavens for that star. I think, sometimes, that star is in our hearts as well."

He talked a little about the wise men, the kings, and the

shepherds who left their flocks. *They were driven.* They had a task, a goal. As men, they were so different, the simple shepherds, the kings, but it's not only rich men who are driven or poor men who follow a calling. They simply responded to a gut reaction, to a mission that had to be fulfilled for their good, for the savior they were compelled to welcome to the world, for the well-being of all. It must have been a driving force, impossible to ignore, though to those around them, it might have seemed foolish. Or even crazy. Imagine these kings packing up and traipsing across the country on some harebrained idea that there was a special infant—coming to save the world, to heal mankind—born in a stable far away. Their servants and soldiers must have thought they had lost it.

Then came the star—guiding them. Leading them.

"Is there something," the pastor asked his congregation, "we feel compelled to do in this season of giving, this season of rebirth? Do people around us suggest we mind our own business or let matters rest?"

His words began to run together and Marcie wasn't sure how much of what she heard was the minister's sermon, and how much her own mind, her own heart. Is there something you are inexplicably driven to *complete* and you can no more stop yourself than you can turn back time? Is this a mission of mercy, meant for goodness and healing? For love and kindness? Because you have to ask yourself that. This is not a season to heal your own wounds at the expense of another—but a time for rekindling love and moving ahead into a better world. Isn't that what the birth of Christ promised? A better world?

Then we have to ask ourselves—do I see the way? Do I see—do I feel the star in the east? Am I being led?

Marcie felt tears on her cheeks and clearly heard the pastor say, "Let's all say a little prayer that gives God permission to guide us in the right direction, in doing good, mending hurts, healing hearts, asking for forgiveness. And then we'll sing."

But she was already praying, and not to God as she was supposed to be. Her prayer went out to someone else.

Oh, Bobby, help! Am I meant to be here? To do this? Because he's everything you said he was—he's strong and invincible, and yet so tender, so sweet. So complicated, so simple. Sometimes I think of irrational things—Jesus whipping the money changers in the temple in fierceness, in battle, and then feeding the hungry masses from five loaves and five fish.... If you could have seen him roar at me like I was the biggest threat, then feed that big buck right from his hand... I swear, the day the mountain lion came to the property, he shot over the cat so as not to harm it, though he could have killed it and maybe should have. He's good, Bobby, and he just can't do something like that without really... Oh, Bobby, if it's wrong for me to invade his world, disrupt his life and make him unhappy, please give me a sign. It's true, I want to bring him home, but I need him to bring me *home! I swear to God, I only want to do the right thing, to feel that things are finally settled so we can all go on to the kind of lives you would have wanted for us. Please, Bobby, tell me! I'll pay attention....*

And while her head was bowed, beseeching her dead husband instead of God, as she'd been instructed, the congregation stood and belted out a hymn. It took her a moment to wipe her eyes and think, I'm crazy as a loon. Praying to a man who's been dead for a year, who was lost to me years before that. Do I really think Bobby's going to give me an answer faster than God? What kind of nutjob am I?

She surreptitiously stole a look across the aisle at Ian. He stood straight and tall, all bushy and proud. And he wasn't singing! Of all the crazy things. This was one place his voice could not only be exercised but appreciated, yet he didn't sing. What a horrible waste. She was filled with a longing to hear him amaze the rest of this congregation with his glorious voice. Yet he was silent.

She sniffed back her tears. Maybe he wasn't all that wonderful. Maybe he was just plain selfish.

She had no idea why this whole episode—so spiritually emotional for her—would make her angry. And she didn't brood over it; she just told herself to get over it and go along as she'd promised. At least until she figured things out.

When the hymn was finished, the benediction read and the pastor led the recessional, she was one of the first out of the church. She shook the pastor's hand and thanked him for a moving sermon.

"Moved you a little much, I think, sister," he said.

"Touched me, yes," she said, guarding herself not to sniff.

"Come here," he said, pulling her into his arms and giving her a hug.

Oh, bad idea. If she didn't steel herself, she'd start sobbing. It was his arms around her—it weakened her. She'd had a million comforting hugs since Bobby finally left them, but her hug tank had been on the low side lately. She desperately needed some reassurance, and as ridiculous as she felt about her prayerful plea to Bobby, it would have come as a comfort to feel his hand on her shoulder, telling her to move ahead, follow her heart....

"Thank you, pastor," she said, withdrawing herself. "Beautiful sermon."

"Then, I thank you. I lack confidence in getting them ready. They're a struggle. Come back and see us."

"Sure," she said, removing herself.

She went and waited by the truck, and while she was there, she watched Ian make his way to the pastor, shake his hand, speak to him, even laugh with him. And she thought—there are two of him! He is that guy who seems so alone and a guy who's made his way in the world just fine. It's just that his world is a different kind of world; it's not that rushing, heavily populated world of demands and connections so many of us have. His is mostly a quiet world and his relationships seemed to be the same. The way he seemed to like it.

When she'd been looking for him, she had asked probably a hundred people if they knew an Ian Buchanan and the answer had always been the same. "Name doesn't ring a bell." Ian probably made his way through life, friendly enough, without anyone asking his name, without him ever offering it.

When Ian got to the truck and fired it up, she asked, "Did the pastor ask you your name?"

"No," he said. "Why?"

So that was part of it. That and the fact he didn't look anything like the picture she'd been flashing around. "No reason, just curious," she said.

"I think we should have a nice, big breakfast. Do you feel like eating before we hit the library?"

"Sure," she said quietly.

"You all right, Marcie?"

She shrugged. "I think I got a little sentimental there for a minute. A good strong cup of coffee should do the trick."

"Well, you're in luck—I know just the place."

* * *

It was a truck stop, of course. Ian was quite proud of the place. There must have been a dozen eighteen-wheelers parked outside and when he walked in, a middle-aged, heavyset, bleached-blond waitress said hello rather familiarly. "Hey, Bub—you doing okay? Haven't seen you in a while."

"Doing great, Patti," he answered. She wore a big name tag so Marcie couldn't assume they were friends. But Ian had been seen around after all—in plenty of places. Coincidentally, none of the places she'd been looking.

Patti poured their coffee and said, "Need a minute?"

"Yeah, give the lady some time to decide," he said.

After Patti had gone, Marcie said, "I guess you must get the same thing every time?"

"Just about. Yeah," he admitted.

"Okay." She studied her menu. "Whenever you're ready, I'll have a cheese omelet."

"Sounds good," he said. He lifted his hand to Patti.

When she arrived he said, "A cheese omelet for the lady, trim it, and for me—"

"Four eggs, side of bacon, side of sausage, hash browns, biscuits and gravy, wheat toast, orange juice and coffee till you float," she finished for him.

He smiled at Patti and it was most definitely a smile. If I were Patti, Marcie thought, I'd think he wanted to ask me out on a date. But all Patti said was, "Gotcha, Bub."

By her first refill of coffee, Marcie started to get right with the world. Nothing straightened her out like caffeine, she thought. Hot coffee, not that stuff Ian left warming on the woodstove when he went to sell wood in the mornings. And this was good and strong. She came around. "So, are you and Patti friends?" she asked.

"Patti's my waitress about once every two months," he said. "She does a good job."

"Why didn't you sing in church?" she asked boldly.

He put down his cup. "I didn't want to."

"Why?"

"Look, don't make me act all conceited. I was in choir in high school. I was in our high school musical—we did *Grease.* I have an okay voice. I don't want to join the choir."

"Who were you in *Grease*?"

"It's not important."

"Who?"

His hand went over his mouth and he mumbled something.

"Who?" she asked, leaning closer.

His eyes came up. "Danny."

"You were the star! You were frickin' John Travolta, except you sing better!"

His eyes shifted around nervously. "You just got a little loud there."

"Sorry," she said. "Sorry. But really… Have you ever studied music?"

"I studied military strategy. I thought you knew that."

"Okay, sorry, brushing up against that forbidden territory. But Jesus, you sing like a god! Wouldn't that be something you'd think about pursuing?"

He was quiet for a long moment and finally said, "I sing for myself. It's nice. It passes time. You're not going to save me, Marcie. You're not going to pull me out of the hills and turn me in to a rock star."

She was speechless. For a split second, that was exactly what she'd had in mind. Not a rock star, exactly, but a famous singer at least. "Well, it's just a stupid crime that you don't even have a radio," she said churlishly.

"No matter where you live, you should have music around you."

And he laughed.

Their plates arrived, along with a check that Ian snapped up. She just stared at his huge breakfast with wide, startled eyes.

"Now what?" he asked.

"Holy smokes, do they see you pull into the parking lot and fire up the grill? That didn't take five minutes!"

He curved his lips into a smile for her. "I like that they're efficient. They work, they get the job done."

"Yeah," she said. "Um—let me split the check. I have money."

"I know. Eighty dollars." He dug into his eggs.

"Really, I'd like to pay my share," she said.

He lifted a sausage patty off his plate and slid it onto hers. "Forget it, I've got it. Try this, it's the best sausage patty you'll ever taste."

"You obviously need a lot of fuel to do what you do," she commented. Then she tasted the patty. "Hmm, right. You're so right."

He plunged his fork into the large biscuit and gravy and held it out to her. "Here. This is even better."

For a second she was still. He was feeding her right off his fork? Then before the mood could drift away, she leaned toward that fork and sampled the biscuit and gravy. She hummed in agreement, let her eyes drop closed in appreciation and when she opened them, he was smiling happily. There was something so intimate, so generous about that simple gesture, it touched her heart.

"I knew you'd like it. I can never finish everything. Help yourself."

"Thank you, Ian," she said quietly.

* * *

When they pulled into the Eureka Public Library, she asked, "Can we browse a little? Or are we in a hurry?"

"How are you feeling? You coughed some."

"I feel so much better doing something. I'd like to pick up a couple of books to keep me busy while you sell firewood. And I'm not sure what I want."

"Take your time. I like to read the papers," he said.

And she did take her time, luxuriously. Roaming the stacks, picking up novels with pretty covers, reading the cover copy and then the first page, having a real hard time choosing. She sat on the floor in the crowded aisles, so happy to be in the midst of entertainment again. She'd been reading classics to Bobby, more for herself than him, but her own tastes ran to newer romances. Deep, emotional romances with happy endings. Where things worked out. Whatever book she chose would have to be the right one; it was the only diversion she had. She had no idea how much time had passed when he said, "You just about ready?"

"Oh! Sure. Can I please have these three?"

"You think you'll read that many before you leave?"

She just smiled at him. "Yes," she said, knowing that was half an answer. Or less.

While Ian was checking out the books and then waiting by the door, Marcie was chatting it up with one of the librarians. They started off talking softly but very soon they were laughing, touching each other's arms as they whispered close. He cleared his throat once and both women looked at him. He treated them to a glower, then they just resumed their conversation, interspersed with soft laughter. It looked as though they'd become best friends in just a short time.

Finally Marcie tore herself away from a hug and

followed Ian to the truck. When they were inside, he was sulky. "You weren't going to get all involved. Hook up with people. All that."

"I didn't," she said.

"Well, that looked pretty cozy, back there. I told you—you're the kind of person people want to get to know, talk to—"

"Don't worry, Ian. I totally protected your anonymity. I told her you were my brother."

"Great," he pouted. "Now she's going to ask me about you. And I told you—I'm friendly and pleasant and then I move on."

"You can do that. She'll find it perfectly understandable."

"Oh? And why's that?"

"Well, she wondered about you. Said you ask for some heavy reading sometimes, but that you didn't make much conversation."

"Oh, really?"

"Yes," Marcie explained. "I said you were brilliant, but not a very social animal. I said she shouldn't expect a lot of chitchat from you, but you were perfectly nice, and there was no reason to be shy around you—you're safer than you look."

"Is that so? And how did you convince her of that?"

"Easy. I said you were an idiot savant—brilliant in literature and many other things, but socially you weren't on your game."

"Oh, Jesus Christ!"

She noted the late-afternoon sky, the sun beginning to lower. "Ian, when was the last time you went out for a beer?"

"Been a while," he grumbled miserably.

"I'd so love to see that Christmas tree in Virgin River

at night. Could we pass through there for a beer? By the time we've had a beer, it might be dark. I should try calling my sister again before she comes hunting me down—and there's that nice little bar there, with a phone I can use."

"Aw, Marcie…"

"Come on. It's been such a perfect day. Let's end it on a positive note. Let me buy you a beer and maybe some of Preacher's dinner—he cooks like a dream."

"Preacher?"

"The cook in that little bar."

"I don't really like big crowds."

She laughed at him. "Ian, if the whole town turns out, there will be fewer people there than in that truck stop or in the church. Besides, you told me that you're around people all the time, you're just not a joiner. So come on. Man up."

It was barely five o'clock when Marcie and Ian entered Jack's bar, and there were about twenty people there. Ian stood by the door and surveyed the new surroundings warily. He noted hunting and fishing trophies on the walls, the dim lighting, the welcoming fire. It didn't look threatening. While there were a couple of tables of people engaged in friendly conversation and laughter, there were also a couple of solitary men having a drink or a meal apart from the crowd. One he recognized as the old doctor, seated up at the bar and hovering over a drink, left entirely alone.

Marcie went right up to the bar, leaning on it, talking with the bartender. Ian spied an empty spot at the far end of the bar in the corner where he thought he'd be comfortable. He approached Marcie's back, meaning to steer her there. As if she felt him come near, she turned and said, "Ian, meet Jack Sheridan. Jack, Ian."

"Pleasure," Jack said. "What can I get you?"

"Beer?"

"Bottle or tap?"

"Whatever's on tap," Ian said.

Jack drew the beer and said to Marcie, "Help yourself to the phone, Marcie. Preacher's back there." Then, she skipped away and Jack put the beer in front of Ian.

Ian picked it up and migrated down to the corner of the bar he'd staked out. Then he watched with interest for several moments as Jack made a few drinks, polished some glasses, exchanged friendly banter with a couple of customers, arranged some bottles, took a tub of dirty glasses to the kitchen, and seemed to completely ignore Ian, the old doctor, and the other lone drinker at the opposite end of the bar. It was probably ten minutes—Marcie must be having a very interesting conversation with her sister. *How is she explaining me?* he wondered to himself.

"How's that beer?" Jack asked, dishtowel in hand, eyeing the nearly empty glass.

"I'm good," Ian said.

"Just let me know," he said, turning away.

"Ah," Ian said, getting his attention but not exactly calling him back.

Jack turned, lifted an eyebrow. Silent.

"She tell you to leave me alone?"

A small huff of laughter escaped Jack. "Pal, the first thing you learn when you open a bar—talk if they talk, shut up if they don't."

Ian tilted his head. Maybe he could stand this place

once in a while. "She tried to explain me to the librarian in Eureka as an idiot savant." Jack smiled and Ian felt an odd sensation—it was a funny story; he liked sharing a funny story. He used to make the guys laugh when he wasn't making them work. "She tell you she was looking for me?"

"She did."

For some reason unclear even to him, Ian did something he hadn't done since finding himself in these mountains—he pushed on it a little bit. "She tell you anything about me?"

"Couple of things."

"Like?"

"Like, you and me—we were in Fallujah about the same time."

"Should've known. You have that jarhead look about you. Just so you're clear—I don't talk about that time."

Jack smiled lazily. "Just so *you're* clear, neither do I."

"Hi, Erin," Marcie said into the phone. "I'm just checking in."

"Marcie, good God, where have you *been?*" she asked.

Marcie could just imagine Erin beginning to pace with the phone in her hand, something she did whenever she was stressed and not quite in control. "You know where I am. Right here, in Virgin River. I'm staying not far from here. Didn't you get my messages? I talked to Drew and Mel Sheridan said she talked to you—"

"Some woman I've never heard of and don't know called, yes," she said. "She says you're staying with him? You're actually *staying* with him? Someplace without even a phone?"

Marcie sighed deeply. "Calm down—he doesn't need a

phone. He lives in a perfectly comfortable cabin on a ridge with an incredible view and he sort of…invited me to stay if I wanted to…"

"Sort of? If you wanted to? Marcie, what the hell's going on?"

"I want you to listen to me, Erin. Listen and stop commanding. I found him, I want to get to know him, I want to understand him. Everything. I want to understand everything. And that takes time. And there's no place I have to be right now."

"This is making me nuts! My little sister, with some crazy stranger on an isolated mountain—"

"He is *not* crazy! He's a good man! He's been very generous with me! I'm completely safe, and there's nothing about this to make you concerned. He goes to work every day and in the evenings when he's back at the cabin, we talk a little bit. We're just getting to know each other. Today we went to church and to the library. Stop hovering—you knew I was going to do this!"

"Let me talk to him," Erin said. "Put him on the phone. I have a few questions."

"No," she said in a panicked gasp. "He can't come to the phone—he's out in the…the…restaurant. I'm an adult, and he doesn't need your permission to invite me to stay in his cabin. You're going to have to trust me!"

"It's not trust and you know it—it's him! I don't know him, I only know that when you were up to your neck taking care of Bobby and Ian Buchanan was out of the Corps, he never even called to ask—"

"He saved Bobby's life," Marcie shot back. "He risked his life to save my husband. What more do I need to know? I want to thank him, I want to—"

"Saying thank you should take about five minutes," Erin interrupted.

"I'm not talking about this anymore. I'll call you in a few days—and work on calming down in the meantime. Erin, do not mess this up for me!" She disconnected the line with an angry poke of one finger.

And looked up into those dark, brooding eyes of Preacher's. Beneath the scowl was a lift of his lips. "Well," Preacher said. "That's a new twist to the story. He saved your husband's life? Hoorah."

"I thought you knew," she said.

"All I knew was you're widowed," he said. "How about this guy? He seem an okay guy?"

She took a breath. "Wild animals will eat out of his hand."

"That a fact?" Preacher said. "I trust wild animals more than a lot of tame men. You should stay for dinner."

"I was hoping to, but why?" she asked, thinking hard on the previous comment.

"It's meat loaf night," he said simply. "It's the best ever."

"Oh."

"And it's a special night. Mel, Jack's wife, she found the perfect topper for that tree and now we can finally return the cherry picker. Half the town's turning out for the lighting. Should've come a lot sooner, but we couldn't do it until she was okay with the topper. The woman looked at every angel and sparkle-ball and star in three counties and rejected them all. But now she has it—so we're going to fire it up. Next year, we'll get it done earlier."

"Cool." Marcie smiled. "What time on the tree?"

He looked at his watch. "About an hour from now."

Nine

Marcie joined Ian at the bar and sat up beside him. Jack was there instantly. "What can I get you?" he asked with a wipe of the bar in front of her.

"I think—I'd like a glass of wine. How about a nice merlot? And two meat loaf dinners. And whatever you do, do not let this guy get the check—I invited him, and it's my treat. My turn. He's been feeding me since I got here."

"You bet," Jack said.

Ian turned toward her. "I'm not sure about staying long..."

"If you have an anxiety attack, we can go. But if you can hang in there a little while, I bet the meat loaf will amaze you. This cook, Preacher? He's unbelievable. I had some of his venison chili when I first got to town and it almost made me pass out, it was so good."

His lips curved in a smile. "You ate venison, Marcie?"

"I didn't have a relationship with the deer," she explained.

"You don't have a relationship with my deer either," he pointed out.

"Yeah, but I have a relationship with you—you've seen

me in my underwear. And you have a relationship with the deer. If you fed him to me, it would be like you shot and fed me your friend. Or something."

Ian just drained his beer and smiled at her enough to show his teeth. "I wouldn't shoot that particular buck," he admitted. "But if I had a freezer, I'd shoot his brother."

"There's something off about that," she said, just as Jack placed her wine in front of her. "Wouldn't it be more logical if hunters didn't get involved with their prey? Or their families? Oh, never mind—I can't think about this before eating my meat loaf. Who knows who's in it?"

Ian chuckled at her. "You're right about one thing. Not a bad little bar here. I never checked it out before."

"Toldja," she said, sipping her wine. "What would you like to talk about?"

"We've talked all day. I haven't talked this much in four years. I think I might be losing my voice."

"I haven't talked this little…"

"I kind of assumed that…"

Just then Jack delivered two steaming plates that he held with towels. He reached beneath the bar and produced a couple of sets of utensils wrapped in napkins and asked, "Another beer?"

"Why not?" Ian said in what was an unmistakably friendly voice. "The lady's buying." And then he put his napkin on his thigh.

Marcie stared at that thigh for a long moment. This was the sort of thing that had her confused. He looked a little crazy, till you got used to him. He could act as if he had needs barely above the animal kingdom, taking roughing it to the next level. When he was in his working clothes, he looked as if he barely subsisted. He could growl and snarl like a lunatic. But he had intelligent diction, good table manners, and while he might not be terribly social and on the quiet side, he had no trouble being around people. He was perfectly cordial.

She had expected a man completely screwed up by his past, by his war experiences, someone hard to reach and nearly impossible to change—a difficult situation, but easy to understand. Instead, what she found was someone pretty normal. It left her with many more questions than answers.

"You're right about the food," he said with a hum and a napkin to his lips and beard.

"Hmm," she agreed, letting her eyes fall closed as she enjoyed mashed potatoes so creamy and wonderful, they were like ambrosia.

Ian finished quickly, sitting back and giving his belly a satisfied rub. Marcie just gave up, pushing her plate toward Ian. "I'm done. Go ahead. Help yourself."

His eyes widened. "You sure?"

"Wait," she said suddenly. She dipped her fork into the mashed potatoes and lifted it to his lips. "Try this."

He lifted his brows, then let her put the fork into his mouth. He savored it. Then he said, "I think you got better potatoes." And he smiled.

"Help yourself, Ian. I'm going to explode if I eat any more," she said.

"Maybe a bite," he said, dipping his fork a couple of times before he, too, had to admit defeat. They sat in silence for a few appreciative moments, finishing their drinks, satisfied. Happy. It occurred to her—they *were* happy.

The contentment was interrupted abruptly. Mel came into the bar with a baby on her hip. Marcie knew she was pregnant, but had no idea there was also a baby under a year old. The baby was all stropped up in a snowsuit, encased from his head to his toes in blue bunting. The smile on her face was brilliant. "Jack! Everyone! It's time. Tell Preach to turn off the stove and get Christopher and come on! Come on, don't make us wait!"

Ian's eyes narrowed as he quizzed Marcie wordlessly. "They're going to light the tree," she said. "I'd love to see it."

"Whatever jingles your bells," he said.

"You're not coming?"

"I'm pretty comfortable right here."

She leveled him with her gaze. "Suit yourself," she finally said. And she got off her stool to follow the people in the bar as they headed outside.

There was a formidable gathering there—cars and trucks double-parked all up and down the street. People were murmuring, laughing, greeting each other. There were lots of excited children running around.

Marcie found herself at the back of the crowd, not out of shyness but because she wanted to see the entire height of the tree and get the full effect. She felt a longing to have Ian at her side, but his reluctance was easy to understand—nothing like the holidays to bring back dark memories of loved ones lost, families in unstable places, loneliness, bittersweet memories.

Mel was suddenly at her side, jiggling the baby.

"I thought you were expecting your first," Marcie said with a bit of melancholy. There had been a time she'd seen a family in her future, but when Bobby was injured, everything went away—all the hopes and dreams and fantasies.

"This is David, my son. I wasn't expecting to be expecting so soon again, but it is what it is. I'm knocked up." She laughed. "You'd think a midwife would have a better handle on things."

"I assume you're happy about it?" Marcie asked boldly.

"It took a little getting used to, but the baby moves now. That seems to change even the most reluctant mommy. How's it going? I see you got Ian into town. Did you finally speak with your sister?"

"I'm doing fine, and yes, I talked to Erin. She's overprotective, but she can't help it. She's seven years older than me, nine years older than my little brother, and when we lost our parents, she took over. Since I was fifteen, she's raised me. Got me through every rough patch of my life. Really, it kills me to defy her like this—but I'm not sorry I did this. Now that Bobby's gone, she'd like me to snap out of it, sense the freedom, do all the things she feels were denied me—go back to school, get a career, marry one of her successful friends or something. She's so conservative—I'm a little too crazy for her. This thing I'm doing—she thinks I'm nuts."

"But do *you* think you're nuts?" Mel asked.

"Sometimes," she admitted. "But every day that passes, I learn more about myself. I don't want to get all gooey, but this is a spiritual journey. I thought it was about Ian, but it might be that Ian is right where he should be and I'm the one who needs to face a few things about my life."

"Aw, honey," Mel said. "That's not gooey. If we had time, I'd tell you about some of the crazy things I've done to try to get myself grounded."

"That would be nice," she said, reaching out to run a knuckle along David's pink cheek.

"Oh, look! It's going to happen," Mel whispered. "David, look," she said, turning the baby's head. "Look at the tree!"

Marcie noticed that Jack was crouched behind the huge tree, a couple of extension cords in his hands. He connected them and the most amazing tree in the world came to life. It was adorned in red, white and blue streamers that ran from the top to the bottom; red, white and blue balls glittered amid white lights—a million white lights. And between them were the gold stars. And patches, visible only by the sparkling gold trim that illuminated them, representing hundreds of military units who stood the watch. But the thing that mesmerized Marcie was the star on top.

It wasn't the typical gold star that often topped Christmas trees—it was a white beacon. And it was *powerful.* It actually cast a glow, as though it was a real star in the heavens. It created a path of light.

Her hand went to her throat to catch the tightness there. It was glorious. "That star," she whispered in sheer awe.

"I know," Mel said. "I had everyone in town looking for something like that. I hope it lights their way home."

"All of them," she whispered. "All of them." And she thought of Bobby, finally home after his struggle. And Ian? Could it light Ian's way home, too?

"How did you get all the unit patches?" Marcie asked.

"Jack and the boys contacted all their old friends. We made phone calls, wrote letters and faxed them. The tree was a sudden decision. Boys from around here have gone into the military—one very close to Jack and me not so long ago. And Vanni's husband, lost to us in Baghdad… He was in Jack's squad several years ago. This is for him, too. And his wife. This just couldn't wait. We had to hurry to get it done, and we did. The whole town pitched in. Doc's clinic was a disaster." She laughed. "He groused, but I think it made him secretly happy."

"It's truly amazing."

The oohs and ahhs subsided and people started to sing. The first carol was "Silent Night," and then "Away in a Manger." Marcie glanced toward the bar, missing Ian, wanting him to be with her to see the star. She smiled to see him standing on the porch of the bar, hands in his pants pockets, looking up to the top of the tree. And she thought—what will be will be. I promise, I won't get in the way of it.

People started drifting away about a half hour later, having been through a repertoire of about ten well-known songs. Mel took her baby into the bar, and it wasn't all that long before Marcie stood in the street with only a few people remaining, all of them looking closely at the tree as Ian continued to watch from the porch. He finally walked down the steps toward the tree and went right up to it, taking a close look at the ornaments and the unit badges. She knew what he would see—a remembrance. A tribute.

Ian didn't poke around at the tree for too long, but he could see in a moment that these military unit patches came from everywhere and there might have been hundreds reaching up to the top of that enormous tree. It made him feel something he hadn't allowed himself to feel in a very long time. Pride.

His reverie was broken when he heard Marcie cough; it came out like a bark. He turned and went to her, taking her hand in his, leading her to the truck. "Did you bring your cough medicine with you?"

"No," she said, coughing again. "Stupid, I know. But I was in a real hurry to get in your truck before you realized that I'd tricked you into letting me come—" She quickly jumped in the truck and when he was behind the wheel, she broke into another spasm. Then she said, "Sorry."

"For what, exactly? For hacking all the way home or for forcing yourself on me all day long?"

She glanced at his profile. Without being able to see his eyes and with all that hair on his face, she couldn't tell if he was amused or angry. "Both."

"I don't think you're coughing on purpose. And I'm not annoyed about the day anymore. It was a good day."

"Really?" she said. "Really? Did you have kind of a good time?"

"Kind of," he relented. "My favorite part was when you told the librarian I was an idiot savant. You think on your feet."

She smiled to herself.

"I think it turned out to be too much of a day for you," he said. "You've been doing so much better, we both ignored the fact that you were real sick there for a few days. You're supposed to be taking it easy."

"I don't have to rest or anything. But I am supposed to take that cough medicine a few times a day, and I let it go all day. Like I said, I wasn't thinking. I'll be fine." She coughed a little more. "I'll take the medicine as soon as we get home. Ian—do you ever get lonely? Up on the mountain?"

The first thought that came to his mind was, *I never used to.* But what he said was, "It's kind of strange how fast you can get used to something, like quiet. Like being alone. I didn't think it would end up being this long."

"Does that mean you planned to come back? Like to Chico? At least out of hiding?"

He turned and looked at her. "Marcie—I haven't been hiding." He looked a little surprised. He looked back to the road. "I mean, when I first got up this way, I didn't tell anyone where I was headed because I didn't know, and didn't tell anyone where I ended up. But I haven't been hiding. I have a driver's license and a registered vehicle. I pay taxes on the property. I do business—even if it's not very official. But I'm not that hard to find. You might have to get used to the idea that no one wanted to find me. No one was looking for me. But you."

"But I checked—I've been to the police and everything. Someone checked to see if you had a registered vehicle, though they said they couldn't give me any information about you if—"

"Did you check in Humboldt County? Because that cabin is over the line—it's in Trinity."

"Oh," she said. "Oh." She coughed a little more; this is what happens when you're fighting the last remnants of a bug, don't take your medicine and get a little tired out. "Can I ask something?" she said carefully. "Why'd you come up here?"

"I remembered the place. I'd come up here fishing with my dad when I was a kid. Before my mom died; before he lost interest. I first came when I was young, then as a teenager. I just remembered it as a place you could hear yourself think. I needed something like that—something low stress. And you admitted yourself, it's really beautiful."

"And it just turned into over four years?"

"It just did," he said. "Something I learned in the Marines—it works for me to challenge myself physically. Push myself. It gives me a look at who I am, what I can do. I was living off the land, roughing it. And I was starting to think clearly. I came up in late summer. I had a bedroll and backpack. Back then, I thought it might be best if I stayed away from people for the most part—thought some things through, tried to get a handle on the ways my life was changed since the Marine Corps. Then all of a sudden, it was snowing and I wasn't quite ready to take the next step. There were options—the GI bill and school, a job, whatever. But I wasn't ready, and the old man, Raleigh, kicked me back to life. Before I knew it, I'd lived with him for months—like two old bachelors going their own way, doing their own thing. Then I was taking care of him, then he was dead. By then, I had a routine and a lifestyle. It was working for me."

"But you didn't have friends…"

"Yeah, I didn't seem to need people. I swore I'd never let that happen. I guess the apple doesn't fall far from the tree."

"Huh?"

He didn't respond for quite a long, drawn out moment. Finally he said, "My dad. When my mom died, I was twenty and had been in the service a couple of years. She'd been sick with cancer. She was only fifty-five, but she'd had a hard fight for about three years. She was ready, but my old man wasn't. It really aged him and he was so pissed off. I mean more pissed off than he had been. He's never been what you'd call happy. He isolated himself, lost interest in things he used to like, slowly left what few friends he had. Every time I came home on leave, he was a little worse. I kept thinking he'd snap out of it, but he didn't. I swore that that would never happen to me, no matter what."

"And it did?"

"Not the way you think. I'm not angry. Not very, anyway. I just turned into a loner because my life was mostly spent alone."

"But don't you ever want more? I mean, like friends? A shower? An indoor john? A full set of dishes?"

He turned and grinned at her. "I have given some thought to the idea of a shower—it's a pain in the ass hauling water. But we mountain men, we don't need a lot of baths."

"Don't you want a TV? A CD player? A computer?"

"See if you can understand this. I want trees that are three hundred feet tall, black bear that poke around my stuff, deer that eat out of my hand, and a view that almost brings me to my knees every morning. I want to work just hard enough to afford my life. I'm sorry I don't have an indoor john and shower for you, especially while you've been sick, but I don't really need one."

She turned toward him and put a hand on his arm. "Aren't you just a little worried you could turn out like that old guy you took care of? Alone on a mountain for fifty years?"

"I've thought about it a time or two," he said. "I plan to keep going to the dentist at least once every other year—I'd like to go out with all my own teeth. Old Raleigh couldn't eat much that wasn't soft. But in all other ways, he didn't have a bad life."

"Okay, wouldn't you rather have a better way to earn money than selling firewood?"

He shot her a surprised look. "I don't sell wood because I'm poor and stupid—I sell wood because it's good money. The trees are free. There's no mark-up. I like cutting 'em down and chopping 'em up. I work at it year-round and make a lot of money when I sell the cut and split logs. I work for the furniture mover in spring and summer, while business is heavy for him. It lets me tend the garden and fish, not to mention get ahead on winter firewood—it has to be seasoned for six months. The river up here is pure and deep. The fish are fat and delicious. It's incredible. Listen, if I needed anything more, I'd work more."

"No regrets then?" she braved.

He snorted. "Marcie, I have lots of regrets. But not about how I live or what I do."

She chewed on her lip for a moment. Then she coughed until it bent her at the waist.

"This truck is too cold for you," he said. "We shouldn't have gone to the bar—we should've gone home. You get straight to the couch when we're home. Cough medicine and bed."

She took a breath. "Do you regret leaving Shelly?"

He glared at her for a moment, putting her on notice that she was getting too close to that forbidden territory again. But to her surprise, he answered. "It didn't go exactly that way. I'm not sure who left who." And then he fixed his eyes ahead again and started up the mountain to his cabin.

"But she said—"

His head jerked back to her. "You *talked* to her?"

"I was trying to locate you," she said weakly, like the wimp she'd suddenly become.

"Okay, this conversation will have to wait. No more."

And that was that. Silence reigned in the truck the rest of the way up the hill and she was afraid she'd made him very angry. She wondered if this was the point at which he'd load her up in his truck—maybe first thing the next morning—and take her to town, to Mel at the clinic, turning her over. This could be the point at which he was through putting up with her and all her talk about what had happened four years ago.

When they made the top of the hill, they each took their turns in the outhouse before entering the cabin. She dutifully took her cough medicine, hacking the whole time, and he turned his back while she got down to just his shirt and her panties and planted herself on the couch. He fed the woodstove, prepared his coffeepot for morning, rolled out his pallet and heavy blanket for bed.

Then he came to the couch. He scooted her over with a brush of his hand and sat on the edge.

"While I was in Iraq, Shelly was planning our wedding. It was set to happen a few weeks after I got back, and while I was gone, it turned into a frickin' coronation. My fault—I'd said, 'Anything that makes you happy.' But when I got back I told her I needed some time, that I was in no shape to be a husband. I was barely in shape to be a marine, which was supposed to be my life's work. I asked her to postpone the wedding—but she was in full bride mode. There are things I barely remember about that talk—something about the dress being fitted, invitations out, deposits made. I tried to convince myself to just close my eyes, lock up my brain for a few weeks and get it done. But I knew I'd be letting her down, letting a lot of people down. I knew I was screwed up and needed to decompress. Also, I knew she had no earthly idea what was happening to me—how could she? *I* barely knew. She said a lot of things, but what I remember most was that she said if I didn't let this wedding she'd worked so hard on happen, I could go straight to hell."

Marcie's eyes were wide, bright green. "Ian, I—"

"I don't want to hear her version," he said, holding up a hand. "I hope she's happy. I hope I didn't screw up her life too much. Believe me, if I'd married her then, it would have been worse for her. Now—you get some rest. I'll be back early in the day tomorrow. Don't do too much. Read one of your books. And take the medicine."

"She's married," Marcie said softly. "Pregnant."

"Good for her," he said easily. "It all worked out, then. Now, tomorrow try to get a handle on the cough."

"Yes," she replied. "Of course, yes."

Ten

Marcie had slept surprisingly well, despite her conversation with Ian right before falling asleep. She could see him in her mind—a thirty-year-old marine, home from some devastating war experiences, still scarred from being wounded—scarred on the inside from all he'd been through. And the love of his life doesn't have a care about any of that as long as she gets to wear a white lacy dress on *her* special day.

This brought some things to mind for Marcie, things she hadn't even considered when she'd gone to see Shelly to ask if she'd ever heard from Ian. Shelly had still been angry and had no interest in knowing whether Ian was all right. But after hearing Ian's side of things, Marcie recalled a conversation she'd had with Shelly when their men were in Iraq together. Marcie had called Shelly, suggesting they meet since their husbands were such good friends. But Shelly was very busy. "Planning a big wedding is a lot of work," Shelly had said by way of an excuse.

"I'd be happy to help," Marcie had offered.

"Thanks, but between my mother, aunts and bridesmaids, I'm up to my eyeballs in help. Still, it seems to take every spare minute I have."

"Maybe you'll come up with a break in your schedule and we could meet for coffee," Marcie said. "Since our guys are best friends and we live not ten minutes from each other."

And Shelly had said, "Give me your number and if I find the time, I'll give you a call."

But she never did. Clearly, never intended to. And for the first time ever, Marcie wondered—would we have been invited to the wedding?

Ian had left a half pot of coffee on top of the woodstove but, while Marcie had slept, the fire had died down. The coffee had cooled. She remembered having that great, rich, steaming hot coffee at Jack's, and it set up a real craving in her. Ian's coffee wasn't bad, but it would be a lot better if it was hot.

She fed the stove, but she didn't have the patience to wait for it to flare and heat that coffee. She eyeballed the little propane stove and thought, that's a quicker option. She took the pot to the stove and studied the dials carefully. Gas on. Simple enough. She turned the dial but nothing happened. She blew on it like she had to do on her dad's old stove. Nothing happened; there was no spark. She smelled the gas however. She gave it a second and said a chant over it—light! Heat the coffee! She turned the knob again—and again there was no spark and the smell of gas was evident. A third try produced nothing.

Then she noticed the matches on the counter and thought, so that's it. Turn on the gas, light the stove! With the pot on the burner, she turned on the gas again and struck a match. And poof! The flame shot about three feet in the air, hitting her square in the face.

She shrieked and whirled, patting her face and hair, running her hands over the rest of her wild red mop to check for fire. She felt the burn on her face. When she looked at the little stove, the flame was just normal, burning nicely under the pot, but her face felt as hot as a poker!

She started to whimper like a baby, all shook up by what could have been a disastrous accident. She rushed to the couch, pulled on her boots and, in Ian's chambray shirt, she ran outside to her car, disregarding all manner of possible vicious wildlife. There wasn't a mirror in the entire house; that much she already knew. She used the sleeve of the shirt to wipe off the little bug's side mirror and took a look. Then she screamed.

Her face was bright red, like a sunburn, and her hairline was singed. Little black squiggles seemed to sprout from her forehead. Her eyebrows, which weren't much to start with and were nearly blond, seemed to be even less significant, and if she was seeing correctly—her *lashes* were shorter!

Ice, she thought. Something cold to relieve the burn before it blistered and swelled.

She ran back inside, turned off the little stove and cursed at it, then started digging around for a cloth. He always laid these things out for her on bath days, but there was nothing handy right now. She was finally pushed to look through the trunks. The first one in which she looked held clothing, but in the second she found some towels and washcloths. She grabbed one, wet it from the chilled water that came straight from the sink pump and pressed it to her face. "God," she said in relief. "Oh, God."

An hour later when Ian walked into his cabin, what he

saw startled him. Marcie was lying on the couch in his shirt and her boots, her legs bare, with a cloth pressed over her face. He knelt beside the couch in a near panic and gently pulled her hands away. "Marcie?" he asked softly.

When she lowered her hands along with the cold, wet cloth, he gasped. "Are you having a relapse? Fever? Should I take you to—"

"It's not a fever!" she nearly shouted at him.

"But your face—"

"Is bright red! I know. And my hair is burned off around my face. And if you bother to look, there don't seem to be *eyebrows* there either, not that I ever had much for eyebrows."

"Jesus," he said in a breath, sitting back on his heels.

"I was trying to heat up the coffee on the propane stove—and apparently I don't know how to use the stove."

"What happened?" he asked. "Are you hurt?"

"Hurt? I'm pretty ugly, but I don't know if it's permanent." She relayed the events of lighting the stove, coming too late with the match or too early with the gas and how it all poofed in her face and scorched her.

His rough finger glanced along the hair above her face and beneath that massive beard his lips twitched slightly. "I have some salve. And this will probably grow back…"

"You're laughing!" she accused. "You are fucking *laughing!*"

He shook his head vigorously but he still showed teeth. Teeth she'd rarely seen. "No. No. It's just that—"

"What? It's just that *what?*"

"I'm sorry, Marcie. I'm sure it's all my fault. I should have showed you how to—"

"You're damn straight it's all your fault! Starting with roaring at me like a goddamn lion and making me scared and making me stubborn and then not showing me how to light the damn stove and then—"

Suddenly he was all teeth behind his red beard. "Making you stubborn?" he asked, barely concealing the laughter.

"Well, I'm at my best when people just do what I ask! And what's so goddamn funny?"

His arms went around his torso to hug himself and he rolled backward onto the floor, erupting into laughter. His mouth opened wide, his eyes squinched and he bellowed. Between gasping and belly laughs, he choked out— "You're bright red! And it's my fault for making you— stubborn! God—you're priceless!" And he laughed himself crazy. She sat on the edge of the couch, boots on the floor, red face staring down at him, glowering.

It took him a while to get himself under control. His laughter ebbed into pants and gasps; he wiped at his watering eyes. Then he finally looked at her.

"I'm surprised you didn't fart from laughing," she said, not the merest hint of a smile on her face.

He huffed a couple of times and said, "It took some doing." He sat up, recovered himself and asked, with a twitch of his lips, "Are you in pain?"

She lifted her chin. "Somewhat."

"Let me find that salve," he said, getting to his feet. He went into one of his cupboards and produced a tin of salve, gently smearing it over her burned face, his lips wriggling in the temptation to laugh the whole time.

"Is it that damned funny?" she finally demanded.

"It's pretty funny, Marcie. There was a perfectly good starter on that stove, but it broke a while back and it was easier for me to light it than get it fixed. See, that's the kind of thing that happens when you live alone—you don't make a house for a family. You get by. It's lazy, I know..."

"But you're not lazy. You work hard!"

"Okay then, it's just one more thing I don't have to do," he said. "Really, it's not that bad, your face..." Then he chuckled.

"I have black squiggles where I used to have bangs."

"I know, honey. But it'll all come back just fine."

Honey? Did he just call me honey? Is he feeling sorry for me? Being sweet to me because I'm scorched? Finally she said, "The salve is good. What is it?"

"Something the vet uses on horses."

"Oh, terrific!"

"No, it's good stuff! Better than what you can get over the counter or from the doctor, thanks to the FDA. I swear." But then he laughed.

"Are you still laughing because I look ridiculous, or because you just got one over on me—giving me horse medicine?"

"I'm laughing because—" he gulped "—how about I grease you up and feed you something to eat? While you're trying to recover from your burn, I could read one of those sloppy romances to you, if you like."

"Read to me?" she asked.

He shrugged. "Sometimes I read to Raleigh, when he was feeling real bad."

"No," she said. "Food, yes. Reading would be nice, but singing would be better. I want you to sing to me."

"Aw, Marcie..."

"I'm a burn victim. Try to be accommodating."

He sighed heavily and went to his cupboard. There were a couple dozen large cans of Dinty Moore beef stew in there. He pulled a couple out and she said, "Good God, are you expecting nuclear war?"

"No," he laughed. "I'm ready for snow. My road to Highway 36 is long. You can get real hungry up here if you're not prepared."

"And you exist on canned stew?"

"It's good," he said. "I'd buy something else if something else tasted better." He emptied it into a pan and put it on the stove. She watched while he lit it. First the match, then the gas. Perfect. Well, that made sense.

So he warmed her stew, scooped it into a big mug, and let her have it. Then he tucked her in, gave her cough medicine, and told her to close her eyes. And he sang to her. Everything was soft but deep and resonant. "New York, New York," the slow version. "When I Fall In Love." "You Don't Know Me," which she tried not to read anything into. She was afraid to open her eyes, afraid he'd stop. There were a lot of old, sweet, mellow Sinatra and Presley songs.

She found herself thinking about Abigail Adams, managing five children and running a farm single-handedly while her husband worked to found America. Marcie had always admired and honored Abigail. Was it so much trouble to go across the yard to the john? Even if you did have to carry a heavy skillet to ward off wildlife? Or heat your water? What *did* she need? One thing she knew for a fact: she sure didn't need an eyebrow wax.

Marcie drifted off to sleep dreaming of Abigail and Ian's voice. In the morning when she woke, the coffeepot was on the woodstove, which had burned low as usual. There was a note on the table.

Don't light the Coleman stove unless you're sure you know how.

And it made her laugh.

Marcie was almost halfway through a novel in which the hero was just about to grab the heroine by the waist, slam her against him and just kiss the stuffing out of her when something occurred to her. Her letters.

In addition to those letters she'd written to Ian about Bobby when Ian was still in Iraq, letters he had answered, she'd written him regularly for a couple of years, to general delivery. They'd neither been answered nor returned. What were the chances…?

She dove off the couch and went first to that little tin box where he put his money every night. She noticed he had stopped locking it. It didn't hold very much—the deed, which she didn't bother with, a few pictures. She was distracted by the pictures. They were very telling in number and subject. A family picture when Ian was a young teen, fourteen or fifteen. A beautiful picture of Shelly, a black wrap over her shoulders, perhaps a college or sorority picture. A picture of Ian and Bobby wearing BDUs, rifle straps over their shoulders, grinning. One with his dad when he was a bit older, his father unsmiling.

It distracted her from her search. A couple of things about them were telling—there were only a few photos, and they were of the most special people he'd had in his life. They marked his passage, from a boy in what looked like an average, middle-class family, to a young man with an unhappy father, to a marine. Then there came the woman, then the friend. Then… Nothing.

Underneath the photos were his medals. The ones she'd

received for Bobby had come in fancy boxes. Ian's were loose. But at least he hadn't thrown them away in a fit of anger or depression.

She tucked everything away very carefully and closed the lid, feeling guilty about going through his things. He deserved his privacy, but there were things she wished to understand. So she went to the trunk that held his clothing and slipped her hand slowly down all four sides. She felt something and gently parted the carefully folded clothes to strike oil. A rubber band held about a dozen long white envelopes, all to him, all from her. All sealed. Never opened, yet saved.

She stared at them in wonder. Now whatever could that mean?

And then she heard a motor. At first, assuming it was Ian returning, she replaced the envelopes and closed the trunk. By the time she got to her feet, she realized it wasn't Ian's truck, so she went to the door.

Well, she might've known. There, in a big, shiny new SUV was Erin Elizabeth Foley. Big sister. She folded her arms across her chest as Erin got out of the car.

Erin took one look at her and froze. She took two steps closer, her mouth agape and said, "Oh my God! What's *wrong* with you?"

Completely forgetting about her red face and burned hair, she looked down at herself. She was wearing one of Ian's shirts and her boots, bare, white legs sticking out between. "The floor is cold. Erin, what are you doing here?"

"I came to see this place, this man. You can't possibly believe I'm just going to let you continue this insanity without knowing what we're dealing with? And it's a good thing I came to get you! Dear God—did he beat you?"

"Beat me? Of course not! And *we're* not dealing with

anything because this is not your deal! You're going to spoil everything!"

Erin came closer, bringing the rich scent of Chanel's Allure with her. She was decked in a tan leather jacket and matching boots with heels—probably Cole Haan, her favorite—and perfectly creased, expensive, chocolate-brown wool pants. She wore thin driving gloves and her strawberry-blond hair fell in perfect waves to her shoulders. There was, of course, gold jewelry and a colorful red, orange and purple Hermes scarf looped around her neck. "What happened to your face?"

Marcie's hand rose to her cheek. It didn't hurt so she had all but forgotten. "Oh. I had a little accident with the stove. It was entirely my fault. But I'm fine."

"Have you been to the emergency room?"

"The what?" She started to laugh. "There's an emergency room a couple of hours from here, but I have some stuff on it. A really good salve they use on horses."

"Oh, for the love of God! You've completely lost your mind!"

"It doesn't hurt," Marcie said, feeling ten years old.

"But your hair. Your beautiful hair! And your…your… *eyebrows!*"

"I noticed," Marcie said. "Really, Erin—why can't you just leave me alone? I did what you asked—I called every couple of days, at least every few or had someone call you, I was careful, I—"

Erin's lips firmed into that implacable "mother expression." "Right. Finding him was one thing, staying with him in an isolated place without a phone and a— Dear God, is that what I think it is?" she said, pointing a finger toward the outhouse.

"The loo," Marcie said, a tad amused. "No bidet."

"I'm going to faint."

"We have a little porcelain pot inside if you can't weather the trek to the head." She decided not to mention it would do well to carry a weapon when one ventured out there.

Erin actually swayed on her feet, her eyes closing briefly. Marcie had to hold in her laughter. If she thought her introduction to this cabin in the woods was interesting, the very thought of Erin slipping on her Cole Haans and trudging out in the morning to the facilities was enough to make her burst into hysterical laughter. "You should see how we manage on bath day," Marcie said, finding it irresistible to bait her a little.

Erin's eyes popped open. "Bath day suggests it's not every day and it's not convenient."

"That would be a true statement."

"And not particularly comfortable…" Erin went on.

"Well, since the only heat is a wood-burning stove, it's quite quick."

"Lord. Get your things."

"No. No, you can look around and lift your prissy little nose and meet Ian if you insist, though you won't like the look of him, I can assure you. And then you can depart before it becomes necessary for you to use the facilities. That's as far as I go."

"At least you'll let me take you to the doctor," Erin said.

"I've seen the doctor," Marcie said before she could stop herself.

"And what did he say about you using horse medicine on your face?"

"Liniments. Horse liniments of some kind that work surprisingly well. But, actually, I didn't need a doctor for that. Turns out the minute I got here and found Ian, I got sick. Flu. He went for the doctor, and the doctor and his nurse practitioner came out to the cabin, gave me a shot and Ian took very good care of me. He made chicken soup and everything."

Erin put her fingers to her temples. She gave a little rub, then recovered herself, giving her head a shake. She glanced at the igloo-shaped mound right beside her big SUV with narrowed eyes.

"My little VeeDub. Not going anywhere for a while, I'm afraid. It wouldn't handle the mountain roads in snow and ice. Things need to dry out a little. If you won't just go away, come inside, Erin." Marcie turned and entered the cabin, leaving the door open for her sister.

As Marcie could have predicted, Erin wasn't impressed. She looked around and though she was quiet, she shuddered. "Where are the beds?"

"As a matter of fact, there aren't beds. I sleep on the couch and Ian sleeps on a pallet on the floor near the stove. I haven't taken his couch—he says he's always used the pallet. It's comfortable for him. The couch is too short."

"There seems to be just the one room," Erin said.

"It's a cabin. It's been inhabited by one man. Not at all unlike the cabins Dad and Drew rented for hunting and fishing."

"This is entirely different, as you well know," Erin said pleadingly. "Marcie, I can't leave you here. I can't."

Another engine ground its way to the top of the mountain and Marcie stepped toward her sister with a look of desperation on her face. "Listen to me—really listen. We haven't talked about what happened to Bobby, about any of that time in Ian's life. We were just barely sneaking up on it, so you are to say *nothing,* do you hear me?" She went to the couch to sit, take off her boots and grab up her jeans to pull them quickly on. "Nothing! Mind your manners, don't insult him and use that sharp lawyer's brain of yours to be political. And I mean it!"

"Really!" Erin said, stiffening.

"You're goddamn right, really!" Marcie sat again and pulled on her boots. By the time she accomplished this, Ian was coming in the door.

He filled the frame. His eyes narrowed. Marcie heard her sister's sharp intake of breath.

Marcie knew it was Erin's presence in the cabin that made his dirty tan jacket look shabbier, his beard wilder. His eyes glittered. He wasn't happy. "The sister, I presume," he said.

Erin stretched her neck proudly and put out a hand. "Erin Foley, how do you do?"

"Doin' just fine, thanks. You?" he said, ignoring the hand.

"Well, thank you. It's nice to meet you. I was just coming for Marcie…"

"I see," he said.

"But I'm not quite ready to go," Marcie said. "Erin just wanted to meet you before she leaves. I didn't call her to come, Ian."

"Don't know how you could," he said, putting his sack of groceries on his small table. "Smoke signals, I guess."

"All right, listen the two of you," Erin said. "I didn't like this idea from the start, Marcie coming up here alone in search of you, especially now—this time of year, the holidays, and almost exactly a year since Bobby's—"

"Erin!"

She cleared her throat. "Well, as you've no doubt discovered, my younger sister is very stubborn and will have her way."

"Can't hardly miss that," he said.

"Finding you and talking to you was one thing—but this is beyond the pale. She can't stay here, Mr. Buchanan. There's only one room, nowhere for sleeping, no indoor facilities, and it appears she's not entirely well. She's sick and burned and… It was very good of you to put her up, take care of her, et cetera, but enough is enough. Marcie should come home to her family. It's almost Christmas. We've all been through enough." She looked pointedly at her sister. "Marcie, really, it's not just me who's anxious to have you home—the Sullivan family is worried about you, too. Maybe you and Mr. Buchanan can stay in touch, meet again after Christmas, somewhere where there's a phone and an indoor—"

"Erin!" If possible, Marcie's face got a little redder.

"Your sister's right," Ian said. "You should be with your family now. We'll be in touch sometime down the road."

"If I'd been ready to go, I would have left! If I'd been determined to leave, I would've hitchhiked—I could have done that," she said firmly. "I was planning to stay as long as you— We were just getting to know each other!"

"You've been here long enough," he said. "And I'm not used to having people around. Good that she's here. You can't get out of here in your car, anyway."

"But, Ian—"

"She's right. Enough is enough. Get your things together."

"But, Ian," she said, taking a step toward him, a pleading expression on her face, "I thought—"

"I think we did just fine together, trapped here by your flu and all. But now she's here to take you home, and I'm ready to have my house back. I'm not used to so many people. You know that." He took a breath. "You'll be in good hands with your sister. She looks extremely..." He gave Erin a glance that was an impolite once-over. "Competent."

"Good," Erin said, rubbing her hands together. "Shall we?"

Marcie looked up into his eyes. Hers were soft and pleading; his were hard. "You don't mean that," she said. "Are you saying you *want* me to go?"

"You should go with your sister, Marcie. She's right. You don't want to worry the family. Sometime later we'll meet up again if you want. But I'm a hermit. And I like it that way."

"You're not a hermit. You sell wood, go to truck stops, churches, the library... I don't believe you want me to go," she said in a near whisper.

"Yeah. You do. But I'm glad you found me. And I'm sorry about Bobby." He dropped his chin. "You'll never know how sorry..." Then he lifted his eyes and met hers. "Go on now. Go home. Where you belong."

"I was starting to feel like I belonged here," she said. He held silent while their eyes were locked. Finally, beaten, she turned from him and gathered up her things. It didn't take long—she kept her clothes in her duffel, along with a few things like shampoo and makeup. In her backpack were maps and notes, and the baseball cards she hadn't yet given him. And she had a purse. She rolled up her sleeping bag. In no time at all, she was done and began to fold the quilt that had kept her warm on the couch.

"I'll take care of that," Ian said.

But she continued. When it was in a nice little square, she stacked her library books on the table. "I didn't finish," she said. "I was just getting to the good part, too. The page is marked. Thanks for everything. I mean, you've done so much for me."

"I didn't do hardly anything at all," he said. "I didn't change anything."

"Yeah, you did. You cooked for me, took care of me, gave me medicine, protected me… But, well, I know I've been a lot of trouble…"

"It wasn't a big deal" was all he said.

"To me it was."

And he didn't respond.

She hefted her duffel, backpack and purse and went out the door, leaving Erin to grab the sleeping bag. She threw her things in the backseat of Erin's car and got in the passenger seat.

She wished he'd roared at Erin and scared her away. But Erin would've come back with the whole sheriff's department unlike Marcie, who just ate a sandwich and nearly froze to death.

"Go into the town—I want to say goodbye to my friends."

"Virgin River?" Erin asked.

"Yes."

"Listen, Marcie…"

"And don't *talk* to me. Don't even *look* at me."

Eleven

Erin pulled up in front of Jack's bar and said, "Don't be long. We'll be driving at night as it is."

Marcie didn't respond, she just stomped inside. Obviously not trusting her, Erin was right behind her.

Jack started to smile, then his smile froze as he took in Marcie's scorched face and fried hair. "Whoa," he said.

She jumped up on a stool. "Broken propane stove. Don't ask."

"I wouldn't dream of it," he said.

"Beer."

"Coming right up."

He poured a draft and greeted Erin. "Hello again. I guess you found the place, no problem."

"Thank God," she said. "Do you have any idea of the living conditions out there?"

He chuckled. "I'm sure it's not that unusual for the mountains. I lived pretty lean while I was building the bar."

"There's no indoor bathroom!"

"Also not too unusual. You have to redig that outhouse

every few years, too. And I suppose you know—we don't have sewer lines that reach that far up and out. It would have to be a septic system, but a man all alone might just brave the cold in winter. Same with cable and electric—you need a satellite dish and generator. There are probably hundreds of cabins just like that out there."

"Then what's the point?"

"Oh, if you'd looked around, you wouldn't ask."

The door opened and Mel came into the bar, David on her hip. She jumped up beside Marcie and passed the baby across the bar to her husband. Then she gave him a little kiss and turned a smile to Marcie. She jumped in surprise.

"I got a little burn," Marcie said.

"Boy howdy. What are you putting on it?"

"Some kind of horse liniment Ian had. It relieved it immediately."

"Ah. Methylsulphonymethane. People around here use it for damn near everything. It's famous for cell repair. I guess Doc's right—you're in good hands."

"Well, not anymore. Mel, meet my sister, Erin. Erin, meet Mel Sheridan. I believe you spoke."

"Yes, of course. How do you do. Nice of you to call for Marcie."

"It was my pleasure. I've enjoyed getting to know your sister."

"And you tended her while she had the flu?"

"With Doc, yes. She seems to be doing just fine—don't worry about that."

Jack had situated David in his backpack so he could serve and handle his son at the same time. Preacher brought out a rack of clean flatware to place under the bar, nodded hello to everyone, lifted curious brows toward Marcie, but then disappeared. Mike Valenzuela came in the back door, went behind the bar to help himself to a draft and was introduced to Erin. When he looked at Marcie, his face froze in surprise.

"The propane stove," she explained wearily. "I turned on the gas first, lit the match second."

"Bet you get that in the right order next time," he said, taking a drink of his beer before going back to the kitchen.

Mel happened to glance down and noted Erin's boots. "Holy smoke, I used to own a pair of those," she said. "I kind of miss them, too. I killed them the first spring I was in this town, traipsing around the ranches and vineyards."

"Is that so?" Erin asked.

"This is rough country. Man's country, I guess, much as it kills me to call it that. I wasn't quite ready for it."

"Well, the men in here are very…"

"I know," Mel said, laughing. "Very pretty, aren't they? But dangerous. Watch out."

"Dangerous?" Erin questioned, wide-eyed.

Mel leaned close. "They shoot deer, play poker, smoke big nasty cigars. And as it turns out—have pretty high sperm counts. You can trust me—I'm the local midwife…"

Jack chuckled, drawing a glance from Erin.

"Where are you from?" Erin asked Mel.

"Most recently, Los Angeles," Mel said. "I was looking for a change."

"A *change?*" Erin asked, stunned.

Mel smiled sweetly. "It snuck up on me. The power of this beauty, the natural phenomenon of unspoiled landscape. What I saw on my first morning—trees that touched the sky, eagles soaring, deer in the yard… Then there are the people here—they're just plain decent folk. I fell in love." She gave her tummy a rub. "Then I fell in love with Jack, who is entirely too fertile for my taste, but still...he has his good points."

"Mel," Marcie said. "I need a lift back to Ian's."

Both women turned to look at her. "Marcie, I won't let you do this!" Erin insisted. "It's primitive! He's primitive! He looks like a total nutcase. A wild man."

"He's actually very docile. Kind."

"There are no beds!"

"I slept on a pallet on the floor for two years while I was remodeling this bar," Jack put in. He scratched his chin. "Didn't shave much either. Used Doc's shower about once every three days or so. We're kind of homespun around here."

"But... But we're not," Erin said.

"Jack," Marcie said. "Call the sheriff. I'm being kidnapped."

"That wild-man look," Jack told Erin. "Not unusual around here. Lotta farmers, loggers and ranchers don't shave in winter. And they don't usually wear Sunday best to chop wood or feed sheep. Ian Buchanan fits right in, and seems like a civil man. I wouldn't worry."

Marcie put her hand over Erin's. "I'm going back and I want you to go home. I'll call and check in, I promise. But I was just barely over being sick, just barely getting him to talk. I'm not done here."

"Marcie—I don't mean to sound cruel, baby, but you're not the only one who lost Bobby. His family, me and Drew..."

"I know, I know. I'm not ignoring that, I promise. We'll be together for Christmas. Please, Erin, don't fight me. Let me do what I came to do. Then it'll be done and I can move on." Tears welled up in her eyes. "Honest, I just have to feel like this is complete."

"What?" Erin asked pleadingly, her voice a strained whisper. "What do you think you're going to accomplish?"

Marcie shot a pleading glance at Mel.

Mel and Marcie connected eyes for a moment. Then Mel looked at her husband. "Jack, take Marcie back to Ian's. Take David with you. I'll tend the bar if anyone comes in, or I can call Preacher or Mike. I think Erin and I should talk a minute."

Jack lifted one brow. "You sure?"

She just nodded and smiled. He leaned slowly across the bar and gave her a little kiss. "I'll be back before the dinner crowd shows up."

When Jack and Marcie had left, Mel went around behind the bar and poured two cups of coffee. "Cream or sugar?" she asked Erin.

"Both. Please. And I don't think you even come close to realizing just how—"

"Almost three years ago, my first husband was murdered," Mel said. With that, Erin stopped explaining herself any further. Mel cleared her throat. "I was a nurse practitioner and midwife in an urban trauma center—central L.A. Mark was an E.R. doc there. He was stopping off at a convenience store for milk for his cornflakes after pulling a thirty-six-hour call and there was a robbery in progress. He was shot. Killed."

"I'm sorry," Erin said softly.

"Thank you. At the time I really wanted my life to end with his. After several months passed and I couldn't seem to get on with my life, I did the craziest thing—I took a job in this one-horse town for almost no money just because I had an instinct that it was different enough to jolt me into some kind of change. I have an older sister," she added, smiling. "She thought I was completely nuts and was ready to kidnap me, drag me to her house to recover. Her way."

Mel leaned toward Erin. "I'm kind of an expert at struggling to move on. It's not easy and it's almost never a clear path. But I can tell you this much—I believe it's necessary to blaze your own trail. And I'm sure Marcie's safe. I don't know if Marcie will work it all out, but I don't recommend getting in the way of a woman trying to settle her life into some kind of order. There are things she wants to understand. We'll try to look out for her, as well."

Erin sipped her coffee slowly. "I know there's a message here, and I appreciate you being so candid, but with Marcie—"

"Yes, Erin—the message is—whatever she feels she has to do to get to that next stage might not make sense, might not work out, might not be practical or wise, but it's what she thinks she has to do. I know you're hurting, too—losing your brother-in-law, having Marcie out of reach right now—I'm so sorry. I remember my sister suffering so much when my husband died—she loved him like a brother. But at the end of the day, Marcie has to feel like she did what she had to do. For whatever reason, working something out with Ian seems to be it. Apparently it's necessary for her. She's been incredibly determined."

"That's true enough," Erin said.

"I wouldn't be having this talk with you if I thought there was any chance Marcie was even slightly at risk. Believe me, I serve the women of this town. I look out for them. Marcie hasn't been real specific, but you and I both know what she's after. She needs to understand why the man who saved her husband's life would run away. Abandon him. Abandon *her*."

"But what if he's only going to do that to her again?" Erin asked, a very sad and concerned look crossing her features.

"That's what she came to find out," Mel said, and she reached across the bar and squeezed Erin's hand. "Let her get to the last page on this story, sweetheart. It's what she's been needing, or she wouldn't have gone through so much."

"But—"

"We don't have to agree or understand," Mel said, shaking her head. "We just have to respect her wishes." Then, very softly she said, "You have to go home. Let her finish what she came to do. You aren't going to lose her."

Erin blinked and a fat tear ran down her cheek. Erin never got choked up. "Do you think she knows how much I care about her? Love her?"

"She absolutely knows," Mel said with a nod. "And you know what? When I see her next, which I'm sure will be soon, I'll remind her."

Back at the cabin Ian paced for nearly an hour. He hadn't been nice to the sister and he regretted that. He could have tried harder with her, reassured her a little so she'd feel okay about Marcie being here. Instead he'd pushed them away.

He shouldn't have let her stay in the first place, Ian thought. He should have told Mel it would be best to take Marcie back to town, to Doc's. Damned little freckle-faced midget. There were a dozen things he didn't like being reminded of. Like, he wasn't a hermit—he was lonely. But he didn't fit in most places, so he kept it to himself. Still, he hated not singing in church when singing felt so good. He didn't like sitting alone in a bar, far in the corner, mute and unfriendly, trying to remain unapproachable. And he hadn't had a good belly laugh in a long, long time. Until Marcie.

For the first time since he hit this county, he wanted things. Like soup bowls instead of mugs and cans to eat soup out of. Things he thought he didn't need, like a few creature comforts. A radio. She was right—a person who loved music should hear some from time to time.

And he wanted someone to care enough about him to try to find him. He wanted someone to love him. It had been so long since anyone had loved him.

But the worst thing she'd made him realize was that this skinny little redhead had held up through Bobby's devastating demise better than he had. And she'd had to work through it every day, every damn day, while he'd merely run away from it. I'm the weak one, he thought dismally, and she's the one with the strength of a thousand soldiers.

He went to his trunk, dug deep, and brought out the stack of letters. He put them on the table under the light. Then he went to the cupboard, reached far into the back and located a bottle of Canadian Mist that had barely been tapped, putting it on the table with the letters. He found a glass, poured himself a shot and threw it back.

And then, without warning, the door to his cabin opened and she walked right in as if she owned the place. She toted all her gear: sleeping bag, duffel, backpack and purse, dropping it all where it had been previously stowed, at the foot of that sagging couch. He hoped all the hair on his face hid the elation that he could feel glow there. "I could've been naked," he said.

She smiled and walked over to the table, pulled out the chair and sat down opposite him. "Ah yes—that would be the thrill of my life, right? We drinking tonight?"

"I decided it was cold enough for a shot."

"Can I join you?"

"Your sister waiting outside?" he asked, getting up to find another glass. He turned up a plastic tumbler and gave it to her.

Marcie poured herself a little splash of the whiskey. "Nah. I sent her home. I had to promise to call every couple of days and get home by Christmas, so I guess I could be some trouble for you. I mean, some more trouble. Sorry."

"What's your mission here? Exactly? You think you're going to straighten me out, clean me up presentable, do some kind of good deed?"

"Oh brother, are you ever feeling sorry for yourself. You probably shouldn't drink if you're that screwed up—this stuff is a depressant, you know." He stiffened abruptly. "My mission, as you call it, is pretty simple. There are these stupid baseball cards. Bobby told me in letters that you were a collector, too—I brought them. Bobby's cards."

She went to her duffel, dug around and brought out an album in which Bobby's collection was carefully preserved. She put it on the table.

"This is difficult to explain. For some reason, the idea of the two of you talking about these baseball cards in the middle of a war, in a desert, staying alert for bombs and snipers was something I never got over." She took a breath. "I want you to understand—they're hard to let go of, only because they were his. He thought they were awesome. He'd want you to have them."

Ian didn't touch the album. "Why didn't you just give them to me right away?"

She sighed. "Because I was sick. And you didn't want to talk about *it*."

"I'm sorry," he said. "I didn't think I could." He stared

down at the table for a moment, then lifted his eyes. "That's it, then? The baseball cards?"

"There was a time, way back, when we wrote, kind of leaned on each other because Bobby got hurt. Then you dropped out of sight. Went missing. So, I came to meet you, or re-meet you, to thank you, make sure you were all right, tell you about your father. And, as it turns out, you seem to be fine. In some ways, better off than me. You live exactly as you like, talk to people when you want and seek solitude when it feels good, have a relationship with nature and aren't burdened with worries or things. You don't carry much of a load, on the outside at least—you have only what you need. And I don't think you need cleaning up presentable. You look just fine."

"You said I looked like a wild man."

"You do." She grinned at him. "I'm used to it now."

"What were you going to thank me for?" he asked, replenishing his glass.

"You're kidding, right? Come on! For saving Bobby's life!"

"You shouldn't do that. You shouldn't even *think* that. I have a lot of regrets, kid, but that's at the top of the list."

"Saving him? Look, we're all sorry he was so badly hurt, that he was a helpless invalid. Beyond anyone's control..."

"You think so? Because I think maybe I knew," he said. "I lifted him and he was limp and heavy. There was a split second when I faced a choice. There was no muscle tension in his body—he was nothing but dead weight. I could've put him down right where he was, covered his body with mine to keep him from getting hit worse and waited it out—the end. And then you wouldn't have been saddled with the burden and pain you've had to carry for three years and he'd have been free. God, you were just a kid. And I knew Bobby didn't want that life—men in combat talk about things like that. But I was selfish. I was thinking about myself—I acted the way I was trained to react, and I just couldn't face letting him go. I was acting like I wanted to be a goddamn hero."

She stared at him for a long moment. "Holy Jesus," she finally said. "Is that how you think it was? That it was up to *you?* And that your actions made my life a nightmare?" She shook her head. "That's not how it was. You should've just read the damn letters!"

He stared down at the pile in front of him. Then he lifted his eyes to hers. So, she'd been into his stuff, found them, knew they'd never been opened.

"Here's how it was—"

"Marcie," he said, his eyes darkening in regret. Pain. "Don't, okay?"

"God, I thought I was the one who needed to understand," she said, taking a delicate sip of the liquor. She made a face and pursed her lips, then said, "You're gonna listen now. We lost our mom when Drew was only two, I was four, and Erin was eleven. Our dad raised us, but when I was fifteen he died suddenly—it was a coronary during a routine knee surgery. Very unusual, very rare. Erin was a recent college graduate, headed for law school, so she stepped in, became the parent, and we all stayed in the house that Dad raised us in and, of course, when Bobby went to Iraq, I lived there with Erin and Drew while he was gone. When we brought him home, that's where we brought him. That's where we were when you visited us—and we weren't very good at that whole thing. We—all of us—were so new to caregiving, it must have looked to you like we weren't going to survive it. It must have looked terrible…"

He remembered; there were days he'd had trouble putting it out of his mind. The house was a disaster, Marcie was skinny and pale and alone, she looked about thirteen. The hospital bed dominated the dining room so it was the first thing you saw when you walked in the house, leaving the family nowhere to have a meal. There was other medical equipment standing around the place—a fancy wheelchair with a head brace, hydraulic lifts, weights for counterbalance when moving that dead weight, a suction machine, oxygen tanks, basins, linens.

"We had to bring him home or leave him in a long-term care facility in another state. After a couple of months we got him into a civilian nursing home—an excellent place, with the military picking up the tab through CHAMPUS. I can thank Erin for that—she wouldn't give up. Bobby had a large family—he was the youngest of seven—and we were all in it together, God bless them. They've been such a wonderful help—family to me in every way."

"CHAMPUS?" Ian heard himself ask.

"It doesn't always work out so good. A lot of wounded soldiers who need long-term care are assigned to military hospitals wherever there's space, and it has nothing to do with where the family lives. I faced leaving Bobby in D.C. or the East Coast or Texas, but… We were very lucky. He had the best. And Ian—he might've looked pathetic, but there was no indication he was in any pain or stress. We pampered him, kept him totally comfortable at all times, and there were so many of us to do that. Bobby's whole family—his mom and dad, six brothers and sisters and their spouses, nieces and nephews, me, Drew, and yes, even

Erin got right in there. He was massaged, read to, kissed and hugged. He was almost never alone. We had a visiting schedule—he was always checked on and covered. Ian—it wasn't torture for me. Losing him hurt, of course, but really, I lost him so long ago that by the time he passed..."

"Relief?" Ian asked reflexively.

"For him," she said. "For me, the end of a long journey. You should've read the damn letters!"

He just shook his head. "I didn't want to know he was dead. Didn't want to know he was still alive."

"He was alive, comfortable, cared for and loved." She nodded toward the letters. "I wrote you about him, but also about me—it was really hard at first, grieving Bobby as though he'd already gone—but then my life became almost normal. I got out with friends quite a bit. I took a couple of vacations—Bobby's parents insisted on it. I wrote you all about them, don't ask me why. Hell, I wrote you *everything*. Every stupid thing. Like you were *my* best friend, not Bobby's."

"But you were still tied to a—"

"No, I wasn't," she said, shaking her head. "I loved Bobby. We knew he wasn't going to recover. Bobby's family tried to get me out, introduce me to people—sometimes male people. If I'd wanted freedom from him, from those obligations, no one in my family or his would have tried to talk me out of it. In fact, there were lots of discussions about things like that—like breaking me loose through divorce so I could pursue another relationship, about pulling the feeding tube so he would just die, but—"

"Why didn't you just do that, Marcie? Why?"

"Because, Ian. Feeding him was part of keeping him comfortable."

"But what if he was thinking in there?" Ian said, a note of pained desperation in his voice. "What if it was torture for him, thinking how much he hated living like that, not being able to move or communicate?"

She smiled gently. "If he was able to think of things like that, then he was also thinking about the legions of loved ones dedicating themselves to keeping him safe and cared for until he could make the last part of his journey."

A long piece of silence separated them. "And none of them was me," he said softly.

"You had your own issues," she said easily, sipping her drink. "Bobby's injuries were physical—yours were emotional. Everyone is entitled to have space to recover. Besides, you gave me the one thing I needed most, and for that I'll be grateful forever. I had a chance to say goodbye. He was real important to me, Ian. Even though he wasn't himself, I really needed to hold him in my arms, tell him I loved him so much, and that it was all right for him to move on—that I'd be fine. Do you have any idea how much that meant to me?"

"Even though you had so much to—"

"I just told you—it wasn't too much. We were busy, yeah. But everyone felt like I did—on different levels. He was his mother's baby—she needed that time. His father's pride—he needed time, too. Bobby was amazing—his brothers and sisters needed that time to say goodbye."

Ian was quiet for a moment before he said, "If I'd read the goddamn letters, I might've been one of the people to pitch in, in case he was thinking in there, counting faces…"

She was quiet for a moment. Then she tipped the bottle over both their glasses. "Want help finding more things to be guilty and regretful about, since your original ideas aren't covering all the bases? As I understand it, you were barely home from a miserable war, broke up with your fiancée, fell out with your dad, left the Marine Corps, to which you thought you'd give at least twenty years. So, Bobby's injuries were just one more thing, and all the family is so grateful you risked your life to try to save him." She took a sip. "Ian, no one's mad at you for not being around."

"Yeah. You sure about that?"

She leveled him with a determined green-eyed stare. Then she snatched the pile of letters and dragged them over to her. "Let's start right here." She snapped off the rubber band and, once she saw they were stacked in order of delivery, lifted the first one and opened it.

"'Dear Ian,'" she read.

> "I hope you're well. You've been out of sight for too, too long and I miss you so much. It would be so nice to hear from you. I want you to know that Bobby's been moved to a wonderful nursing home. His entire family and my entire family work together to be sure that he's always around loved ones. We help with some of his care, but there's an awesome staff here. He's not in pain. Really. Of course we don't know everything, but doctors have run every test imaginable and examined him a hundred times—he feels nothing from his neck down. And he never exhibits any symptoms of tension or anxiety. I've been told he could make tears if he felt suffering. Ian, there are no tears. In fact, even though they say I'm crazy, I think sometimes I see the closest thing to a smile.
>
> "My life feels strangely normal. I work at the insurance company—same job, same friends. I don't

make a lot of money but my boss is real flexible; he's a great guy—he brings his yellow Lab to work with him every day. Bobby's wonderful mother insists I have nights out with some of the girlfriends who were keeping me busy while the two of you were in Iraq—we even go dancing sometimes, but a couple of them are pregnant so more often we do movies, dinners out, picnics in summer and parties with our gang in winter. I seem to have inherited a really large family and huge group of friends, almost all married with families. They're the same friends I've had for years—there are three girlfriends from high school I've known forever and four women from work I've known since I started there. You'd think working together every day, we'd get sick of each other—but we still drive the boss crazy talking and laughing all the time.

"I like to take my time with Bobby in the early mornings before work—but not every day. Most days, though, when he's just coming awake, I like to be the first person he senses. Don't laugh at me now, but I think he can smell me. He turns his head toward me and I can tell he knows. Then I like the evenings. Reading to him relaxes us both. I've been reading Bobby *Ivanhoe*—it's just amazing how much I get into this story by reading aloud. I have no clue if he's hearing me, and I'm sure he isn't understanding me, but I almost can't wait to get to the nursing home and start the next chapter. Bobby has read more good books since he was injured than he ever did before. I get right up on the bed with him to read and sometimes he turns his head toward me and seems to nuzzle me, burrow his head into my shoulder...."

Marcie read on, through a dozen letters, every once in a while replenishing her glass and his. At one point she got up and fixed herself a glass of cold well water, but continued on. Eventually, the letters contained more about her and less about Bobby, because of course he remained unchanged. She had written all about her trip to British Columbia, about the charm, the landscape, the friendly people. Then there was an all-girls cruise for four days, three nights. She took Ian through two years of her life as the wife of a disabled marine, as a sister, a sister-in-law, daughter-in-law, friend. There were family gatherings, new births, weddings, things that were *normal.* She had a falling-out with a close girlfriend that alienated them for a few weeks and in the next letter explained how they worked it all out. She told him about a bad haircut, about her younger brother Drew's plethora of girlfriends and his careless ways with them. She even reported on the VW's broken fuel pump.

The letters were more about Marcie's life than Bobby's. And Marcie's life was not the torture he'd envisioned. But the thing that had him riveted was that she wrote to him as if he were an old friend. An important friend. And she always included her phone number, asking him to call her collect anytime. And she always closed with *"Miss you..."*

Then came the most recent letter, written last year, telling him that Bobby had passed, sweetly and quietly, and as divine luck would have it, she had been there. Since she was only there for a couple of hours a day and took some days off on occasion, she considered this a small miracle. She was cradling his head in her arm, reading, when she realized he hadn't moved his head or eyes or mouth in a long while. She felt for a pulse, put her face against his to see if he was breathing. "'And I knew right away.... Not from the absence of pulse or breath really... It was as if I felt his spirit leave him. I don't know if you'll understand this—it was a great relief to know that all this time his spirit had been there while we all loved him so well. I had always thought it possible that his spirit had gone home long before his body would release its hold—but I swear to you, I had a fullness in my heart as though he'd passed through me as he departed. And I said, "Goodbye, darling Bobby. We'll all miss you." And I was so happy for him.'"

It was quite late when she'd finished reading that last letter to him. The level in the bottle was considerably lower, but they hadn't killed it. She plunked the last envelope down on the stack and they were quiet. Ian sniffed quietly once or twice, then wiped impatiently at his eyes.

Finally Marcie said, "I might need an escort to the loo. I'm a little drunk."

It broke through his sadness, changing his mood yet again. "You think?" he asked, smiling.

"Well, I don't exactly have your height and girth. And I'm a small drinker—couple of beers or wines or fruity things. Truth is, I'm worried about standing up...."

He laughed at her. "No one held you down and poured it down your neck."

"It's awful reading letters you've written. All the bad sentences, terrible spelling, stupid remarks... I bet when you go to hell, they just read every letter you ever wrote out loud."

He chuckled and stood. He said, "Come on, lightweight, I'll take you out." But what he thought was, they were beautiful letters. If he'd actually read them, they might have helped him get his head straight a little quicker. The one thing he'd been missing in his life—someone who cared about him—she'd offered him a long time ago.

He walked her to the outhouse, stood outside while she took her turn, then escorted her back to the cabin before making his run. She flopped on the couch and rolled over on her side without taking her boots off, without pulling up the quilt. He shook his head at her. "You're going to sleep good." Then he pulled her boots off and covered her.

"Hmm. That's the last time you get me drunk, Buchanan."

"Like I said, I didn't hold you down."

"I sense a problem. I got real used to the taste." And then she hiccupped.

"I'll be gone when you come out of it," he reminded her. "I've got some wood to deliver in the morning."

"Right. Yeah, I know that. Do I still have my library books?"

"You think I could get to the library in the hour you were gone today?"

"Oh, never mind. Good night, my sweet bear."

Oh, God, how that made his heart swell and lurch. Before he could stop himself, he bent his lips to her temple and placed a soft kiss there. Her hand came up, stroked his hairy face, and she hummed. "The only problem with this is that I can hardly tell when you smile. I so love it when you smile."

"Good night, lightweight."

While Marcie slept the sleep of the drunk, Ian paged through the album of baseball cards. He imagined Bobby's fingers on every one. Tears ran out of his eyes, washing the remorse and pain out of his soul. She might never know how much this simple gift meant.

Twelve

When Marcie finally opened her eyes, there was a marching band on parade in her head—a dull thumping that seemed to have a beat. Whoa. She'd sipped her way through twelve or fourteen letters. Bad idea. But she knew where Ian kept the aspirin.

She sat up carefully. The room was in order, as Ian always left it. Even the letters were tucked away; the baseball card album still on the table where she'd left it. The coffeepot rested on the woodstove, which needed a couple of logs. She fed the stove first, then put on her boots and took a trip out back, and when she returned she just about chugged the thick, black coffee even though it wasn't quite hot enough. A glance at her watch told her that Ian wouldn't be back for a while, and having now learned the ways of stoves, she decided to take advantage of his absence to freshen up. She heated the water for her hair first, then the tub. Then she went through the tedious process of emptying the tub, which was more trouble than filling it. By the time she was done with all that, she was actually tired, which had more to do with staying up late and drinking than the flu. In fact, she had hardly coughed at all.

After washing her hair and bathing, she took her manicure scissors to her damaged bangs and managed to snip away the charred ends, combing it into some order. Her small makeup mirror showed she had a slight, healthy glow; the burn was healed, or nearly so. She applied a little makeup, something she hadn't bothered with since arriving. But she'd forced her presence on Ian over and over again—it wouldn't hurt to be presentable. She gave some attention to her eyes, lined her lips. She opened one of those cans of stew, ate about half, then she settled on the couch with her book, a new woman.

Without warning, the new woman vanished. Suddenly she knew—it was a year ago today. Funny, she hadn't thought of that even once while she was reading through all those letters—not even the one with the date of Bobby's passing in it. December 17, a week before Christmas.

It had been a very odd experience. Once she'd known Bobby was gone, she stayed right where she was, holding him. She didn't cry; she didn't call for a nurse or aide. And while she held him she communicated with her heart, telling him to be happy where he was. It was at least an hour before anyone came into the room—a sixty-year-old nurse's aide, bringing around linens for the morning shift. "You're here late," the woman said.

And Marcie was stroking Bobby's cheek, running her fingers through his hair, holding him close. She didn't respond. She knew once she let go of him this time, she wouldn't be able to hold him again. Something about the way she was touching him must have tipped off the aide because she came over to the bed and put her fingers to Bobby's neck. "Mrs. Sullivan," she said gently.

"I know. I'm having a little trouble letting go..." Marcie murmured.

"I understand. I'll call someone for you. That usually helps. Someone will come and—"

"Could you put that off for just a little while? Could you give me just a little more time with him?"

"I'll finish my rounds with the linens and then I'll have the charge nurse make a call. Would you like it to be to his parents? Or maybe to your sister?"

"Call his parents," she said. "They should be the first to know. Then would you please call Erin?"

"Sure." Then she smiled sweetly and gave Marcie's brow a loving stroke. Surely she'd seen every bizarre reaction to death in this place. "Take your time here. Take all the time you need."

And when the aide left the room, Marcie had picked up the book she'd been reading to Bobby and continued to read. She read aloud to him for almost another hour—his body had grown cool to the touch. He was so completely lifeless, it rather amazed her. She would have thought there wouldn't be much change in him, in his body, since he was so still even when he was alive, but the change in him was remarkable. She had never sensed tension in him until he passed, and then a complete relaxation settled over his facial features and he looked positively beautiful. Ethereal. Complete peace took over. And then he became so quiet. Cool. Hard. Still. Gone.

Mr. and Mrs. Sullivan came into the room and rushed to her. They found her with Bobby in her arms, the book open on her lap. "Marcie? What are you doing?"

"I wasn't ready to leave him," she said softly, her voice clear, her eyes dry.

"She's in shock," Mrs. Sullivan said to her husband. "We should call the—"

"I'm not in shock," Marcie said. Then she laughed lightly. "Good Lord, I've been expecting this for three years. But now it's here, I know I won't touch him again and I'm having a little trouble giving him up…."

The book was pulled out of her hands, she was drawn off the bed, to her feet, away from him. His parents kissed him goodbye and the sheet was pulled over him. Marcie went to him and pulled the sheet back. There was no reason to hide him—he looked as if he was asleep. She smoothed back his soft, dark hair.

"Marcie, the mortuary was called. They'll be here soon."

"I'm in no hurry," she said. It wasn't as though there were decisions to make—all the arrangements had been made a couple of years before. They'd take him away, he'd be cremated and there would be a memorial for him. But until they took him, wasn't he still *hers?*

"He belongs to a higher authority now." It was her sister's voice. "You can let go of him without the slightest worry. He's in good hands."

"Did I say that out loud?" Marcie asked. "Did I?"

"Say what, sweetheart?"

"That until the funeral people came for him, he was still mine?"

"No, baby. You didn't say anything. I could tell, that's all."

"I just want to be close to him until they come…."

"We can stay here, just like this, as long as you like. To hell with funeral people. They can wait."

"Thank you," she said softly, sitting again on the bed. She touched him, kissed his cheek and brow, whispered to him. Her in-laws thought she was losing it, but Erin held them off. Marcie heard Erin in the hall outside the room. "Cut her some slack. It's a lot to give up. She'll be fine."

And when they came to take Bobby away, Marcie gave him one last kiss and let him go. Then she embraced her in-laws, told them she was sorry for their loss, and went home.

She felt tears on her cheeks, but she didn't feel pain. Just that loneliness that sometimes plagued her. That sense of no longer being attached to Bobby, a feeling of having no purpose.

It was another hour before Ian came home. And when he walked in, she knew what had taken him so long. His hair and beard were dramatically sheared, clipped short and neatly trimmed. He had grocery sacks in his arms. He tried not to, but it was obvious, he was smiling.

"Ian!"

"It's me. You expecting someone else?"

She looked up at him and forgot everything. "What have you done?"

He walked straight to the table and put down his sacks. "I have more stuff to get, so sit tight." And he left the cabin again. When he returned with a couple of boxes stacked high on top of each other, she was sitting in the same place. He put those on the table, as well. Then he finally turned toward her, letting her look him over. She stood and took slow steps toward him and her hand rose to touch his cheek. Where there had been a good five or six inches of bushy beard was now less than a half inch of brownish-red beard, combed into place, soft as down. Even his neck was shaved.

"Where is my wilderness lunatic?"

He frowned at her and touched her cheek gently. "Have you been crying?"

She glanced away. "I'm sorry. I had one of those days."

He put his thumb and forefinger on her chin and pulled her eyes back to his. "What's up?" he asked softly. "Need to talk about it?"

"No," she said, shaking her head. "I know you don't want to—"

"It's okay. What made you cry? Homesick? Lonesome?"

She took a deep breath. "It was a year ago today. Snuck up on me, I guess."

"Ah," he said. He put his big arms around her. "That would make some tears, I guess. I'm sorry, Marcie. I'm sure it still hurts sometimes."

"That's just it—it doesn't exactly hurt. It's just that I feel so useless." She leaned against him. "Sometimes I feel all alone. I have lots of people in my life and can still feel so alone without Bobby." She laughed softly. "And God knows, he wasn't much company."

He tightened his embrace. "I think I understand."

Yeah, she thought, *he might.* Here was a guy who was around people regularly, yet completely unconnected to them. She pulled away and asked, "Why did you do this?"

"I thought I could clean up a little and take you somewhere."

"Wait. You didn't think I needed you to do this for me, did you? Because of Erin?"

He laughed, and she could actually see the emotion on his face, given the absence of wild beard. "Actually, if you'd asked me to, I probably wouldn't have. You really think you can match me for stubborn? Probably not. I kept the beard because of the scar," he said, leaning his left cheek toward her. "That, and maybe a bit of attitude of who cares?"

She gently fingered the beard apart to reveal a barely noticeable scar. "It's hardly there at all. Ian, it's only a thin line. You don't have to cover it. You're not disfigured." She smiled at him. "You're handsome."

"Memories from the scar, probably. Anyway, tonight is the truckers' Christmas parade. A bunch of eighteen-wheelers in the area dress up their rigs and parade down the freeway. I see it every year—fantastic. You think you're up to it? With it being that anniversary?"

"Maybe it's a good idea," she said. "Getting out, changing the mood."

"We'll eat out and—"

"What's all this?" she asked, looking at the bags and boxes.

"Snow's forecast. It's just what you do up here. Be ready. But this time I got some different things, in case you're sick of stew. And I never do this—but you're a girl, so I bought some fresh greens. And fresh eggs. Just enough to last a couple of days. No fridge; and they'll freeze if we leave 'em in the shed."

"Ian, what about the bathroom? What will we do about the bathroom if there's a heavy snow?"

He laughed at her. "No problem. We'll tromp out there fine—but I'll shovel a path. And I'll plow out to the road, but it's slow going and if the snow keeps coming, it's going to be even slower."

"Wow. Is it safe to leave tonight? For the parade? Will we get back in?"

"We don't have blizzards, Marcie. Snow falls slow, but steady. Now, I'm thinking bath day. How about you?"

She put her hands on her hips and looked up at him with a glare. "All right, be very careful here. I've had my bath. And a hair wash. I'm wearing *makeup,* Ian. Jesus. You wanna try to clean me up?"

His eyes grew large for a moment. Then he said. "Bath day for me, I meant. I knew. You look great." His thumb ran along her cheek under one eye. "Just a couple of tear marks, but you can take care of that. Let me put this stuff away and get my water ready. You have something to read? Or are you looking for the thrill of your life?"

"I have something to read," she said. And, she thought, at the end of the day, they all turn out to be just men.

Ian had in mind an Italian restaurant in Arcata, a place he'd been a time or two. When he'd been before, he always just ate at the bar, alone. This time, at a table with a glass of red wine each, there was talking. It was hardly possible to remember the man who merely grunted or complained that he didn't need to have people around. Marcie made no comment about the change; tomorrow would mark ten days. One more week would bring Christmas.

He wanted to know what kind of little girl she had been.

"Bad, very bad. I took the term *tomboy* to the next level. I didn't have any little girlfriends, just the boys. I could take all of 'em, but even though I thought I was a boy I fought like a girl—biting, hair pulling. I went from slingshots to spitballs and my dad got called to school a lot. I was a bratty little carrottop, the smallest, meanest one in my class."

He grinned largely. So beautifully. "How does this not surprise me? You're a little better mannered now, but not much."

"Then the cutest boy in ninth grade got a crush on me. My first thought was—bet I can take him. My next thought was, bet I can get him to kiss me. It turned me into a girl overnight—a total transformation. *Bobby.* Erin Elizabeth was prissy from the day she was born and you can't imagine how it killed me to ask her for advice on looking pretty. She was so damn smug about it, too."

"Bobby? Since ninth grade?"

"Uh-huh. We went steady all through school, married at nineteen. Barely nineteen."

He just shook his head. "Awful young."

"Awful," she said. "Our families wanted us to wait, but it didn't take too much convincing—we couldn't keep our hands off each other. I think everyone went along with the wedding just to cool us down. But there were a lot of bad jokes—like I was wearing training pants under the gown. That sort of thing."

"And did it? Cool you down?"

"Kept us from pawing each other in public, at least," she said with a grin. "Now you have to step up, Buchanan, and tell some things—you were star of the high-school musical. You probably had girls all over you. Huh?"

One corner of his mouth lifted. "I was pretty much a slut," he said, making her laugh so loud that people's heads turned in the restaurant.

"No morals," she interpreted.

"Few," he said. "I was on my way to getting some girl I barely loved in trouble."

"Barely loved? Did you tell them you loved them to get in their pants?"

"Be fair—I was a teenage boy!"

"You did! You're such a dog!"

"I was a pup, that's what I was. The Marine Corps was my dad's idea, but the joke was on him. Not only did I take to it, but spruced-up marines have no trouble getting girls."

"My little brother, Drew, I think maybe he's a lot like you. He's a gorgeous little devil. Smart and so funny he can make you laugh till you leave a little wet spot on the floor—and he has a different girl every month. He's such a screw-off, it's hard to believe he's going to be a doctor."

"Doctor?" Ian asked, mouth full.

"Uh-huh—he's a med student now. My sister's a lawyer, my brother will be a doctor and I barely made it out of high school."

Ian swallowed. "Come on—I bet you were an honor student."

"Nope. I was pretty much a B average on a good report card. But then I had other things on my mind—like fun, Bobby, et cetera. I'm much more serious now."

"I wish I'd known you then—you must have been a real loose cannon. So what kind of doctor do you think your little brother will be?"

"At this rate? A gynecologist."

The bantering went on all through dinner. For Marcie it was wonderfully pleasant and fun, but not different than her life had been—being with someone, talking, laughing. She suspected it was very different for Ian, at least lately. By the way his eyes grew more golden than brown, she assumed it felt good.

The truck parade happened after dinner, when it was good and dark. They parked along a high road and watched from the truck until that wasn't good enough and they got out and sat on the warm hood. The trucks were, as he said, magnificent. The flashing, sparkling lights, Santas perched atop, even Nativities, snow scenes and Christmas trees set up on long flatbeds. Every color under the rainbow was represented and, for good measure, the drivers blasted their horns in response to the gallery of viewers who waved and applauded.

After standing out in the cold for a while, then riding

back toward home in a truck with a poor heater, Marcie was shivering. So Ian suggested they swing through town before heading up the mountain. If it wasn't too late, they could get a quick toddy to warm them up.

The tree lit their way into town, so majestic, that star creating just the right path. When they walked into Jack's there were quite a few people, the lights dimmed, the fire in the hearth blazing. They chose to sit up at the bar in front of a grinning bartender. "Evening," Jack said.

"I wonder if I might use the phone, since I'm here?" Marcie said. "I should check in, make sure Erin had no trouble getting home."

"You bet. Can I set you up something to come back to?"

"How about a brandy," she said, jumping off the stool. "Something nice and smooth."

"You got it." And when she'd gone to the kitchen, Jack said to Ian, "And you?"

"Schnapps, thanks."

Jack put a couple of drinks on the bar. "You take advantage of the holiday special at the Haircuts R Us store?"

"Funny. I thought you talked when they talked, shut up when they didn't?"

"We read faces, too. You're completely un-miserable—a new look for you."

"I took Marcie to see the truck parade," he said. "You ever see that truck parade?"

"Couple of times. Mel and my sister took the baby over, but I had a full house tonight. That damn tree—been bringing 'em in from miles away. I'm expecting the wise men to pop in here any second."

"It's not a bad-looking tree," Ian said.

"Thanks, but it's going to be smaller next year. Mel's set

on a big tree like that, but you have no idea what a pain in the butt it was. Almost had to rent a flatbed to bring it home."

Ian chuckled and took a sip of his drink. "What got you up here, Jack? To Virgin River?"

"After twenty in the Marines? I was just looking for some peace and quiet so I could catch my breath. And think."

"That a fact? And here I thought it was an original idea."

Jack laughed. "Well, then Melinda showed up, and now peace and quiet is a thing of the past."

"That's a rough spot you got yourself in," Ian observed.

"Yeah," Jack said. "Beautiful blonde in my bed every morning when I wake up. I'm telling you, the suffering just won't end." There was a quick flash of a grin, and before Ian could think of a comeback, Marcie was sitting up beside him.

"All's well," she reported. She took a slow sip of her brandy and made a sigh of pleasure. "Very nice, Jack."

"I don't know when you're headed home, Marcie, but there's a Christmas Eve thing going on here. Since there's no church open in town and Preacher closes up on Christmas Day to have it with his family, on Christmas Eve the townsfolk are having a candlelight gathering around the tree."

"Really? What time?"

"Won't be a midnight mass, that's for sure," he laughed. "Mostly ranchers and farmers around here—they start early in the morning, even on Christmas. Last I heard it was scheduled for eight o'clock for about an hour. I'm taking the family to Sacramento for the holidays, so we'll miss it. But if you're still here, stop by."

"I'll keep that in mind," she said.

The brandy and schnapps didn't keep them warm all the way home and when they arrived, Ian first stoked the fire, getting it going before walking Marcie out to the facilities. They both remained in jackets and boots until the cabin heated up a little. Marcie finally spread her sleeping bag over the couch. She took off her boots, but left her clothes on, wrapping herself up in her bag to try to generate some warmth.

Ian was just unrolling his pallet and about to pull off his boots when she said, softly, "Thank you for a wonderful night, Ian. It's the best night I've had in…years." And then he heard her yawn.

He didn't move; couldn't breathe. There was an odd sensation filling his chest, a gathering of moisture in his eyes. He wanted to say, No, thank *you!* But he couldn't trust himself to form the words. She had no idea how it changed him inside—in his head and heart—just to have someone to talk to, to laugh with. The scrappiest little girl on the playground, like an angel come to draw him out, made him feel for the first time in such a long time, as if he was living instead of merely existing. It was a gift he was sure he didn't deserve, especially after sealing himself off from the world as he had. And after trying to scare her away.

Trouble was, he didn't know if he could go back to his old, silent, anonymous ways. And yet, he didn't have anything else. The reality was, he had this cabin and about a couple thousand dollars that would have to last all winter. There was no hidden bank account, no benefit checks, no retirement. He could put the property up for sale, but there probably wouldn't be a buyer, maybe for years. He didn't have things to sell or barter.

He could beg her to stay, but he wasn't sure he'd ever be able to even build her an indoor bathroom. He'd let himself get down to practically nothing, enjoying the deprivation on some screwed-up level. Then Marcie showed up and suddenly he felt like a rich man.

Just when he felt ready to open his mouth to say something like, *No, Marcie—it was you who made it perfect,* he heard a soft snore come from her side of the room. It made him shake his head and chuckle silently. She slept well on that lumpy sofa; she was at peace here when she should be annoyed by all the inconveniences.

They were alike in that way, he realized. She was as able to make do as he was, yet in Marcie's life there was so much more—family, work, friends, real living.

Quietly he traded his jeans for sweats and got down on his pallet in front of the fire. But sleep was far away. All he could think about was how real his life had suddenly become, how vast and full of possibilities when just two weeks ago an unending sameness had stretched out in front of him. Forever. It had been so long since he'd even thought about what might come next for him, and sometimes it seemed there never would be a next.

Old habits die hard—he thought this might be a good time to ignore her, reject her, hope that he'd get beyond this emotion real fast. But he knew he wasn't going to do that. No. He would allow this to happen to him for a little while. She'd fill him up with goodness before she left; he'd tackle what to do with all those feelings later. Ian decided he could think of her as a Christmas gift. A beautiful little glimpse of what life could have been.

It was a long while before he slept. Not long after he nodded off, he felt something and opened his eyes. She was beside him on the floor by the stove, wrapped in her sleeping bag, red hair all crazy from sleep. "I got cold, even with the sleeping bag," she said.

"I'll feed the fire," Ian replied, sitting up and slipping a couple of logs into the stove. Then he lay back down, giving her room on the pallet beside him and, pulling her close, said, "Come here, little girl. Let me get you warm."

"Hmm. That's what I need."

"And what I need," he said, giving her a kiss against her temple.

"Can I tell you something?"

He laughed. "Marcie, aren't you tired of talking yet?"

She completely ignored him. "It's about that whole wedding thing," she said. "You know, with Shelly?"

"I'm not thinking about that right now," he said, pulling her closer against him.

"I know, but I just wanted to say—I've been in four weddings, including my own. Brides—all of them, at one point or another—have that moment, that meltdown, when it's all about them and their wedding. It's easy to forget it's about the marriage, but not about the wedding. But reality sets in real quick." She yawned. "Some brides are worse than others, but Shelly probably didn't mean what she said."

He was quiet for a moment, not even able to conjure a memory or image of Shelly. He asked, "Four?"

"Hmm?"

"Four weddings?"

"Uh-huh. And a godmother twice, and I'm going to be one again in March—my friend Mable is having a boy, her first."

He gave a snort of laughter. "You have a friend named Mable?"

"Uh-huh. She thinks it was her mother's revenge for making her sick during pregnancy. We all call her Maybe. She's married to William, who we call Will. They're Maybe Will to everyone."

"You're connected to a lot of people. That makes me happy, knowing that," he said.

She snuggled closer. "And now I'm connected to you, too. That makes me happy." She yawned again. "But here's what I wanted to tell you, Ian. That thing with Shelly? I think maybe you dodged a bullet there."

He laughed softly, pulled her closer still. *Oh yeah,* he thought. He wasn't meant to end up with Shelly.

"I'll be quiet now," she said.

"Good."

When Ian had allowed himself to think about Marcie, his vision had been one of loneliness and despair. That's because he didn't know her as Abigail Adams, the sassy, indefatigable, positive woman she was; because he'd never let himself know.

He couldn't see as far from the top of his mountain as he thought he could.

Thirteen

Marcie felt something on her hair and woke to look into Ian's rich brown eyes. Dawn was barely lighting the cabin and he was running his big hand over her curls. "Morning," she said sleepily.

He didn't say anything. He just lowered his lips to hers and touched them gently, sweetly. She felt the brush of his beard, the soft flesh of his lips and let her eyes drop closed. He moved over her mouth for a moment. She moaned and slipped an arm around his neck, holding him there.

He pulled back just a little and whispered, "We're snowed in, honey."

"Good."

"I was jealous of Bobby, you know," Ian said, petting her hair back along her temple, moving it over her ear.

"Be careful, Ian—you're talking about 'it.'"

"I'm ready to tell you anything you want to know. We were all a little jealous of Bobby. He had something real special with you. You sent him panties."

Her cheeks warmed in spite of herself. Her eyes got very round. "He *showed* you?"

Ian chuckled. "He showed everyone. Very skimpy panties. I think they were lime-green with black lace or something."

"I cannot believe he showed you!"

"He was proud of them. He kept them tucked in his inside pocket like a good-luck charm."

"They were perfectly clean, I'll have you know."

"Aw, that almost comes as a disappointment," Ian said, chuckling. "They should have had your scent on them."

"They had Tide and Downy on them!"

"And you sent him that picture—on the motorcycle."

She put her hands over her face. In muffled tones she muttered, "I'm mortified." He pulled her hands away and lightly kissed her again. "So the night I almost froze to death was actually the second time you've seen me in my underwear."

"Technically, I've seen your underwear a ton of times. I came home a couple of times to see your cute little rump sticking out of the covers, not to mention all that underwear on my tub, drying out," he said. "And I'd trade my life to see you in your underwear again."

Her eyes got round for a minute, but then she smiled slightly and a little laugh escaped her. "I've heard some interesting come-ons in my limited experience, but that's a new one. Tell me, do I have to shoot you after you peek?"

"What if I told you, you might have to shoot me to stop me? Would that scare you?"

"You don't scare me, Ian. I know you'd protect me from anything. Even yourself."

He pressed kisses all over her face and she held his face

in her hands while he did so. His breathing came faster, rougher. "I want you to know something," he said in a whisper. "Something like this happening with us—it didn't cross my mind until—"

She waited. Finally she said, "Until?"

"Until you came back. This doesn't have to happen, Marcie. Tell me if you don't want to—"

"Oh, Ian." She laughed. "You talk too much!"

The gold flecks in his eyes gleamed and he came down on her mouth harder, slipping an arm under her while he kissed her with heat, slipping his tongue into her mouth. Her other arm went around him, pulling him against her and, with a will of its own, her body arched against his, hungry. Not just starved in general, but for Ian, to whom she'd bonded herself in so many ways.

Without breaking their kiss, his hands began to rove over her breasts, hips, thighs. He slipped a big hand under her sweater to touch her breast and sighed against her lips as he did so. Then he helped her out of her sweater and his big hands were on the snap of her jeans, slipping them down over her hips, her knees, until finally they were off. He tugged his T-shirt over his head, leaving him in just those soft sweats, and he stared down at her small body. "God above," he said in a reverent whisper.

"Is this how you looked at me when you were saving my life? When you got me out of my clothes and warmed me?"

He shook his head, a naughty smile on his lips. "There was no funny business. This time, there's definitely going to be funny business."

"Good," she said, letting her eyes drift closed again. "Good."

He kissed her around her neck, shoulders, chest, biceps,

tummy. All the while he ran a thumb under the elastic of a very small panty. "How do you feel about me chewing off your underwear?" he asked.

She sucked in a breath, shuddered. "I can always get new underwear…"

It made him laugh deep in his throat. This was what he loved best—her playfulness. Or maybe it was her small body, appearing fragile, but not. Or was it the fire on her head and the flashing green eyes? It might be quicker to list the things he didn't love, if he could think of any at all.

He made the bra disappear first, finding her nipples with his tongue, loving the sounds she made as he pampered her. Then he dropped his head to her belly and taking the elastic of her panties in his teeth, he dragged them down over her hips. He pulled them the rest of the way with a trembling hand and had his lips against hers again. He kissed her deeply, filling his hands with her hips, her smooth butt. "A natural redhead…"

"Ah, how could you doubt me?" she asked breathlessly. "Especially after a couple of weeks in the woods…"

"Marcie, baby, I gotta have a taste. I have to."

She arched slightly. "Oh, my," she said. "Well, if you have to, you have to…" And her legs came apart slightly, making him growl.

He went down, parting her legs, burying his face in those red curls until he felt her fingers lock into his hair, felt her lunge against him and heard her panting cries. He rose somewhat reluctantly to capture her mouth again. "Honey, you're ready for anything…"

"You," she whispered. "You're what I'm ready for."

With one hand and a kick of his long legs, he was free of his sweats, planting himself between her legs. He tried to take it easy, finding her and entering slowly. But Marcie was in a hurry and lurched against him, pushing back. For a moment, when they were locked together, everything went still. With their eyes upon one another, their lips barely touching, they were quiet, motionless, just the breathing and the hot gaze between them, savoring their moment of joining. Then her eyes slowly drifted closed and her hips moved beneath him.

Ian covered her mouth in a hot, deep kiss and pumped his hips, holding on, waiting, moving gently, then fiercely, until he felt it all happen at once—her fingers on his shoulders, digging in, her pelvis thrust against him, her insides pulsing in a fabulous joy that left him drenched in hot liquid. And he made the moment count, letting it all go, being with her through the ecstasy.

He held her for a long, quiet time, his lips on her neck, her lips on his shoulder, their bodies rising and falling with rapid breathing, moist with perspiration, calming down, recovering. Finally she whispered in his ear, "What were you thinking while that happened, Ian?"

Before he could come up with an answer, the truth came out. "I was thinking, thank God I didn't forget how that was done."

She laughed, rubbing his back.

"What were you thinking?" he asked.

"I was thinking, thank God he didn't forget how that was done."

But he wasn't laughing anymore. The look on his face was dreamy. He brushed her hair away from her brow. "You're real special, Marcie," he said. "I never saw this coming, but..." He couldn't finish.

She put her palm against his cheek. "That's nice, Ian.

You're awful special, too. And I let you get me naked when I'd been with you ten days."

"You let me do more than that."

"I wanted you to make love to me. You must think I'm a bad girl—"

"You *are* a bad girl, the best bad girl that was ever born," he said. "The meanest little carrottop on the playground. You're the best thing that ever happened in my life, Marcie. I was dying—you knew that. You made a difference. It's what you always intended to be—a difference." He grinned. "Like Abigail."

"Aw. That's the nicest thing anyone ever said to me."

He brushed her lips with his. "Am I crushing you?" he asked.

"No. And don't move. I don't want to lose the feeling of being part of you."

He wanted to tell her she'd be a part of him for the rest of his life, but that might frighten her more than his roar. "I'd just like to spoil you for a little while, if that's okay."

"Sounds interesting. Just how will you spoil me, if I might ask?"

"Well, I'll start by not digging us out of here too fast," he said. "How does that sound?"

"Like heaven. Pure heaven."

Ian and Marcie dressed somewhat reluctantly and headed outside to check out the snow and make a run to the outhouse. It was still coming down, softly, slowly, but not too deep on the ground yet.

She got her turn first, and she made it quick. Then Ian was allowed the facilities. When he came out, he found himself alone. She must have gone back to the warmth of the cabin in a hurry and he began to follow. Before he got five feet, a snowball hit him square in the face. He wiped it away to see her leaning out from behind a big tree, laughing. "Did I mention I was good in softball?" she asked through her laughter. "I pitched!"

The chase was on—Ian took after her with a roar that was answered by giggles. He was stronger and more sure in the snow, but she was agile and quick and managed to get off a few snowballs while he was in pursuit. She ran around trees, rounded the shed at least once, took a few snowballs in the back and retaliated. But the chase ended when she tripped on something under the snow and did a face-plant right into the soft white powder.

He rushed to her side, scared, and rolled her over to find her laughing and spitting snow. He just looked down at her in wonder—did nothing disturb her? Scare her? Panic or worry her? He covered her mouth with his for a long kiss, and when he let her go she said, "Before we go inside, we should make snow angels."

"I'm not making snow angels," he said. "What if Buck sees me? It would ruin my reputation forever."

"Just one, then. Yours would be so big—like Gabriel, for sure."

"Then will you go inside with me? No more screwing around?"

"Aw—I thought that was your favorite part?" she asked, taking a handful of snow and shoving it in his face.

With a growl, he got to his feet, lifted her off the ground and threw her over his shoulder, carrying her back to the cabin. He stood her in front of the door and brushed the snow off her before letting her enter, then did the same himself.

"You've forgotten how to play," she accused him.

"You play around enough for both of us," he said. Without shedding his jacket, he got water heating on the propane stove and the woodstove. "I'll give you a little time alone while I shovel a path to the john and hook the plow blade onto the truck. Think you can manage these big pots on your own?"

"Are you going to dig us out so soon?" she asked, clearly disappointed.

He smiled at her. "Not exactly. I'm going to make a couple of passes at the road—but no one has to know about it. I just don't want to get us too buried. Do me a favor? When you're done with your bath—start my water cooking?"

"Sure, Ian," she said. "And if you're very nice—I'll scrub your back."

Winters had always been a huge burden to Ian—the shoveling and plowing a necessary evil to give him access to the road, the john. But not on this particular winter day—this time it was a godsend. He'd like to keep Marcie boarded up in his cabin for a couple of weeks, but in reality, a day and night would be all he could really afford.

After making sure there was a path to the outhouse, he fitted the plow onto the truck and loaded the bed with firewood to make the truck heavier. He covered the wood with a tarp and drove down his access road. A couple of feet of snow wasn't a big deal and if he cleared it today, tomorrow wouldn't be as bad.

There was an old guy a couple miles down who had neither a plow for his truck nor a working tractor. In fact, it didn't appear the tractor had been in use since Ian migrated to this mountaintop. The old boy's road to Highway 36 wasn't real long and tomorrow Ian would check on him to make sure he had a clear road and food. They weren't friends; they'd hardly spoken. But Ian had been aware of him for a long time and just couldn't stand the thought of him freezing or starving to death, stranded. It was a small thing; he only had to make the short pilgrimage a couple of times a winter.

When he finally made his way back to the cabin, she said, "Well finally! I've been wondering if I should come out and lend a hand!"

He pulled off his gloves. "We're clear to the road if we have to get out of here. But there's no reason we have to. Is my water hot?"

"Yes, and if you're nice, I'll make you eggs before they spoil."

He took his jacket off and draped it over a kitchen chair. "You going to read your book while I take my clothes off and wash up?"

She grinned an elfish grin. "Not on your life."

It was only two nights and a day, but for Ian it was healing and for Marcie, pure magic. They ate well, made love, napped in front of the woodstove, talked. The end of the snowy day found them together on the couch, Ian leaning back against the arm, stretched out, holding Marcie between his long legs, enjoying her closeness and their conversation. Her head rested against his chest and he stroked her soft hair, catching it between his fingers.

"I want to know more about Erin," he said. "You two seem nothing alike."

"Nothing," she confirmed. "There are three different Erin's. If you really want to know, get comfortable."

He chuckled at her. "I'm comfortable."

"Well, while we were growing up and she was so much older, she was just a bossy big sister. I think that's the natural order of things, but it's magnified when a mother is lost—the oldest daughter sometimes assumes the role. A giant pain in the butt. But then we lost Dad and she tried so hard to take care of us. We were beyond being taken care of, you know. A thirteen- and fifteen-year-old—we coped in our own ways, had our own lives. I had Bobby, and Drew had sports and buddies. I feel really terrible about that—we weren't there for Erin at all. And she was just beginning law school, which demanded so much of her. But we were stupid kids—we didn't know anything."

"You told her that, of course," he said. "Once you realized it."

"Of course," she said. "I was next to mess up her tidy little life, but at least she was already a lawyer in a nice practice when I hit her with getting married. She tried to talk sense to me, but I had only one thing on my mind. There were fights and tears between us, but in the end Erin did what Dad would have done—she gave me a wedding…"

"She did?" he asked.

"Or Dad did, depends on how you look at it. When Dad died, there was a house, insurance, stuff like that. Erin guarded it for things like educations. I wasn't interested in all that—I wanted to marry Bobby. Since there was no stopping me, she did the only thing that would make me happy. And although I knew she was miserable about it, she beamed the whole time. She wasn't upset about it being Bobby—she loved him and his whole family—it was just our youth.

"Then Bobby came home to us as an invalid. My big sister, who I'd spent so many years resenting and resisting, was the best advocate I had. She worked her legal brain for months to get us the best benefits available from the military. You know how it is getting stuff out of the military—you have to be a bulldog—relentless. Some people just luck into things like larger base housing or CHAMPUS for off-base medical care—but most people have to wait till stuff is available and then better be first in line when it is. That takes constant energy. She made phone calls, wrote letters, and I think she even got our congressman involved. And she was the one who found the perfect care center. And my glamorous sister? She got right in there, got her hands dirty, helped to wash him, change linens, brush his teeth, put salve on his eyes... She held him and whispered to him like the rest of us. She came through in every way."

Ian felt his throat tighten. He tried to imagine that uppity broad who came to take Marcie away getting down and dirty like that. He couldn't even get a picture in his mind of her taking a hike out to the "loo," as they were fond of calling it.

"That's the three Erins?"

"No—that's the first two. The bitchy big sister, the dominant mother figure. Then there's the one you met—she's a very successful attorney. Very well-put-together, makes a good living, makes her clients happy and the senior partners proud. Her main concern is still me and Drew, making sure we have whatever support we need. But she's thirty-four and alone. There have been a few very short-term boyfriends, but we've all lived in the same house together since Dad died, except that little while I lived with just Bobby. Erin has no life but us. She's given us everything. She comes off looking domineering and maybe cold and calculating, but really she's sacrificed everything, even her personal life. She should be married or at least in love, but she spent every free second making sure we were taken care of—me with Bobby, Drew with college and then medical school—you have no idea how much energy and expense is involved in just getting into medical school. Drew couldn't have done it without Erin, just as I wouldn't have known what to do about Bobby without her. Really, I owe her so much. I fight her when she bosses me, but I owe her big-time."

He lowered his lips and kissed her head. "It sounds like you do."

"That's why I promised to be home by Christmas," she said. She turned her head and looked up at him. "I could stay here forever, but I promised. And it's not just for Erin—Bobby's family thinks of me as a daughter, a sister, after all we did together…"

"I know. You held up pretty good in this place—it's hard living here."

"It's not too hard for me. It's cold on the butt when nature calls. And now I carry that skillet with me everywhere I go. But I'd take my frostbitten butt to see you feed that deer out of your hand any day."

"That deer-feeding trick would get old after a while." He twirled a red curl around his finger. "When you decided to come up here, what did you think was going to happen?"

"Not this." She laughed. "In fact, I'd have bet against it."

"But what did you want?"

"Peace of mind," she said. "For both of us. I wanted to tell you what had happened in your old world, and I wanted to know that you were all right so we could both move on with peace of mind." She sat up and turned around, kneeling between his long legs and sitting back on her heels, facing him. "Ian, why did you do it? Why did you stay here so long without getting in touch with anyone?"

"I told you, I was camping and—"

She shook her head. "There was more to it. I understand about how you stumbled on this place and ended up staying, but did something traumatic drive you away?"

He frowned slightly. "Do you think it had to be like that? Jack told me he came up here to get some space so he could think…"

"But he went into business. He has a lot of people in his life who depend on him. It doesn't seem like the same kind of thing. Was it Shelly? Did that whole thing about the wedding—"

"Marcie," he said, touching her cheek. "It was everything. Too much at once. It was Fallujah and Bobby. Then it was Shelly and my father…"

"Tell me about letting Shelly go," she said.

He glanced away, then back. "Let me ask you something—did Shelly ever call you? Visit you and Bobby? Or were you the one to make contact with her?"

"I was looking for you…" she said.

Enough of an answer. "I had suggested to Shelly in letters, before the bomb in Fallujah, that she call you. You lived in the same town. Bobby was my friend," he said.

"But, Ian—"

"I know. But what happened to me and Bobby was one of the biggest reasons I had to take a time-out to recover. Shelly knew what had happened. She knew Bobby was an invalid and you were taking care of him. She knew you'd been to Germany and D.C. and finally home—yet she never even wrote you a letter, never called you. A girl from your town, her fiancé's best friend, my life in the balance getting him out…" He made a face. "Marcie, I didn't know she was that kind of person. I thought she was more the kind of person who would—"

"Ian, once we were back in Chico, I didn't contact her again either," Marcie pointed out. "Not until I was looking for you."

His expression changed. "Again?" he asked.

Caught. She looked down. "Before the bomb, I called her." She looked up. "Because you and Bobby were good friends, I thought we could get together. She was very busy. She took my number and said if she ever had any free time, she'd get in touch."

"And she never had any free time," he said. "She never told me that, but somehow I knew." He inhaled and let it out slowly. "You were busy taking care of Bobby, and Shelly had a wedding to plan. The difference in that scared me. It turns out Shelly had tunnel vision—she could only see one thing. I'm not sure I was even a part of what she saw." He ran his finger along her cheek. "You aren't kidding—I dodged a bullet there. I didn't fully realize it, but I knew something wasn't right."

"Ah," she said. "Ah. On top of everything else. And with your father? What did your father do?"

He looked away uncomfortably, but he knew he was going to be honest with her. "Nothing he hadn't done my whole life." He looked back. "My dad was always tough to please. He thought pushing me would make me a man, but I was never man enough. All I ever wanted from him was a word of praise, a proud smile."

"What about your mother?"

He smiled tenderly. "God, she was incredible. She always loved him, no matter what. And I didn't have to do anything to make her think I was a hero. If I fell flat on my face she'd just beam and say, 'Did you see that great routine of Ian's? What a genius!' When I was in that musical, she thought I was the best thing to hit Chico, but my dad asked me if I was gay." He chuckled. "My mom was the best-natured, kindest, most generous woman who ever lived. Always positive. And faithful?" He laughed, shaking his head. "My dad could be in one of his negative moods where nothing was right—the dinner sucked, the ball game wasn't coming in clear on the TV, the battery on the car was giving out, he hated work, the neighbors were too loud… And my mom, instead of saying, 'Why don't you grow the fuck up, you old turd,' she would just say, 'John, I bet I have something that will turn your mood around—I made a German chocolate cake.'"

Marcie smiled. "She sounds wonderful."

"She was. Wonderful. Even while she was fighting cancer, she was so strong, so awesome that I kept thinking it was going to be all right, that she'd make it. As for my dad, he was always impossible to please, impossible to impress. I really thought I'd grown through it, you know? I got to the point real early where I finally understood that that's just the kind of guy he was. He never beat me, he hardly even yelled at me. He didn't get drunk, break up the furniture, miss work or—"

"But what did he do, Ian?" she asked gently.

He blinked a couple of times. "Did you know I got medals for getting Bobby out of Fallujah?"

She nodded. "He got medals, too."

"My old man was there when I was decorated. He stood

nice and tall, polite, and told everyone he knew about the medals. But he never said jack to me. Then when I told him I was getting out of the Marine Corps, he told me I was a fuckup. That I didn't know a good thing when I had it. And he said…" He paused for a second. "He said he'd never been so ashamed of me in his whole goddamn life and if I did that—got out—I wasn't his son."

Instead of crumbling into tears on his behalf, she leaned against him, stroked his cheek a little and smiled. "So—he was the same guy his whole stupid life."

Ian felt a slight, melancholy smile tug at his lips. "The same guy. One miserable son of a bitch."

"There's really no excuse for a guy like that," she said. "It doesn't cost you anything to be nice."

He lifted his eyebrows. "Oh?"

"Really. He ought to be ashamed. Everyone has the option to be civil. Decent. I knew when I met him he was mean and ornery."

"Next you're going to say I won't be free of that till I forgive him," Ian said. "They always say, not for the person who has been horrible, but for yourself."

"Not bloody likely, coming from me," she said. "Now if he *asked* for forgiveness…"

"Hah. Not in your wildest dreams," he said.

"I wouldn't expect so. I met him, remember. None of what you told me surprises me."

"Marcie, I don't hate him, I swear to God. But I can't see why I'd want to say, 'I'm perfectly okay with you being the coldest SOB I've ever known.' And I'm sure not looking to be around that again. What's the point?"

She leaned forward and laid her head against his shoulder. "Hmm. Why would you? It's not likely he'd change. Ian, there's nothing you can do to change him. Now I understand. Now it will be all right."

"What is it you think you understand?"

She held him close. "You were battle scarred. You'd lost your best friend, even though he was still alive—technically—a complication that probably made things even worse for you. Your relationship floundered. That happens so often after a soldier gets out of a war zone—been happening since World War I and earlier, I'm sure. Too bad that happened, but I don't think you could have helped it.... You had to have a little time..."

"I know I could've used some help, but if anyone had offered to help me, I'd have broken his jaw," Ian said.

"I'm sure. You probably had a lot of rage stored up at that time. Well-deserved rage. The least a person can do is try to empathize. Be patient. Your loved ones—"

"It turned out I didn't have loved ones," he said in a quiet voice.

"Well," she said, lifting her head and looking into those lovely brown eyes. "You do now. And thank you—I wanted to understand what happened. That's all I wanted, and you didn't have to tell me, but you did."

He pushed some of that wild red hair over her ear. "You had some fantasy about what would happen when you found me, admit it."

"I did." She grinned. "I tried to keep it to myself, and it didn't include fabulous sex. I fantasized that I'd find you, tell you some things that would ease your mind and then I'd take you home."

"Home?"

"To Chico, or wherever home is to you," Marcie said. "A lot of your old squad checked in on Bobby, asked if I knew where you were. You're not as alone as you think. But you'd have to go to some trouble to find them now. You went missing too long. When people think you don't want them, they let you be."

"Not all of them." He laughed.

"Well, I told you—I can match you for stubborn."

"So, tell me about this forgiveness thing you don't get," he prodded.

"Oh, Ian—I'm in the same spot as you. If someone did something horrible to me and never apologized or asked for forgiveness, I wouldn't break my neck trying to forgive them. Those insurgents in Fallujah? I'm not working on loving them like brothers. If that's what I have to do to be an okay person, I'm going to remain the baddest little carrottop on the playground."

"What about God?"

"God understands everything. And even He made a mistake or two. Look at the size of avocado seeds—way too big. And pomegranates? Too many seeds. What a waste of fruit!"

He laughed loudly. "So what do you do to come to a peaceful place about those horrible people?"

She lifted her head and looked into his eyes without mirth. Her green eyes were warm and soft. Her smile was gentle. "We accept them as they are. And if we can't love them like brothers, maybe we can understand and let them be their own problems. Holy Christ, isn't that enough of a challenge? Accept him as he is, Ian—a miserable old son of a bitch who was hardly happy a day in his life, and it really had nothing to do with you."

Though he fought it, he felt his eyes glisten with tears. Long seconds passed in which she met that clouded gaze fearlessly—not afraid of his roar, his rage or his tears. "How does someone so young and bad and wild get wisdom?" he asked in a whisper.

"Wisdom? What I get is struggle. I haven't had it as bad as you, as hard as most people. I just do my best, that's all. But I want to tell you something. I didn't love you with just my body, Ian. My heart got in there. I hope you know that."

"I know that." He touched her lips briefly. Then he asked, "So, what's wrong with him? My father? You said he was sick."

"Not critical—but his maladies will get him sooner than later. He's being treated with chemo for prostate cancer, he has Parkinson's, had a mild stroke and I believe some dementia is settling in. But, be warned—he could have years." Then she grinned.

"You—are—amazing."

"You could come home with me, Ian. For Christmas."

He was quiet for a moment. "No. I couldn't do that."

"Why not? Will the good people from the towns around here be without firewood? Would the cabin get snowed in?"

He smiled at her. "Baby, I'm not going to kid you—you changed my life, and all in ten days, but not enough to clean me up and take me back to Chico. Listen to me," he said gently. "This is nice, you and me. But I think it's a tryst that might never be anything more. This thing that happened between us—it wasn't supposed to."

"But you're not sorry," she said.

"You know I'm not sorry. I'm grateful."

"I think if I stayed a little longer…"

"What? You'd get through to me? Transform me into

some other kind of guy? Pluck me out of my run-down cabin and make a civilized man out of me?"

She shook her head. "Nothing like that ever occurred to me. You're more civilized than most of the men I know. But lately I've been thinking if I stayed longer you'd laugh more. You'd sing to people instead of just to wildlife. You'd probably ask that librarian out for drinks."

"Yeah," he laughed. "After I found a way to convince her I'm not an idiot savant."

"If I came back here to see you, would you lock me out and make me sleep in my car?"

He laughed and shook his head. "No." But he thought, *she might come back once, maybe even twice.* Then it would stop, because he and this place wouldn't change much. And he didn't deserve her; she should have so much more than some beat-up old marine with issues who'd stuck himself in the woods.

"Since you won't come back with me, I'm staying till Christmas Eve. I won't leave at the crack of dawn, but I'll get home in time for dinner. It's just a few hours away."

"Erin isn't going to like that," he said. "She's ready for you right now."

"She'll have to wait. I'm doing the best I can. I don't want to leave you. Ever."

Instead of talking about it anymore, he asked her, "Is it too soon to make love again?"

"No," she said, smiling.

He pulled her against him. It was better this way, he thought, that he not add the words *I love you* to the mix. This was hard enough on her. Instead, he kissed her as well as he could, his hands running over her body in a way that promised more loving.

In the morning when she woke, he had gone. He left a note. "Sweetheart. Selling wood, plowing some roads. I won't be too long. Ian."

"Sweetheart," she whispered to herself. She folded it in half and quarters and found a safe place in her wallet to preserve it. Forever.

Fourteen

Ian unloaded his entire supply of firewood in short order and took delivery orders for three more half cords, which would take him another day to load, deliver and unload, giving people their cozy fires for Christmas. And his supply of cut and cure wood was running low, which was the plan. He'd cut and split and cured all spring, summer and fall and then, with luck, sell off his wood in a matter of weeks.

He was in Virgin River before noon. He parked by the bar, but he didn't go in. Instead he walked up to that huge tree, taking a closer look at some of the unit badges. He looked around; he was alone. Then he pulled a few things out of his pocket. He'd fixed them up with short wires so they'd hook onto the branches. His unit badge—the same as Bobby's. A Purple Heart and a Bronze Star—medals awarded for the highest bravery and valor. He fixed them onto the tree. It took him just a few moments.

"I'll see those get back to you," a voice said.

He whirled around and found himself facing Mel Sheridan. Her coat was pulled tight against the cold and occasional snow flurries, her hands plunged in her pockets. "I won't be here at Christmas—we're going to Jack's family. But I can tell Paige—Preacher's wife—to make sure when she rescues some of the badges that she holds on to your medals. It wouldn't do to lose them. They're important."

"I'm not worried about what happens to them. I don't have much use for them now."

She laughed a little. "I've heard that before."

"Oh?"

"My husband, for one. You guys, you're peculiar in that way. You train to do the things that bring awards, then won't display them. Jack—he was going to get rid of his until his father confiscated them to keep them safe. Jack said it wasn't the medals, it was the men. So—if you can remember the men with the medals, good enough. I'll see you get them back."

"Thanks," he said weakly. "I think they're better off here."

"For now," Mel said. "I guess Marcie will have to head home, but in case you're around Christmas Eve..."

"I heard," he said. "A town thing. I don't know..."

"Well, the town's kind of easy—no RSVP required. If you get the itch." She shrugged and smiled.

"That's nice," he said. "I have to go. There's an old guy, neighbor of mine, who doesn't have a plow..."

"Good of you to look out for him, Ian."

"I don't really, I just—"

He stopped abruptly at the sight of Jack, Preacher and Mike coming out of the bar in a big hurry, jacketed up, carrying rifles and duffel bags.

"Jack?" Mel asked.

He continued toward his extended cab truck. "Travis Goesel wandered off yesterday. Didn't make it home.

Family's been looking all over their farm and grazing land." He threw a duffel in his truck bed. "David's with Brie."

"Wandered off?" Mel asked. "Travis wandered off?"

"He was tracking a cat. Mountain lion killed his dog, so he grabbed his rifle and he went after it. Kid's a good tracker and excellent shot. And too smart to be out all night in this snow."

"Where's the Goesel farm?" Ian asked before he could stop himself.

"You know the Pauper's Pond area?"

"Sort of. The river that runs past my place feeds a couple creeks and a pond out there. I'm east of their property a few miles. That cat's been around my place."

"What makes you think it's the same cat?" Jack asked.

"Aggressive one—he didn't run off like they usually do."

"That a fact? You must know that area. Any chance you could lend a hand?"

Ian wanted nothing so much as to get back to the girl. Especially if that cat was out there with blood lust.

"The kid's sixteen," Jack went on. "He's big and strong. But I agree with his father—this isn't good. I don't know what's worse, the mountain lion getting him or the cold."

"Okay," Ian said. "If the boy's smart, he's not walking uphill toward my place. I can start at the base of the mountain and work west. You can start in the west and work east. Will that help? A kid that age could walk miles."

"His father, brothers and some neighbors are all over that farm—we can work the outside acreage." Jack pulled his duffel out of the truck bed. "Preach and Mike can go together on the west side of Goesel's farm, I'll go with you on the east."

"I don't have hardly any heat in that truck," Ian said.

"Yeah, but you got a plow. I love the plow. That could come in real handy. I'm gonna get one of those to mount on my truck. I have myself a long road into our new house."

Ian looked at Mel. "I left Marcie early this morning when I went to deliver firewood. She won't know why I'm not back. If she tried to get to town in that car of hers..."

"When David lies down for his nap, I'll run out there and tell her what's going on. Would that help?"

"Tell her she's going to want to stay in. She doesn't like that. She doesn't like making do and not traveling to the outdoor facilities. You'd better tell her about that mountain lion, that he's around and he's not getting any more shy."

"I'll do that. You just be real careful out there. Jack!" she yelled. "You be careful!"

Jack grinned at Mel. "I'll be back real soon, Melinda. Travis has presents under the tree—we have to get him home. You just keep that little bun in the oven warm. Come on, Buchanan. Let's do it."

The men left town in two trucks—Ian took Jack and Preacher took Mike. They headed out the same highway, and then at a fork that led to the farm, Mike and Preacher took their truck off to the left while Ian and Jack kept going past the farm. "How much land you have sitting under that cabin?" Jack asked Ian.

"Six hundred and sixty acres," Ian said. Jack whistled. "It's all mountain and trees in a restricted-logging area. So it's a lot of nothing."

"Nothing but quiet and pretty."

"There's a stream," Ian said. "Good fishing. Good hunting. And I harvest the trees for firewood, a little here and there. I think the old man, Raleigh, homesteaded."

"How'd you know him?" Jack asked.

Ian laughed. "I was wandering around the mountains, camping, hunting rabbit, on a fool's mission, when winter hit the mountains real sudden. Raleigh was older than God already and couldn't hardly chop his own wood, so he gave me a roof for some help on the land."

"Good deal for you!"

"Yeah, the joke was on me. He got real sick and what he needed was a nurse in addition to everything else."

Jack grinned at him. "You must'a stuck it out if you're in the cabin."

Ian shrugged. "I never saw that coming—he wrote some kind of will that old Doc had to witness. If he hadn't done that, I might've figured out what to do with myself by now."

"Nothing wrong with having more than one choice, man. We should probably park along the road up here pretty soon and go back on foot."

"There's a road that'll take us almost straight back around the hill another couple of miles—it'll get us farther in there. Tell me about this boy? Why would he do this?"

Jack turned and looked at him. "Ever have a dog?"

"Yeah," Ian said. "Velvet—a black Lab." Velvet had been his best friend when he was a kid. The old girl made it till she was fourteen, till her back was so slumped and her hips so painful, it hurt him to look at her. But he couldn't let go; seemed like he had a long history of that. He was seventeen to her fourteen when he heard his father's early morning curse while he was getting ready for school and he knew—Velvet had had an accident in the night. She was tired and weary; she couldn't always remember to do the right thing. "That dog has to be put down," Ian heard his father say.

Afraid he might come home from school one day to find her gone, he cut school and went alone to the vet and held her while she drifted off, painless. He couldn't stand the thought she might go alone; he wouldn't put it past his father to take her, drop her off, leave her to die by herself. God, her face was more peaceful and rested in death than it had been for the last year of her life. Seeing that, it should have made him feel glad for her, relieved—she wasn't going to last much longer anyway.

He couldn't let Velvet go alone. He had needed the time to say goodbye, and he didn't want to come home and find her gone. He needed to be with her—like Marcie had needed to be with Bobby. He swallowed hard.

But his memory drifted back to Velvet, remembering the whole loss, how it tore him up. He'd gone off to private places where he could cry like a girl, unable to let his parents or friends see he had that amount of emotion.

"That mountain lion's been bothering their property—stalking," Jack said. "The dogs have been running it off, keeping it away from the goats and hens."

"How old was the kid's dog?" Ian asked.

"I don't know, exactly. Six or eight—a border collie, a herder named Whip. They had a half-dozen farm dogs, mostly herders, outdoor animals, but Travis raised that one himself. He picked her out of a litter and for a while she was a 4-H project. Goesel said he couldn't keep the damn dog out of the kid's bed. You know farmers and their dogs—they don't get overly sentimental as a rule. I don't know how the cat managed to get to the dog—they usually aren't looking for that kind of a fight."

Ian ground his teeth. "Think I'd go after the son of a bitch, too."

"Yeah," Jack said. "Yeah, I had a dog growing up, too. Big dog—Spike, no kidding. He was almost a perfect animal. But he let my sisters dress him up. That used to make me sick, I'm telling you. The way he let himself be humiliated like that."

Ian shot him a look and a big grin. He was picturing a German shepherd in a tutu and a disgruntled teenage boy. A laugh shot out of him.

"It wasn't funny," Jack said.

"I bet it was," Ian said. Then he pulled off the road at a sharp left. "Gimme a minute here." He jumped out of the truck, got some tools out of the box in the bed and went around to the front. He loosened up the brackets on the plow hitch, pulled the plow with all his might to angle it, then lowered it and tightened the brackets. It wasn't the kind of plow fitting that had hydraulics inside the vehicle to move the blade, it was all manual, old and old-fashioned—but it got the job done. He threw his tools back in the box and got behind the wheel.

"I don't see a road. You see a road?" Jack asked.

Ian laughed. "I know where the road is."

"How?"

"I can feel it. Relax."

Jack braced a foot against the floorboard, a hand against the dash and said, "I'll relax when we're not in a ditch. Go slow."

Ian laughed at him. "So," Ian said, maneuvering slowly, "if the kid's smart, we'll be looking for some kind of recent tracks, shelter, or…"

"A body," Jack supplied.

"If he was lost, he might've followed the river or the road. About the time night was falling, he might've seen any one of several old logging roads," Ian said. "You're not going to see the road with the snow, but you'll know it's there by the tree line. Like I'm doing now."

"I'm not convinced there isn't a big hole right in your path, hidden by snow. You could go slower," Jack said, tense.

"You could relax. I've been all over this place." Then after a bit, he stopped the truck. "Want to head out from here?"

"Let's do it."

They exited the truck at the same time. Ian took a rifle out of the rack in his truck and a flashlight out of the glove compartment. Jack was digging around in his duffel.

"I only have one flare gun, but I have an extra stocking mask and a scarf—put this around your neck. We'll start down this road together, but when we separate, if you find anything, just fire a couple rounds. With me?"

"Gotcha." Ian buttoned up his jacket and thought, *I didn't have any reason for the long underwear this morning, damn it.* He wrapped the long plaid scarf around his head and neck, partly covering his face. He missed the heavy beard right now. "See, I think the dog wasn't as scrappy as the other dogs because she was a little spoiled by Travis," Ian said, speaking as though he knew Travis and the dog. "That could've been working on him at the same time."

"I know," Jack said. "How's your flashlight? You need batteries?"

"To tell the truth, I'm not sure."

Jack pulled some extra batteries out of his duffel as well as a hand gun he tucked in his waist. He tossed Ian the batteries, then two bottled waters that Ian put in each pocket. They walked down the road, looking right and left, and hadn't gone far when Jack said, "Okay, I'm going this way into that stand of trees."

"I'll head this way," Ian said, and they separated.

Ian walked toward the river, eyes trained on the ground, on the landscape, and occasionally up into the branches just in case that big cat was having a little game of hide and seek. And he thought some about the kid remembering himself at sixteen; he'd been a hothead, devoted to a few things in his life, and his dog was one of them.

He'd also been pretty angry with his father in general. His dad was a passive-aggressively cruel person—he wouldn't leave a tip, drove real slow in the passing lane, withheld affection. Every birthday card or holiday gift was signed "Mom & Dad" by Ian's mother. Every word that came out of the old man's pie hole was a criticism.

After Velvet, Ian had stopped pretending it didn't matter; he was bigger and stronger than his father and got right up in his face, giving it back to him, something he soon realized was tearing his mother up. His mother begged him to lighten up, let it go, ignore being snubbed or criticized virtually every minute. "How do you stand it?" he had railed at his mother. "He should kiss your feet, and he acts like you're his slave!"

And his sweet mother had said, "Ian, he's faithful and he works hard to support us. He might not be romantic or doting, but he gave me you. If that's all I ever get from him, it'll always be the world to me."

Not enough, Ian remembered thinking. Not enough. Joining the Marines seemed like a smart and safe way to go—got him the hell out of there and to a place where he could be in touch with his mother and not have to put up with his father.

Then came his mother's death, then more active duty leading up to Iraq. His father was the only family Ian had left and he was woefully inadequate. After Iraq, after a few scrapes that even he knew had all to do with some PTSD, he feared he was turning into the old man. There were random fights with guys he had no real quarrel with. Things set him off and he just lost it. Even if the Corps could look the other way for a while, Ian couldn't. He'd been a strong leader who'd turned into an asshole who just couldn't cope. That's when he got out, hoping he could get back to the man who was admired. Followed.

And Ian's father said, "You are no son to me if you quit. If you run away."

Ian said, "I never was a son to you."

Talk about a standoff.

He scanned the ground, looking for any sign of the boy—broken shrubs or tree limbs showing that someone had passed, marks on the ground including drops of blood, recent footprints in the snow.

He also thought about Marcie. When she'd infiltrated his life, his first thought hadn't been that she was beautiful and sexy. In fact, his twentieth thought wasn't even that—she was sick, pale, listless…frankly, homely as a duck. Vulnerable and anything but pretty. Still, it wasn't the pretty that got to him when she started to get a little color on her face—it was the pure contrariness. The fight in her—he'd always appreciated anyone with that kind of gumption.

She was just about well in less than a week and her eyes had started to regain that little spark that said she'd have her way, speak her mind and damn the consequences. How more like him could she be? He was able to appreciate her and give her credit—though not out loud—without getting captured by her.

Then slowly, he began to *like* her. No matter she fully

intended to get in his business and mess up his life, she had a kind of drive that he couldn't help but admire. She wasn't doing any of it just for herself, but for herself and everyone from her dead husband to his family to Ian…to his cranky, isolated father whom Ian had been absolutely determined not to be like…but was.

It was when she defied her classy big sister and came back to his dusty little cabin that he fell. Aw, damn, what determination she had to be with him, to see it through, whatever it was she felt she had to do. Even she didn't seem entirely sure what she was doing there—but she wasn't ready to give up on him. And she had this insane idea that everything could be all right! Somehow, she was going to pull him back into the man he'd been to her dead husband; the brave leader, the fearless and committed man. Not someone who just dropped out of sight and isolated himself out of a kind of self-hatred. Into the man his father had never had the sense to be proud of.

Oh, God, I can't have turned into my father so soon!

He forced his mind back to Travis Goesel, scanning the ground, the shrubs, the lower branches of the trees. He looked at the old watch that still worked. He'd been trekking without a sound from Jack for two hours and it was approaching four o'clock. They only had two more hours of daylight at the most, so he called, "Travis! Travis! Make a sound! Move something!"

He walked a little faster, scanned the terrain with concentration, and it came to him that it was good to belong to something. Even though Jack was out of sight and the other men where on the west side of the farm, he felt as if he was a part of a unit of men who had a purpose again and, until Jack piled in the truck with him, he hadn't felt that in a long time. He'd been so anxious to sever himself from the pain of war, he'd forgotten how much the pleasure of brotherhood filled his soul. This, he had to admit, had all occurred because this feisty little redhead had come into his life. She forced the issue. She pushed him out of his cocoon while he was still raw, growing new skin.

If she'd left her disabled husband in the hands of his family three years ago to come after him, would she have succeeded in pulling him up out of his self-indulgent withdrawal any sooner? Probably not. He'd licked his wounds for such a long time that he got used to the taste of his self-pity.

Ian grew wearily cold, craving long underwear. He'd been out in the woods for hours. He ate snow rather than drink the bottled water, in case he found the boy and needed it for him.

Then he saw a smear of blood and some tracks, partially covered by a new blanket of snow. By the width and weight of the trail, it was the cat, wounded. He followed the trail just a short distance, realizing the cat was dragging itself heavily. A moment later Ian realized that Travis would have intelligently gone in the opposite direction to this bloodied trail. So Ian did also.

Ian made it to the river and was looking left and right along the edge as night fell. He'd have to head back to the truck soon, at least to confer with Jack and discuss the plan for searching at night. Part of such a plan would have to include long underwear and dry socks. But he just couldn't make himself stop.

Darkness fell in earnest. He shone the flashlight on his watch and saw it was nearly six o'clock and he yelled for the millionth time. "Travis! Travis!"

Then as the light from his flashlight fell upon the snow,

he noticed a drop of blood here, a drop there. Travis was hurt and doing just what Ian expected a smart kid to do—he was following the river home. Using the flashlight to scan the ground as darkness thickened around him Ian saw something. Not far away from the river's edge was a pile of dead pine needles and brush, covered with a little new snow. A mound. It didn't look like much, but he gave it a slight kick with his boot and when some of the debris fell away, he saw a sleeve. He was instantly down on his knees, digging. In mere moments he uncovered a boy, his face white, his lips blue, his eyes closed. Ian shook him vigorously, not knowing if the boy was dead or alive.

"Travis! Travis!"

The boy's eyes finally came open, and he blinked not knowing where he was. He smacked his dry lips. He looked up at Ian with a dazed expression. "Sorry… Dad…"

"Aw, Jesus, Travis!" Ian said, relieved beyond words that the boy was alive. "You're going to be okay, buddy." Then he rolled him carefully onto his side and saw that the back of his jacket was shredded and he was bleeding. The damn cat had got him from behind but, thanks to Travis's clothing, the mauling had not gone deep and, with the help of the snow, his bleeding had been stanched.

"You get him, son?" Ian asked.

"I don't think so. I'm sorry, Dad."

He was delirious, probably more from cold than his injury. Thank God he'd buried himself under dead leaves and pine needles to preserve his body heat. "I'll get you outta here, son, hang on," Ian said, now running on automatic. He stood and fired twice into a thick tree—three shots were the signal that you were lost, two was a standard response from a search team, and one shot could be mistaken for a hunter. You never sent a bullet into the air with the possible outcome of it returning to earth to find a living person or innocent livestock.

Then he put the rifle strap over his shoulder and scooped up Travis in his arms. Immediately he remembered doing the same for Bobby. But this time it was different—there was muscle tension in Travis's body. He was responding to the pain, maybe from the cold, maybe from having a mountain lion's claws in his back.

"Wake up, Travis! Wake up! Did the cat get you, huh? Tell me," he panted, walking as fast as he could. He hoped he wouldn't fall. His torso was okay—he had on a T-shirt, sweatshirt and jacket, but his legs, knees and feet were now soaked with ice and snow. "You with me, buddy?"

"Who…you…?"

Ian laughed in spite of himself, just hearing the kid's response. "Your guardian angel, my boy! You shoot at the cat?"

"I…think…"

"He left a bloody trail—you get a shot off?"

"I…I couldn't a hit 'im," Travis answered, his tongue thick.

"Yeah, bet you got lucky. He's bleeding way worse than you. Good for you," Ian said. "Talk. Keep talking. Tell me."

His speech was slurred and labored, but Travis did as ordered. "Got me…from…the tree…I saw him…I had him…bastard got Whip…"

"Keep talking," Ian said breathlessly, now laboring heavily under the weight of Travis combined with the difficulty of moving through the snow. "Almost there," he said, but in fact, he wasn't sure how far it was. He kept tromping. And tromping. But he knew the woods, knew the river's edge that ran by his property. "Talk to me! Tell me about your girl!"

And the boy tried. He named her—Felicity. Must be the next generation's girls' names, Ian thought, almost laughing if he'd had the breath. "Keep talking!" he demanded. "This Felicity, you in love with her or something?"

"She's a good girl..."

"That bites," Ian said. "Sucks she couldn't be a bad girl. You don't know, bud—those bad girls, they get right under your skin. She pretty?"

"Pretty," he said.

"Atta boy, keep talking," Ian said, laying the boy carefully on the ground. "I'm going to fire a couple shots to let them know we're coming." And Ian quickly put another two in a fat tree, just to be sure there was some backup on the way. The kid was in rough shape so, if he had to, he'd take him out of here and come back in the dark of night for Jack, but it would be better if—

"Hey!" Jack shouted. "What you got?"

"Your boy," Ian said in a weak breath. Then he saw the truck about a hundred yards down the road.

"Lemme help," Jack shouted.

"I've got him. You drive."

"I don't know this road," Jack said. "I can't *feel* it."

Ian let a laugh erupt. "I fucking *plowed* it for you! Let's get going!"

When they got to the truck, Ian balanced Travis on his thighs and pulled the keys out of his pocket, pitching them to Jack. Then he climbed into the cab with a boy the size of a man on his lap. Travis's head was lolling back and forth and he was struggling to keep his eyes open. Before Jack had the key in the ignition, Ian had ripped open

Travis's jacket and shirt, tearing his undershirt open, then he did the same with his own three layers. He pressed Travis's bare chest to his own and hugged his body close, warming him with his own body heat.

Jack carefully turned the truck around and headed out. "The plow is down. Should I stop and put it up?"

"Nah. The county should thank us."

"Could hurt the plow blade."

"Who cares?"

"Where we headed?" Jack asked.

"I don't know. We need medical help. You tell me. We can call his parents from wherever…"

"Virgin River, I guess," Jack said. "It's just as quick to drive him straight to town where Mel and Doc can look at him as to call them from the farm. Besides, they have the Humvee ambulance. What's his condition?"

"He tried to bury himself to keep from freezing to death, and he did a good job of it. But another couple of hours and we'd be outta luck," Ian said. He absorbed the boy's cold into his body. "He also got mauled by the cat, but the temperatures were low and the bleeding doesn't look serious—but then what do I know? Plow faster, huh?"

"You got it, sir," Jack said.

Ian settled back in the seat and pressed Travis's face against his bare shoulder, feeling his carotid pulse picking up as he held him chest to chest. Momentarily, he felt him stir on his lap. Within fifteen minutes the boy's eyes had drifted open. Surprise dawned on his face. "Who are you?" he asked weakly.

"The Christmas fairy," Ian said. "You're going to be okay, kid." Ian pulled the bottle of water out of his jacket pocket and held it to Travis's lips. "Take a little drink. Slow and easy." Finished, Ian's arms came around him tight, holding him against him. "I'm gonna get the heater fixed in this truck, if it's the last I do. I think you got that cat, boy."

"I shot at him, but he still lunged at me and I butted him in the head hard as I could. He just ran…"

"He was bleeding good. You must've hit him plenty hard."

"I didn't get him," he said slowly. "Scared him away long enough to bury myself."

"I had a dog," Ian said. "My best friend for years. She used to sleep on my bed. She was a good dog…"

"Whip was a good dog," he said.

Ian ruffled the kid's hair. "I loved my dog. I'd have done the same as you. That cat's a bad cat. I've seen it around."

"You've seen it?"

Ian nodded. "I should've killed it. This is my fault—I should've shot the cat. He had my girl trapped in the outhouse for hours, in the cold, but I shot over its head to run him off. I'm sorry, kid. I should've killed the cat."

"I should've, too," the kid said, sleepily, laying his head against Ian's shoulder.

"Drink another couple swallows," Ian said, holding up the water for him.

A few minutes later Jack drove into Virgin River pounding the horn in long, urgent blasts that brought people out of the bar, including Mel and Doc Mullins. Jack pulled right up to the Hummer while Ian, bare-chested, carried Travis out of the truck and, as they were accustomed to doing, Mel and Doc sprang into action. They lifted the hatch on the Hummer, pulled out the gurney and Ian placed the boy there.

After a quick check of his vitals, Ian told them about the lacerations on his back from the mountain lion he'd been tracking. Mel rolled him onto his side while Doc lifted the jacket and glanced at the injury. "Not so bad. Hypothermia. Melinda, you get in back—start an IV and get him warmed up while I drive. Valley Hospital can deal with this, no problem. The boy's going to pull through fine." To Jack he said, "Call the farm—tell his parents."

"Will do," Jack said. "Then I'll go out and fire a flare for Preacher, Mike, and the rest of the search party. You saying we're home free?"

"Good as it gets," Doc said. "Come on, Melinda! You slowing down on me?"

"Oh, shove it, you old goat," she snapped, climbing in. "Jack—mind the baby."

He grinned largely. "You bet, my love."

Through it all Ian thought, *I'm part of a unit.* Even out here in the middle of nowhere, there were people to belong to. He'd always known that, but never thought he'd slip into their fold.

Jack just stood there, looking at Ian. He lifted one brow. "Your girl, huh?" he asked.

"I was just talking to the kid," Ian said.

"Uh-huh. You better head for home, pal."

Fifteen

By the time Ian walked into his cabin, it was after eight at night. He was so tired and chilled, he thought it would be half the night before he'd warm up, much less be able to load the pickup with the next day's firewood. He didn't even have the door closed behind him when he heard a wild shriek and Marcie leaped at him, her arms around his neck and her legs wrapped around him.

"Hey," he laughed, holding her clear of the floor. "Hey. You're on me like a tick."

She leaned away from his face. "Are you all right?"

"I'm freezing and hungry. Were you scared?"

She shook her head stubbornly. "Did you find the boy?"

"He was found," Ian said. "Hurt and cold, but he's going to be all right. Can you warm and feed me? Would Abigail Adams do that?"

"She would, and in between, she'd plow two fields and give birth." Marcie grinned at him.

God, she's so alive, he thought. It would be a travesty

to hide her away on a mountaintop. But for now, having her on top this mountain was like the answer to a prayer.

Ian had to dig his way out to the john early the next morning, shoveling a path for Marcie to use when she woke. Then he loaded up the back of the truck with firewood, feeling better than he had a right to, since she hadn't let him sleep that much during the night. Then, rather than going straight to that intersection where he liked to sell firewood, he drove in the opposite direction a couple of miles, adjusted the blade on the plow, and cleared a path up to his neighbor's house.

He didn't like what he saw upon pulling up. There was no homey curl of smoke from the chimney; no sign of life. His first thought was—if I have to hold another ice-cold body against my chest…

But the front door creaked open. The old man stood there in the frame, wearing his boots and coat.

"I cleared your road, in case you need someone to get in or need to get out."

"Obliged," he said.

"Listen—how you fixed for firewood? You got some canned food you can open up while the snow's heavy?" Ian asked.

"I'll get by," he said.

Typically, that's when Ian would give him a small salute, then turn and head out down the drive to Highway 36, to get on with the things he had to do. Instead, with a muffled curse, he lifted up the tarp covering his load and filled his arms with split logs. He walked right up to the front door with the wood and the old guy barred the way. Ian stared down at him. "Come on," he said. "I brought you wood for your stove."

After a moment's hesitation, the guy let him in, grimacing. On his way to put the logs beside the stove, Ian caught a whiff of something disgusting. He kept his mouth shut, having an idea what the problem might be. When he crouched to stack the logs by the stove, he pulled off a glove and touched it. It was ice-cold. He stood and went back out the door and loaded up another big batch of logs. On his way to the door he glanced along the property and saw what he expected—the outhouse was buried in a couple feet of snow and there was no path. The old boy couldn't split his own logs, if he had any to split, and he either couldn't get to the outhouse or was worried about falling in the snow and not being able to get up. As for shoveling, he likely just didn't have the stamina. He'd been making far too much use of some indoor make-shift chamber pot that he'd empty when he could get to the john. It was horrid.

Ian delivered a third load of wood and said, "Get your fire going. I'm going to clear your path for you. Where's the shovel?"

"Don't bother. I'll—"

"Don't argue with me about it—where's the damn shovel?"

He tilted his head out the door. Ian went out, looked around to the side of the house and found the shovel leaning against the house, nearly buried by the snow. Well, he was missing his usual firewood crowd and he was in a hurry—so it would have to be a narrow path. But this had to be done. Only a damn fool would let pride cause him to freeze to death in his own filth.

And that won't happen to me, because I won't let it. Just like he'd always believed he wouldn't let himself turn into his father? It gave him pause…

When he'd cleared the path, he pounded on the man's door. "You like Dinty Moore beef stew?" he asked shortly.

"Why?"

"I have a surplus. I thought I'd leave some off later."

"No need to do that."

"Come on, man—it's a friendly gesture. The woman at my place hates that stuff and won't eat it—I'll leave by a few cans. If it's not going to be too big a burden for you to take it off my hands."

He shrugged. "You grow weed over there on that ridge?"

"Hell, no. What makes you ask that?"

"What you do over there?"

"I cut down trees and sell firewood out of my truck. I fish some. Lately I shovel and plow a lot. I don't know your name."

"We're even," the old boy said. "Since I never knew yours."

"Ian Buchanan," he said, not putting out his hand.

"Michael Jackson," the old boy said, and Ian let a burst of laughter escape. The old man frowned darkly and Ian realized, too late, that this fella probably hadn't seen television in decades, if ever.

"Nice to meet you," Ian said. "Mr. Jackson."

"You sure you don't grow weed? Because I don't get mixed up with growers for Dinty Anything."

"I'm sure," Ian said. "I'll drop some canned goods by later on, but for now you can get to the john and heat up the house."

Ian went back to his truck, adjusted the plow so it wouldn't scrape on the highway and turned around to leave. There was no thank-you, no pleased to meet you. But then, Ian had been taking care of the old guy's drive for over two years without any exchanging social graces.

But, no doubt about it, things were declining some for the old man. Mr. Jackson had been able to plow his drive till now, but now he couldn't even make his way out back to the toilet and it was possible there was no food in the house. Remembering how Doc checked on old Raleigh at the end, he decided he would mention this situation to Doc. He couldn't have Michael Jackson on his conscience; his conscience was pretty full right now.

It took him longer than usual to deliver his wood. He had to wait for both his customers to go to their ATM's to withdraw cash as he couldn't afford to take a bad check at this point. By the time he got back to his cabin, it was afternoon and he'd been gone eight hours. When he came in, Marcie had his bath water simmering on the stove. "Well, Abigail," he said, smiling at her. "I see you're ready for me to come home. Tell me, do you have the back forty plowed?"

"And the barn rebuilt," she said, smiling. "You took a long time today."

"Some days are easier than others," he said. "I have to make a quick run. Not fifteen minutes." He walked over to his cupboard. "How much of this beef stew you willing to part with?"

"Why?"

"I don't think the old man next door laid in his supply." He started pulling out large cans and stacking them on the table till he had eight of them. He went to his trunk to get a duffel and loaded it up with the cans.

"That's nice, Ian. Sharing with him like that."

"Nah. I just don't want a bad smell drifting over to my property. Keep my water going, will you? I'll be right back."

When Ian pulled up to Mike Jackson's house, he found the man no more friendly or receptive than earlier, but he didn't put up a fuss about the stew. He took it, nodded, and closed the door.

That moment was an epiphany. You can have it either way out here. You can get bonded with your town, your neighbors, belong to each other and have a connected existence where mutual reliance got you through the hard times. Or you could have it like this. If you never let anyone get near you, they soon got the message you wanted to be left alone. Out here, where neighbors were separated by miles, hills, big trees and, too often, hardship, no one fought for your friendship or your companionship. You'd have to at least meet people halfway.

Ian hadn't given much of anything to the people around him here in Virgin River. He was just like his father. Thank God Marcie had ignored that... He'd have to change things—or he'd end up like his old neighbor, like old Raleigh.

Ian went home, where he had Marcie playing Abigail, and it was cute. There were just a few days left to them and he was going to make the most of the time they had together and, because he knew it was hard for her to go and bring an end to this mission of hers, he'd make it as easy on her as he could.

So he bathed, he ate, he held her against him for a little while and read aloud the spicy part of her romance novel, which was positively nothing compared to the real thing that followed. Then they spruced up a little and drove into Fortuna together to do some laundry. It was there that he told her his plan.

"Tomorrow, when I get home from delivering wood, I'm going to dig out your car for you and tow it into town, park it at Jack's, put some chains in the trunk and show you how to put them on so you're safe when you're ready to head home. Please don't get a wild hare while I'm not around and try to leave without a goodbye. It's not safe for you to take the bug down the mountain without chains. Promise?"

"Promise," she said.

"I want to be sure you're safe. Taken care of."

She looked down as he knew she would. Sad. Quiet. Marcie was hardly ever quiet.

With the sound of jeans clacking in the dryer and the hum of machines droning in the background he held her arms and turned her toward him. He lifted her chin with a finger. "We still have time, Marcie—time for you to be sure you've asked me everything on your mind so you feel right about going home. So you have peace of mind."

"And you?" she asked him.

He ran a knuckle down her cheek. "My mind hasn't felt this peaceful and calm in years. We'll make the most of the time you're here." He gave her lips a little kiss. "I was so angry when I first faced you. I'm not angry anymore. You made things good for me."

"An awful lot more passed between us than I ever imagined," she said. "But I'm glad."

"Then let's fold our jeans and head back to town. I think we can get a toddy with Jack and Preacher before they close. Then we'll go home, stoke the fire and if you want me to, I'll read the dirty part of that book to you again."

She slapped his arm. "Please, it's not dirty! It's romantic."

"Yeah," he grinned. "Very." He pressed his lips against her forehead.

They went by Jack's to find it was his last night in town before taking the family back to Sacramento for the holidays, so Mel was there, as was Jack's sister, Brie, and her partner Mike Valenzuela. The mood was festive. Jack's son, David, was asleep in Preacher's quarters behind the bar and there was a lot of excitement about traveling for Christmas. Ian and Marcie ordered up beer and were pulled into the upbeat mood.

Doc didn't seem to be around, so while Marcie used the kitchen phone to check in with her sister, Ian took a moment to speak to Mel about his neighbor and suggested he might not be doing well. She just smiled and said, "Thanks, Ian. Before I leave in the morning, I'll speak to Doc and he'll check on things out there. If he needs assistance, Doc will do what he can. But be warned—some of these old-timers don't change their ways. They're pigheaded about things like help, medical intervention, that sort of thing."

"You don't have to tell me," Ian said. "I was with old Raleigh when he went."

"Then you already know." She smiled. "Have a nice Christmas, Ian."

"You, too," he said.

He hadn't celebrated Christmas in a long time. The last time had been with Shelly before he left for Iraq. He'd given her a ring and suddenly the holiday became all about getting engaged.

His father had never been much about Christmas. It was Ian's mother who made the holiday real, decorating, baking, fixing up gift baskets for everyone she knew, buying gifts that she'd given a lot of thought to. His dad always came up with something lame for his wife—a subscription to a women's magazine, a sweater too ugly for words that she'd gush over, a couple of cookbooks. He was famous for caving in to something the house needed like a washer or vacuum cleaner and saying, "All right then, it's an early Christmas present." After his mother died, Christmas disappeared entirely. The tree didn't come out, the lights didn't go on the house, there was no special dinner. Ian was glad not to be around.

But on the Christmas Ian had given Shelly the ring, he'd also given her a necklace and a beautiful peignoir. He remembered the details now—that was when he decided he was *not* going to be like his father. He was going to be thoughtful.

For Ian, there still wouldn't be a real Christmas this year, yet his spirits were higher than they had been in years. He didn't have any decorations and would probably end up opening a can of Dinty Moore for his dinner. He was sorry he didn't have a present for Marcie and relieved she'd had no opportunity or means to get one for him. But he liked that the town was not only getting into it, they were honoring the men and women who stood the watch. That in itself made it a joyous holiday.

To his surprise, he was starting to think in terms of things changing for him. *Because I've had these unusual, unexpected, illuminating weeks of Marcie.* She opened his eyes in so many ways. And then he started to laugh to himself, because his mind turned to septic tanks. What would it take to buy and have a septic tank installed, a hot water heater, an indoor bathroom? It would start with money—real money and not the hit and miss income of selling firewood in winter and moving furniture part-time in summer.

The guy who owned the moving company had offered him full-time work a couple of times because Ian was strong and fast, but he'd said no thank you. He now considered getting in touch with that guy and getting his name on the list for full-time. Maybe he'd even look around, see if there were other interested employers—he was fit and not afraid of work.

Then a little voice reminded him that he hadn't filed a tax return in four years because he just didn't care. He had slipped out of the functional world; could he really expect to slip back in?

For the right reasons, he thought. She'd taught him to laugh again. Just that alone warranted getting a full-time job and buying a septic tank, not because it would matter to Marcie. Because it would be good to improve, to live rather than exist. And hell—it had been a long time since an honest-to-God shower.

At that moment, she came out of the kitchen and hopped up on the bar stool beside Ian, and she wasn't wearing her happy face. "Erin Elizabeth is getting a little pissy. She's ready for me to get home. She's past ready."

"You can't be surprised," Ian said. "You did promise her."

"I kind of put off telling her I'm staying here till Christmas Eve. It's just a four-hour drive, or so."

He slipped an arm around her shoulders and kissed her temple. "It's the right thing to do, Marcie. Your family loves you, needs you. You don't want to take that for granted."

"I know. Right now I just have too many *right things* to do. Heat your bath water, plow your fields…"

"Make me laugh…"

"Make you roar." She smiled at him.

"No matter what you think right now, you'll be glad once you're home," he said. "Familiar and comfortable and… Listen, when you told my father you were going to look for me, what did he say?"

"I told you," she said, focusing on her beer. "He said I was probably wasting my time."

"I know him too well—what else did he say?"

"Really, he was just a crotchety old—"

"Come on—you never hold back. The truth."

She turned wide, innocent, troubled green eyes up to his. "He… He said if I found you, I should tell you he left the house and car to the paperboy."

Unexpectedly, Ian erupted in laughter. He threw his head back and howled. Marcie just stared at him while he laughed until his eyes watered. His lips were still curved in a smile when he got it under control.

"That is *not* funny," she said. "I think it's awful."

"But it's so him," Ian said. "I wonder if he burned all my baseball cards and letter jackets, or just gave them away."

"Well, he doesn't deserve you," she said in a pout, taking a sip of her beer.

"So, no talk about me going back to Chico to see him one last time before he dies?" he teased.

She looked startled. "Ian, I never wanted that. I'm pretty sure you wouldn't see anything you didn't see four or five years ago."

"You deny that you wanted me to see him one last time…?"

"Ian, no! No, not that! I wanted *him* to see *you.* I wanted him to know you were all right—that no matter how mean he was, no matter how cruelly he treated you, you were good. Strong and good. Or, more specifically, I wanted you to let him know you were all that. I swear."

"Why?" he asked, completely confused.

She put her hand over his. "Because of the kindness you have in you. He doesn't deserve it, he's done nothing to earn it, he'd never even thank you for it—but he's on the decline and it would be a good thing to do—to let the old guy know that in spite of everything, you're still a good and strong man with a heart and you're not like him. You'll never be like him. That's all. I thought maybe someday down the road you'd think of that anyway, and I just didn't want you to think of it when it was too late." She smiled at him. "Not for him, for you."

"You think you know me that well?"

"I do," she said. "I've been watching you—with the wildlife, with the neighbors, with everything—it's natural to you to do anything that takes heart and generosity. I bet that was the hardest thing for you to give up."

On the morning of Christmas Eve, Ian didn't get up to deliver wood. He could have loaded the truck and made one more sale and delivery before Christmas and get a better-than-usual price. Instead, he made the coffee and served a hot cup to Marcie. "It's morning, sunshine. It's a big day for you."

"You're not selling wood?" she asked sleepily, sitting up.

"Not today. Your coffee's hot at no risk." He grinned at her.

"Hmm," she said, taking the cup. "You make a very adequate Abigail."

"Tell me what I can do to make this easier for you."

She sipped her coffee and thought for a moment. "Two things."

"Name them."

"Take me to town and leave me. Say goodbye to me and just go—don't linger, don't watch me drive away."

He gave a nod. "If that's how you want to do it."

"And can you tell me—do you feel anything for me?"

He put his big hand against her wild curls. "I feel everything for you. But that won't change the facts. We're strangers from two separate worlds that won't easily merge, and I'm still a guy with what you call issues—piles of them. Not really ready to make any rapid-fire changes, though I think I made some small ones in spite of myself. I have a lot less hair, for one thing."

"You've come along nicely." She gave him a little kiss. "I think if I had more time…"

He stilled her chin in his hand, commanding her attention. "Listen. I won't kid you—you changed everything. Come back sometime if you feel like it. But if you don't, I won't hold it against you. Remember what you told me—that after you did this, after you found me and thanked me, asked me some questions and told me the things you had to be sure I knew, you were going to be free to move on. It's okay, Marcie. Even after what passed between us. *Especially* after what passed between us—you can move on if you want to. I expect that."

"And what if what I want is you?" she asked him.

"The only thing in the world that could possibly make me sad is if I couldn't make you happy. That's what scares me the most—that you would want me, and I'd let you down."

"Why do you even think that way?"

"Just a sorry old habit," he said.

"I bet you could break that habit if you'd just let yourself."

He smiled. "That's one of the best things about you—your eternal optimism."

"Oh, Ian, that's not optimism. It's faith. You should give it a try sometime."

Sixteen

At one o'clock Ian drove Marcie into town to where her little green VeeDub was parked. He showed her how to put the chains on her rear tires if she ran into snow. But right now the roads were clear as was the sky, and she was good to go if she left within the next couple of hours. Then he put his arms around her and gave her a long, loving kiss. He didn't even look around to see if they were being watched. And he said, "Thank you, for matching me for stubborn."

"I'm not all together about this," she said. "This is really hard."

"When you get closer to home, you'll start to feel good about being with all of them. They were always there for you," he reminded her.

"Good—"

He put a finger over her lips. "Shhh. Don't say it. Drive carefully."

"If I write to you, will you answer?"

"Absolutely," he promised.

"Well, that's progress," she said weakly. "I… Ah… I left

you something. I slipped it into your clothes trunk when you weren't looking."

"Aw, Marcie—you shouldn't have done that."

"It's not a Christmas gift or anything. Something I meant to give you, but the time was never right. And then I decided you should have it in private. I'll see you again, Ian." She gave him a tremulous smile and a tear ran down her cheek. "Saw and chop carefully," she said. "And take good care of Buck."

"I will," he said, touching her lips once more. "Till later."

"Okay, then. Till later."

She walked up the steps into the bar while he went to his truck. She heard that rough, loud motor as he drove away. She realized he hadn't asked for a phone number where he could reach her if he got crazy and decided to call. She'd leave her number with Preacher, and Ian had her home number in those letters he hadn't read. But she had little confidence that Ian would be hanging around the town after she was gone. In fact, she worried that he would pull deeper into himself.

The bar was quiet at this time of day—only a couple of locals finishing up their lunch. Preacher came out of the back and said, "How's things, Marcie?"

"Fine. Good. I'll be heading back to Chico in a little while. Could I grab a cup of coffee first?"

"You bet. You okay?"

"I guess. I said goodbye to Ian. I hate to leave. Who would've believed I'd find him and get so close to him?"

"But you found him," Preacher said, pouring her coffee. "And I suppose you took care of all your unfinished business."

"Yeah. We talked a lot. It's all good," she said, lifting her eyes bravely.

"That's what I like to hear. He seems like a stand-up guy. He found that boy, you know. Travis Goesel. Saved his life."

Marcie's eyes shot open wide. "Ian did?"

"Yeah. Dug him out of a shelter he'd made to keep himself from freezing, carried him over a mile. The kid's about six feet tall and built solid, heavy. Ian tore off his shirt to warm him.... Really, another hour or so, it would've been just a body. Kid's doing just fine. He'll be opening presents with his family tomorrow morning."

"But he told me— Ian said he'd been found. He wouldn't take credit for anything. Listen, Preacher... Jesus, I don't know how to say this, but could you sometimes try to draw him out a little? Ian? It doesn't have to be anything big—but while I was here, he came off the mountain a little bit and—"

"Sure, kid. We like having him around."

"And I want to leave you my number in Chico, just in case." She pulled a bar napkin toward her and wrote her name and phone number on it. "If you ever need to reach me for any reason, that's my home phone. It's got a machine, you can leave a message." Then she pulled the napkin back and wrote some more. "Cell phone," she said. "I want you to be able to reach me if you— Well, you know."

"Absolutely. Sure." He folded it and put it in his pocket. Then he put the coffeepot at her side. "Listen, with this candlelight thing going on tonight, there could be a crowd, so we're working in the kitchen—I gotta get back to Paige and help out. If you need anything, like a sandwich or anything, just stick your head in the kitchen and holler."

"Go ahead. I'm fine. I'll take off after a cup of coffee, thanks."

So, he found the boy and saved him. And then took all his canned stew to the old man next door. Either Ian had changed dramatically or he'd always been the kind of man who was drawn to helping out when he could. She'd seen a few changes in him, but what she suspected was that this life alone was not really who he was. He hadn't run off so much as he'd been abandoned—by the Corps, his girl, his father, his brothers in arms. So he isolated himself for a while until he could get his bearings, figure out where he was going and how he was going to live. It was possible that the information she brought him about Bobby's last three years and passing helped him find some closure in that. That's what she came to do. If she'd done that, then that was all she could ask.

As for closure for her, the opposite had happened. She loved him. She wasn't sure she could give him up. But for now, she had to return to her roots, her home. She couldn't give up those people either.

The door opened behind her but she never even turned. "You!" she heard. "Young woman!" She turned to see Doc standing there. "Can you drive a Hummer?"

"Of course not," she said. "I own a *Volkswagen.*"

"Then you'll learn. Melinda's gone and I got a head injury I have to get to Valley Hospital. I can't drive and tend that. Come on."

"But I'm leaving…"

"Now!" he snapped, turning to go.

Marcie sat for a second, thinking. The door opened again. "I said *now!*"

"Oh, for God's sake," she muttered, grabbing her purse and following Doc.

* * *

Ian went back to his cabin and fed the stove. He thought about splitting some logs or shoveling or checking on the old guy next door, but instead he sat at his table and did nothing. Nothing, except remember every expression on her face, every sentence she'd uttered. Then he pulled her library book in front of him and reread that romantic passage she loved, the one that got them going. He really couldn't remember loving that sweet in his whole life. Was it just because it had been so long? Or was he right when he considered that, for two people without much practice, they sure learned how to please each other well in a short period of time.

This was good, he told himself, that she had gone. She needed to go home, where she belonged. It wasn't his home anymore and hadn't been since his father put the final nail in the coffin of their relationship. Ian had faced the reality—there was no one there for him anymore. No one.

Except Marcie, the girl who'd made him laugh and love.

But that had been here, where circumstances forced them together. Once things settled back into place, what they had together here wouldn't be the same.

Still, he wondered what it would feel like to see the old man one more time before he was gone, before it was too late. Ian had no illusions; his father wouldn't have become warm and fuzzy. In fact, he'd probably be worse, given age and illness. He was rigid and unforgiving and always had been. It had been impossible to impress him and make him proud back when he was in the Corps, it would be impossible now, after the last four years.

But, maybe facing the old man was the cure to becoming him. Marcie might be right—Ian didn't have to forgive his father so much as forgive himself for hating his father, for letting his father's disapproval and meanness shape him into an angry man. It might be the passage out.

How could a goofy, stubborn little redhead be so incredibly insightful? It just didn't work in his head. It didn't add up.

Ian remembered the *something* she'd left for him, but he didn't want to see what it was; he wasn't sure he was up to it. But then the other part of him thought if he just had something concrete to remember her by, it might bring joy to his days. He went to the trunk and there, right on top, was an envelope. It was addressed to Marcie. On the back of the envelope she had written something.

Darling Ian,
It was my plan to show you this letter. I didn't think I could part with it, but as it turns out I want you to have it. You'll see why. And I meant what I said, Ian. I fell in love with you. Marcie.

He stood by the woodstove and began to read the letter and then had to sit down to finish it. It was a letter to Marcie from Bobby. It was written on that thin military-issue letter paper that you fold into its own envelope—thin, pale blue tissue with the image of an American Eagle on the page. From the date on the postmark, it was very likely Bobby had been sitting right next to him while they both took a couple of minutes to dash off letters to their women in time to make the postal pickup.

Hey, Marcie, baby. I miss you, girl. I think about you every minute of every day and I'm counting the sec-

onds till I feel you up against me again. Thanks, baby, for being so tough through all this shit. I couldn't be with any other kind of woman. Some of these guys—their girls write 'em these terrible letters about how bad life is for them while their guy's away and I couldn't take it if you did that. How'd I know you were the one when we were fourteen? I must be a frickin' genius!

I have to tell you something. I'm not chicken, telling you in a letter instead of when I get home—I just can't wait, that's all. See, I want this forever. You probably think I'm out of my head to say that, now especially. I mean, this place is awful. We haven't had that much trouble, but other squads have been fired on, ambushed, run into suicide bombers, all that crap, and we know it could be us any second.

One of the reasons it hasn't been us yet is Ian. The man's unbelievable. I've never known anyone like him and I've known some real awesome people, especially in the Marines. This is one helluva jarhead, baby. He knows what he's doing. He can lead you into hostile territory and make you think you want to be there. He's the person who keeps everyone from feeling sorry for themselves. I've seen him put himself between a young marine and gunfire. We had an injury on the road—kid stepped in a hole and broke his ankle and Ian carried him all the way to camp, must of been five miles. Wouldn't hand him off or share the load. I offered to take the kid for a mile, but Ian said, Keep your eye on your business, marine, so I don't end up carrying two of you.

We found a couple of armed insurgents on a door-

to-door search and I watched Ian take a guy down bare-handed. An hour later I saw Ian holding a little Iraqi baby and talking to the mother, smiling at her, reassuring her. I don't know how he does that—goes from the strongest, meanest guy here to the sweetest. And then at the end of the day, when everyone's pissed off and dirty and tired, he talks to every man, makes sure they have their head on straight. He doesn't want anyone too shook or scared or lonesome not to keep themselves alive if we have trouble. One of the guys got a Dear John and he was pathetic. Ian could have told him to get a grip and act tough, but instead he kind of talked him through it and when the guy cried, Ian didn't make fun of him or anything. He just kept a hand on the guy's back, solid, and talked to him real soft, told him there weren't a lot of guarantees in life and some things took a while to get past, but if it was any consolation, his brothers wouldn't ever leave him. If the girl couldn't stick, Ian told him, better to find out early. It takes a real special woman to put up with a marine.

He's right about that, baby—and you're it. I don't know if you're up to it, me taking on the Corps for a career, but I hope so. Thing is, if I could be half the leader and friend Ian is, I'd be a frickin' legend. I can't wait till you finally meet him. You're going to admire the guy as much as I do. And then you're probably going to coldcock him for making the Corps look so good to me. Ha ha. He won't be surprised—I told him all about you, that you might be a little bitty thing, but you aren't afraid to stand up and speak up.

I miss you so much, baby. I'll be back before you know it. I love you, Marce.

Ian took a few deep breaths and then read it again. What was this? How could Bobby think that much of him? It was goofy hero worship and Ian didn't feel he deserved that. Ian was just doing the job he was trained to do—it wasn't anything special.

He was sure right about Marcie, though. She was a little pistol. A beautiful little pistol who brought sunlight and laughter with her everywhere she went. One determined little girl. She didn't quit early; she'd have made a good marine. Bobby was lucky he found her in the ninth grade. It wasn't easy to find a woman that strong, that powerful, that sure of herself and what she wanted.

After all she'd been through, after everything they'd shared, what kind of a guy doesn't at least say "I love you, too"?

Doc took Marcie on a wild ride out to a farm in the foothills and snapped at her to help him with the gurney. Then Doc climbed in the back to administer to their patient, a farmer who'd taken a donkey's hoof in the head. His head was split open and he was seeing double, but he was conscious. So while Doc took care of his patient he yelled at Marcie about her driving, which she couldn't understand because she thought she was doing very well considering she wasn't used to a vehicle that size.

When they got to Valley Hospital they had to wait around for X-rays before Doc would leave the farmer. Then Doc made her drive back to Virgin River so she could experience this vehicle without the yelling in the background. By the time they pulled into town, she was a wreck.

"Come on," Doc said. "I'll buy you a drink. You earned one. You did just fine."

"Well you'd never know it from the way you yelled at me," she grumbled.

"Nah, you were half as good as Melinda—which is good. She's had practice. She slings that thing around like it's a skateboard. Come on. It's time for a drink."

"Really, I was going to be out of here five hours ago."

"Well now, don't you feel good that you were able to help? Lend a hand? If you hadn't been sitting right there, I'd have had to take Paige or maybe the patient's wife, who wouldn't have been able to keep her eyes on the road. It was a lucky break for all of us. Have a drink and some dinner. You can drive in the dark, can't you? We'll fill you with food and soak you up in coffee before you go."

"Yeah," she said wearily. "Sure. Why not. I'm already too late for Christmas Eve dinner in Chico."

"There you go. Another break."

"My sister might not see it that way…."

"What would be even better," Doc said, "is if you had two drinks and spent the night in the spare bed at my place. That would be even better."

"No," she said. "Really, I have to go. I can't hang around here. It just makes me sad."

"Whatever you think you have to do," Doc said. "It's an open offer."

The bar was packed with people, gathering for their little program around the tree. There were trays of snacks sitting all around—from hot hors d'oeuvres to Christmas cookies. People whom Marcie had never met introduced themselves, asked her where she was from and if she would stay for the carols. She did accept a brandy from Preacher, then sampled the snacks and finally she migrated to the kitchen and called Erin. "I apologize, but I'm running late…"

"What?" Erin nearly exploded. "What are you thinking? You promised to come home!"

"I'm coming," she said. "Listen, there was an emergency—a guy from town got kicked in the head by his donkey and Doc needed someone to drive to the hospital so he could tend the head and… Well, I got delayed by five hours and I'm sorry. So I'll be catching Santa in the act, but I'll get there."

"It's dark! I don't want to worry about you!"

She took a breath. "I drive in the dark all the time, but go ahead and sit up and worry if you want to. I'm going to have some food and some coffee—then I'll be on my way."

When Marcie migrated back into the bar, she was worn down. She felt as though she had disappointed everyone, not the least of whom herself. She'd grown tired. No doubt it came from the long day, the emotion of leaving Ian, the wild ride with Doc. But most of all she felt the disappointment that the thing she'd started with Ian didn't seem destined to go further.

But then, what could she expect? That they'd laugh together, love together for a week or so and he'd change everything about himself? And for all her big talk—that she'd stay in that cabin forever—she wasn't at all sure that after a year of that she wouldn't be out of her mind. Besides, she had brought him some relief, but she hadn't healed him; he had lots of healing left to do. And he probably knew what he needed—to split and sell his logs, feed the deer, sing in the morning and ease slowly back into the world.

Inside, she began to grieve. She couldn't help that her heart ached. But she reminded herself that what she wanted most was for Ian to see his own way, to find peace and happiness. With or without her. Marcie knew she had her faults, but being selfish was not one of them.

People were starting to move out of the bar and gather round the tree. She followed. On the porch someone said, "Here, Marcie," and handed her a candle. She thought it wouldn't make much difference if she stayed to sing a couple of carols before starting her drive.

The tree was splendid; it sparkled and shone in the clear night. The star beamed a path down the street. There were many more people gathered outside than there had been in the bar. Clearly they'd been arriving for a while. There was a lot of mingling and chatting, laughing and lighting candles. No one seemed to be in charge. Then someone finally said, "Away In The Manger." Slowly, haltingly, singing began—a little clumsy at first. By the time they were halfway through the first verse, and this was only a first-verse kind of crowd, their voices had become stronger. Then someone else shouted, "Silent Night!" and they began again. Next, "We Three Kings!" and then came "Silver Bells," which they stumbled through badly until everyone, including Marcie, was laughing. There were a lot of mumbled suggestions and milling around when a voice, clear and strong and beautiful, came from the back of the crowd. Softly. Slowly. Mellowly.

Oh holy night
The stars are brightly shining
'Tis the night of our dear Savior's birth!

Marcie's heart leaped; her eyes filled with tears as she whirled around, only to find a crowd of people behind her also turning to his voice. She handed off her candle, breathless, blurry-eyed, and pushed her way through the crowd, separating them so she could pass. By the time she got through the people, she saw him there, standing across the street. The light of the star fell on him, and she hardly knew him. He was clean shaven, dressed in his good pants, shirt and denim jacket. And beside him on the ground was a duffel. Packed.

Her hand rose shakily to her throat, which was constricted and tight. Tears ran down her cheeks. He smiled at her only briefly, then his eyes rose to the star as he sang.

Fall on your knees
Oh, hear the angel voices
Oh, night divine
Oh, night when Christ was born
Oh, night divine
Oh night, oh night divine

His was the angel's voice.

Fall on your knees, indeed. It was all Marcie could do to stay upright. But Ian didn't stop singing; he gave the hymn everything he had, then another chorus, loud and moving. There was not so much as a murmur within the crowd and no one joined in, so stunning was the voice, the passion. And when he finally came to the end of the hymn, he just let his chin drop in reverence, looking down.

First there were gasps of delight, then applause began, but Marcie just walked toward him, her eyes shining, her legs weak. When she reached him, she put a hand against the cheek that bore the long, thin scar. And his hand was against her soft, red curls.

"What are you doing here?" she asked softly.

"Practicing that singing for people instead of wildlife," he said. "You're the one who shouldn't still be here. I thought I'd stop by for a carol or two, then head out."

"Long story. But where are you going?"

"Chico." He smiled at her. "There's a girl there I have business with."

"You'll stay with me?"

"Maybe one night, since it's getting so late. Then I'll check with the old man's paperboy and see if I can get a let on a room."

"Oh, Ian…" She threw her arms around him and he held her off the ground. He kissed her soundly, to the cheers of their audience.

But then he put her on her feet and held her upper arms. "Listen, Abigail—there are some things you have to know. I have fourteen hundred and eleven dollars to my name and I need gas. No savings. I haven't filed a tax return in four years. If I can't pay the taxes on that mountain in the spring, it'll just go away, and I can't pay the taxes if I don't find a job. I haven't had a real job in a long time. And my father—I don't have any illusions about it being a tearful reunion. He'll probably just kick me to the curb. So go into this knowing it's still a mess. Just because I sang out loud doesn't mean—"

"You think I'm a wimp?" she asked, incredulous. "You think after everything I'm *weak?* Then why are you coming? I know how you hate weakness!"

"To see if there's anything to us. Marcie, I wouldn't hurt you for the world, so tell me you're up to this if it all falls apart. Because going in, there's a lot on the minus side, starting with me. I could be a huge disappointment to you in the end."

"Did you return my library books?" she asked.

"I didn't," he said, shaking his head. "There were only so many things I could do if I was going to get to you before Christmas."

She smiled up at him. "Well, I never did know quite where I was going. But there was this light... And I followed... I told you, I love you. Ian, I love you so much. I'll start there and take everything else as it comes."

"And I didn't tell you," Ian said. "I didn't want to mess you up, let you down. But I can't remember ever feeling this way before. I love you, Marcie. I'll try anything."

"Okay, then. Why don't we just start with faith and we'll go from there?"

He grinned at her. "Erin Elizabeth is going to be a little disgruntled when she sees me."

She patted his cheek. "She won't even recognize you for a couple of days, at least. You look so magnificent. Who's going to feed Buck?"

"Buck's on his own for now. We'll catch up with him when the snow melts. Does that work for you?"

"Perfect," she said. And she thought, if these mountains are beautiful in winter, they must be heart-stopping in spring with the promise of new life. Like hers.

Like his...

Like theirs...

* * * * *

Please turn the page for a sneak preview of SECOND CHANCE PASS, the next book in Robyn Carr's widely acclaimed VIRGIN RIVER SERIES.

Not only will you meet some old friends in this wonderful new book, you'll make the acquaintance of several newcomers as well.

SECOND CHANCE PASS will be available in bookstores everywhere on February 1, 2009.

Enjoy!

SECOND CHANCE PASS available February, 2009
TEMPTATION RIDGE available March, 2009
PARADISE VALLEY available April, 2009

One

Vanessa Rutledge stood in front of her husband's grave, her coat pulled tightly around her against the crisp March breeze, red hair billowing in the wind, and said, "I know this is going to seem a very strange request—but I just don't know who else to ask. Matt, you know I love you, that I'll always love you, that I'll see you in your son's eyes every day. But darling, I'm going to love again, and I need your blessing before I can move on. If I have that, I'd like you to give the man who is to be my future a little nudge. Let him know it's all right. Please? Let him know he's not just—"

"Va*ness*a!"

She turned to see her father standing out on the deck behind the house, holding the baby. It was time to go—she had an appointment with the nurse-midwife. Little Matt had been born six weeks ago and this morning they were both seeing Mel Sheridan for their first checkups since his birth. Her father, retired general Walt Booth, was driving them into town so that he could watch the baby while Vanessa had her exam.

"Coming, Dad!" she called. She looked back at the grave. "We'll talk more about this later," she told the headstone. She blew a kiss in that direction and hurried down the little hill, past the stable and up to the house.

The last place Vanessa had ever expected to find herself was in a little town of six hundred. When her father chose this property a couple of years before his retirement from the U.S. army, she'd thought of it as an ideal getaway spot—somewhere she and Matt might escape to for a week of riding, fishing, shooting skeet. Then her world changed abruptly when Matt, a marine, got orders for Iraq. She must have gotten pregnant days before his departure. And a couple of months before the baby was born, he was killed in Baghdad. She'd been alone a long time now, and even with her dad and brother's support, sometimes she was so lonely.

There was a time, years before Matt, that Vanni had envisioned herself as a high-powered news anchor; her degree was in communications. On a whim, she'd decided to spend a year or two as a flight attendant before pursuing that career, but had ended up loving the work, the travel, the people. She'd still been working for the airline when Matt left, but a combination of loneliness and advancing pregnancy had sent her packing to Virgin River. Even then, she had thought it temporary—she'd have the baby, wait for her husband's return from war and move on to his next assignment with him.

She didn't cry so much anymore, though she missed him—missed the laughter, the long late-night talks. Missed having someone hold her, whisper to her.

Walt had the diaper bag slung over his shoulder already and was headed for the car. "Vanessa, it bothers me that you spend so much time talking to that grave. We should've put him somewhere else. Out of sight."

"Oh dear," she said, lifting a curious eyebrow, the corner of her mouth twitching. "Matt hasn't been complaining that I'm bothering him, has he?"

"Not funny," he said.

"You worry too much," she told her dad, taking the baby from him to put him in the car seat. "I'm not brooding." She fastened the baby in. "There are some things no one but Matt should hear. And gee, he's so handy…"

"Vanessa! For God's sake!" He took a breath. "You need girlfriends."

She laughed at him. "I have plenty of girlfriends." Close girlfriends from flying days, and even though they didn't live nearby, they were great about visiting and staying in touch, giving her every opportunity to talk about Matt, about grief, then about the baby and recovery. "You'll be happy to know Nikki's coming up for the weekend," she said. "A girlfriend."

Walt hefted himself into the driver's seat. "We've been seeing a lot of Nikki lately. Either she can't stay away from the new baby or things aren't going so well with her and that…that…"

Walt couldn't finish and Vanessa laughed at him. "She can't stay away from the baby and no, things aren't going so well with Craig. I smell a split coming," Vanessa said.

"I never liked him," Walt said with a grunt.

"I know. He's been real unlikable lately," Vanni said. Her best friend, stuck in a relationship that was going nowhere, wanting a partner and family, and yet almost as alone as Vanni.

Vanni had other friends besides fellow flight attendants. She'd begun to grow close to some of the women in town—her midwife, Mel; Paige, who worked alongside her husband in the only bar and grill in town; Brie, Mel's sister-in-law. Still, there were some things only Matt would understand.

When you lived in a place like Virgin River where the doctor's office made appointments only on Wednesdays, it was a pretty good bet there wouldn't be any waiting around. Sure enough, Mel was standing in the reception area right inside the door waiting for them to arrive. Her face lit up in delight as they walked in and she immediately reached for the baby. "Ohhhh, come he-e-e-r-re," she sang. "Let me look at you!" She lifted him as if weighing him. Then she cuddled him close. "He's looking good, Vanni. Getting nice and fat on the breast." She looked at Walt. "How's Grandpa doing?"

"Grandpa could use more sleep," he grumbled.

Vanessa just laughed. "There's no reason in the world he has to get up. He certainly can't help me nurse the baby."

"I wake up, that's all. And if I'm up and Vanni's up, I might as well see if she needs anything."

Mel smiled at him. "That's a good grandpa," she said. "He'll be sleeping through the night before you know it."

"When did David sleep through the night?" Vanni asked of Mel's one-year-old.

"The first time or the last time?" Mel asked. "You might not want to ask that—we have sleeping issues at our house. And now Jack lets him in the bed with us. Take my advice, don't start that!"

Vanessa peered at Mel's growing tummy. David had just turned a year and their second baby was due in May. "I hope you have a really big bed," she said.

"There will be plenty of room when I kick Jack out of it. Come on—let's look at Mattie first and take care of his shots." Mel carried the baby back to the exam room with Vanessa following behind.

Mel had delivered little Matt right in Vanessa's bedroom, and their bond had grown deep and strong. It didn't take long to determine the baby was at a good weight, in excellent health, and Mel gave him his shots. "I'll take him out to Walt while you get into a gown, how's that?"

"Thanks," Vanni said.

A few minutes later Mel was back. "Your dad took the baby over to Jack's for a cup of coffee. And some male bonding, I suppose."

Vanni had taken her place on the exam table. Mel checked her heart and blood pressure and got her in the position for a pelvic. "Everything looks great. You had a wonderful delivery, Vanni—you're in excellent shape. And boy, did you lose weight quickly. Isn't that breast-feeding a miracle?"

"I'm not back in my old jeans yet."

"I bet you're close. Go ahead, sit up," Mel said, offering a hand. "Anything we should talk about?"

"Lots of things. Can I ask you something personal?"

"You can always ask," Mel said while writing in the chart.

"I know that before you married Jack, you were widowed…."

Mel stopped writing. She closed the chart and looked at Vanni with a sympathetic smile. "I've been expecting this conversation," she said.

"How long was it?" Vanni asked, and Mel knew exactly what she was referring to.

"I met Jack nine months after my husband's death. I married him six months later. And if you confer with the town historian and gossips, you'll learn that I was at least three months pregnant at the time. Closer to four."

"We have a town historian?"

"About six hundred of them," Mel said with a laugh. "If you have anything you'd like to keep secret, you should consider getting out of here fast."

"Matt's only been dead a few months, but he's been gone almost a year.... It's been a really long time since—"

Mel touched Vanni's knee. "There's no rule of thumb on this, Vanessa. Everything I read says that when people enter new relationships relatively soon after losing a spouse, it indicates they had happiness in their marriage. Being married was a good experience for them." She shrugged and smiled.

"I didn't even know for sure I was pregnant when Matt left for Iraq last May. We buried him six months later. I'm not thinking about another marriage, of course," Vanni said. "But I am thinking about— Well, what I'm thinking is that I don't want to be alone forever."

"Of course you shouldn't be alone forever. You have a lot of life to live."

"It's not as if there are any prospects in Virgin River..."

Mel laughed softly, brightly; her eyes twinkled. "Yeah. That's what I thought."

Vanni smiled. "Should I be thinking about birth control?"

"We can talk about that. You wouldn't want to be as unprepared as your midwife. Especially with having a baby to take care of. Believe me." She took a breath and ran a hand over her big belly. "I wouldn't *let* myself think ahead! I remember when my sister said, 'I know widows who have remarried, and are happy.' I almost took her head off. I was appalled. I wasn't at all hopeful life could go on."

"It sure went on for you," Vanni said.

"Boy howdy. I came here absolutely determined to live

out my days lonely and miserable, but that damn Jack—he ambushed me. I think I fell in love with him the minute I met him, but I fought it. As though I might somehow be unfaithful to my husband's memory by moving on, which was absurd. I had the kind of husband who would have wanted me to have love in my life, and I bet you did, too."

"You don't send a man off to war without talking a few things through—my parents taught me that. One of the first ways Tom and I figured out the general was headed for a possible deployment—the paperwork came out. Wills, trusts, et cetera. Not just in case something happened to him, but what if he was away in some jungle or desert war zone and something happened to Mom?" She smiled a bit wistfully. "Matt didn't dwell on the worst-case scenario. It was quick and to the point. He said I wasn't the type to wallow and he'd be disappointed in me if I did. He had a few requests—where to be buried, what to do with his favorite personal items, if we had children and something happened to him, to make sure his parents got regular visits. And—if a good man showed his face, I was not to hesitate." She took a breath. "My requests of him were almost identical." She straightened. "If I'm lucky enough to run into another man half as wonderful as Matt, I should be ready."

"Absolutely. It's not at all impossible, even in little old Virgin River. Let's get you something reliable while you're considering all this. You want a pill you can take while breast-feeding? Can I hook you up with a diaphragm or IUD? Have you given the options any thought?"

Vanni smiled gratefully. Of course she'd thought about it. "Yes. IUD, please."

"Let's go over the models," Mel said. Then she smiled. "By the way, you're all cleared for intercourse. Should you find…"

Vanni laughed. "Thanks," she said.

"You have good judgment. Make sure there's a condom involved. We don't want the transmission of any—"

"I have good judgment," Vanni repeated. "And extremely good taste."

There *was* a man on Vanessa's mind, precisely the reason she found herself imploring Matt's grave for help, blessings. Was it too soon? Should she feel guilty? She was afraid to allow herself to think about him too much. Matt's best friend; her best friend. Paul.

He had happened to be in Virgin River helping to build Mel and Jack's house when the news came that Matt was dead. He stayed on, supporting and comforting her, spending Christmas away from his parents, brothers and their families. They spent a lot of time talking about Matt, crying about Matt, lost in hours of sentimental remembering. Without Paul's strength she'd never have gotten through the worst of it. As the weeks passed, the miserable sobbing gave way to just missing him. While she had been tremendously fond of Paul since the day she met him, they grew so close after Matt's death, their relationship intensified. At least in her mind.

She asked him to be with her, standing in for Matt, when the baby came. He had to be coerced, but in the end he was as present, as involved as any husband could be.

Their relationship went back much further than that, of course. It wasn't as though they became friends because of Matt's death. In fact, that night long ago when she met Matt, it was Paul across the room who first caught her eye. He was so tall, his legs so long and hands so big, it was hard for him not to stand out in a crowd. There was that sandy, willful hair that had to be kept short because it would defy any kind of styling. Not that Paul was the kind of man to fuss with hair; it was obvious even from a distance that he stuck to basics. It was his masculinity she noticed; he looked like a lumberjack who'd cleaned up to go into town. He had an engaging smile; one tooth in front was just a little crooked and he had a dimple on the left cheek. Heavy brown brows, deep chocolate eyes—details she got a bit later, of course. She hadn't even noticed Matt....

But it was Matt who put the rush on her, swept her off her feet, made her laugh, made her *blush.* While Paul hung back, shy and silent, Matt charmed her to her very bones. And shortly after the charm, he made her desire him madly, love him deeply. He was hardly a consolation prize—he was one of the best men in the world. And a devoted husband, so in love with her.

Vanni hadn't pined for Paul for ten minutes—she had been so happy with Matt. Paul was their best man; Matt had asked Paul to be sure Vanni was all right if anything went wrong in Iraq.

She loved Paul before Matt's death, grew to love him more deeply afterward. It was like the natural order of things that Paul should step in now. But there was no indication from him that he felt anything more than a special friendship. She had no doubt he loved her, loved little Matt, but it didn't appear to be the kind of love that could warm her on cold nights.

She'd talked to him a few times since the baby's birth, since he'd returned to Oregon; polite and entertaining conversations about the baby, the town and his friends here, about her dad and brother, even sometimes about Matt. But he never betrayed any longing. Not a whiff of desire came through those phone lines.

She felt like a fool even wanting him. But there was no denying it—she missed him so much. And not the way a young widow misses having a man in her life. The way a woman longs for a man who stirs her, moves her.

When Mel walked Vanni out to the front of the clinic, Vanni spied her younger brother's girlfriend waiting there. "Brenda!" Vanni said, going to her, giving her a hug. "I guess if there are only appointments on Wednesdays, there's a good chance you'll run into all your friends here," she said with a laugh.

"I guess." Brenda shrugged, blushing a little.

"I have to rescue my dad. He's got the baby at Jack's. I'll see you later. Probably tonight at dinner."

"Sure," Brenda said. "Later."

Vanni blew out the door and Brenda sank into her chair. The waiting room was small and she was the only patient. It had been the old house's front room and was decorated exactly so. Heavy cream-colored velvet draperies covered the front windows. They were pulled back with sashes and always remained open. An ancient sofa and settee, upholstered in burgundy velvet, were flanked by two wing-back chairs with curved wooden legs. The fabric on the chairs was yellow brocade that had long ago lost its lustre. A few Gisele chairs with cane seats were spotted around the room which, itself, was rarely full. There was only Mel and Doc Mullins to see patients, so unless someone wandered in, the appointments were spaced comfortably apart.

Brenda had an elbow on her knee and her forehead rested in her hand. "Whew," she said weakly. "Of course I'd have to run into Vanessa. Crap."

Mel grabbed Brenda's chart. She just chuckled and went

to her, pulling her to her feet. "Don't worry about that. Come on, let's check you out."

"But it's Tommy's sister! What if she asks me why I was here?"

"Brenda, Brenda, that's not going to be a problem." Mel pulled her along to the exam room. While Brenda stood by the door, Mel stripped off the exam-table disposable paper and refreshed it. Then she handed Brenda a gown. Mel flipped open the chart and said, "So—you're here about concern over heavy periods."

"Yeah, but…"

"I know," Mel said. "Except they're fine."

"Fine," Brenda said shyly. "I need birth control pills…."

She looked down and Mel just lifted her chin with one finger.

"Sure. I know," Mel said. "But if Vanessa ever asks you why you were here, you just say you were concerned about your periods and I checked you, told you everything was just fine. How's that?"

"Really?"

"I don't talk about patients' business," Mel said. "Put on the gown. We'll have a checkup. We'll talk about why you're really here. And, Brenda—everything is going to be fine."

"My mom doesn't know I'm doing this," she said. "She thinks it's my periods."

"Okay," Mel said, and she was thinking that Sue Carpenter was pretty sharp. Chances were good she knew exactly what was going on. After all, Tommy and Brenda had been steadies since the start of school and there was no question they were really serious. "I'll be back in five," she said, leaving the room.

Few seventeen-year-old girls felt comfortable discussing birth control with even the closest of mothers. When

Mel returned and Brenda was gowned and ready, she said, "I'll need to update your Pap, and if you don't mind, I'd like to do a check on you for STDs to be sure there's nothing we should treat. Should we talk about emergency birth control?"

"Huh?"

"Have you recently had unprotected intercourse?"

"No," she said. "Thing is, Tommy won't come near me without my own birth control, even though he has...you know..."

"Condoms," Mel supplied.

"Yeah. He says that's not good enough."

"Well, God bless him," Mel said. This darling girl, a gifted student who would very likely get lots of offers for full-ride scholarships, had been the victim of a sexual assault less than a year ago, before Vanessa and Tom had moved here. She'd gone to a beer party in the woods with a bunch of teenagers, intending to have one sneaky beer, and three months later discovered she was pregnant, without having the first idea how that could have happened. If that wasn't bad enough, Brenda had had a raging case of chlamydia, which may have contributed to a spontaneous abortion, miscarriage—something Mel wanted to be sure was completely and successfully treated.

Mel performed her examination, did some tests, wrote a prescription and said, "I want to commend you for taking care of your health, Brenda. I know it can be scary to ask for this kind of help when you're young. But you're wise to take precautions."

"What if my mom asks you about this?"

"She probably won't, but if she does, I'll tell her that you're doing just fine."

"You think that'll do it?"

"Oh, honey, I've gotten very, very good at not telling things. Ask Jack," she added with a laugh. "You can start taking these right now, but they won't be effective for two weeks. Try to remember to take them at the same time every day—like right before bed or as soon as you get up in the morning. That will increase the reliability."

"He's going away, you know," Brenda said a little emotionally. "Right after graduation he goes into basic, then West Point."

Mel put a hand against the girl's soft, pretty hair. "First of all, you wouldn't want any other kind of boyfriend—he's an overachiever and will be a huge success. Cream of the crop. Second, just because you have pills doesn't mean you have to do anything that you're not ready for. With me?"

She nodded.

"He'll be back for leave and vacations. There will be lots of letters between you—wonderful letters."

She nodded again, but said, "E-mails."

"Just as good. These pills are for your health and safety, Brenda. You don't have to send him off with something to remember. Don't be pressured."

"Oh, I'm not. I understand what you're saying," she said softly. "Tom would never pressure me. Besides, I love him."

Mel smiled. "How nice for you. He's a very special young man. And you, my dear, are a very special young woman. You're completely in charge of your body—always remember that."

Nikki Jorgensen pulled up in front of the Booth ranch and gave the horn a toot before getting out. When she let herself into the house, Vanni was sitting on the floor beside the baby. Little Matt was lying on a small baby quilt with toys he was entirely too young to enjoy spread around him.

"Hurry up," Vanni said. "He's *smiling!*"

Nikki threw her purse on a chair and knelt on the floor opposite Vanni. They were so unalike—Vanni being a statuesque redhead and Nikki small and dark, her black hair falling down her back almost to her waist in a straight, silky sheath. They spent a few minutes making stupid faces at the baby until Vanni finally said, "I can't wait to tell Paul he's smiling for real."

And that alone plunged them into silence. "Have you heard from Paul?" Nikki finally asked in a gentle voice.

Vanni shook her head, looking away. "Well, I call him at least every week. But he's only called here a couple of times."

"Oh, Vanni," Nikki said, sympathetic.

"Never mind. I'm just being stupid. He's probably so relieved he doesn't have any obligation here anymore…."

"I'm sure that's not it," Nikki said, giving Vanni's soft red mane a stroke.

"I should probably be embarrassed by my feelings for him."

"Now, why would you say that?" Nikki asked.

"Matt hasn't been gone that long."

"Almost a year, dead several months, and who is more likely for you to be attracted to than someone who misses him as much as you do? Who loves little Matt as much as Matt would himself? Besides, it's not as though you just met him—he's been around since the day you met Matt! You know him better than anyone. You certainly don't have to wonder what kind of man he is."

"I'm just afraid…. I guess I worry that everyone will think it's too soon for me to have those kind of feelings."

Nikki laughed. "Vanni, you're a kick. I'm just so relieved you *have* feelings. You're a little young to give up, don't you think?"

Vanni gave her a thankful smile. "So. How are things with you and Craig?"

Nikki's smile vanished. "The same. Not good. I gave him an ultimatum. Commitment or quits. He just keeps saying he needs time. How much time? It's been five years. He knows I want a family, and my clock isn't standing still."

Vanni shook her head. "He'll never give you up."

Nikki lifted a thin, dark brow. "Oh yeah? You a betting woman?"

"Nikki, do you mean it? Really?"

Nikki touched the baby's foot. "I'm not going through life without at least a shot at this," she said. "I'm a selfish woman. I want it all."

Paul had been back in Grants Pass almost six weeks, since right after the birth of Vanni's baby. He had gone to Virgin River in the fall to finish Jack's house, and because of Matt's death, stayed on until February. All that time he concentrated so hard on holding it together for Vanni, he was jammed up inside. When he got back to Oregon, a little out of his head, he let off some steam. Not anything particularly wild—just a few nights out with some of the boys, his brothers and some construction crew. And he took out this woman he'd been with a couple of times before. The usual for them—a casual thing. Terri. He'd been very, very needy. She was funny, cute, young. Eager. Sexual. Safe.

Or so he thought.

She came to him at work and asked him if he could sneak away for a conversation. He folded his long legs up into her little Toyota in front of his office, and through some tears she explained that she was pregnant and hadn't been with anyone but him. He thought he was going to die on the spot.

"Pregnant?" he repeated. "Pregnant?"

"Yeah," she said. "It happened that night after you got back to town. You remember. God, I hope you remember, Paul. Because I sure do."

"How in the world did that happen? You said you were on the pill. I wore a condom."

"I don't know," she said, sniffing. "It's probably my fault. I'm sorry."

"Your fault?" he asked. "How?"

"I haven't had a boyfriend in so long, I got a little sloppy with the pills, missing them sometimes. Your call—it came as a surprise. I hadn't heard from you in such a long time and I just couldn't pass up seeing you. But you had the condom and I was sure we'd be okay.... I don't know what went wrong. It must have been me missing pills, you having a faulty condom. I can't think of any other explanation...."

"Aw, man," he said. He took a breath. "Okay," he said, getting a grip on panic. "Okay, tell me what you need," he said, taking her hand and holding it in both of his.

"Any possibility marriage might come to mind?"

He didn't even have to think about it. "Terri, we can't get married—we're barely consenting adults. This relationship we have isn't much of a relationship."

"That's a little beside the point right now," she said.

"We don't know each other. Not really."

"We know each other well enough that I'm pregnant."

"I take this to mean you've decided you want to have the baby?"

"I'm almost thirty," she said, bristling. "I'm not getting rid of it."

"Okay, okay, good," Paul said, relieved in spite of common sense telling him this could be wiped away; it could disappear. He did *not* want to be in this position, but inexplicably, he didn't want this baby erased. "I can help financially. I can do my best to support you emotionally. But, Terri, anything more than that would be a mistake for both of us."

"Why?" she asked, tears springing to her eyes.

He put an arm around her and held her against his shoulder as much as he could, given the console that separated them in the front seat. "Lots of reasons, starting with before anything happened between us, we had a conversation about us—neither of us was looking for anything serious. We've been together—what? Three times in a year? Four? God, I'm sorry, Terri, but there's not that much to us. We're just not in love."

"How do you know I'm not?" she asked.

"We've spoken once in the last six months. If you had those kind of feelings, I never suspected."

"What if you'd known I felt like that?" she asked him.

"Terri, Terri. It would've changed everything," he admitted. "I wouldn't have wanted to mislead you about how I felt. Far as I knew, we were on the same page. Marrying you now would only get in the way of you finding what you really need. And believe me, you don't need me."

"What am I going to do?"

Selfishly he thought, what am I going to do? "Whatever you want to do, I'll help in every way I can. I'm sorry, honey, but you deserve a husband who loves you as much as you love him."

"But I'm having your baby!" she said desperately.

"Whatever I can do, Terri, except marriage. It wouldn't last. It could make us enemies and we have to do better than that. At least it's early and there's plenty of time to look at all the options."

"Options," she sniffed. "Sounds like you'd prefer I have an abortion—"

"Absolutely not," he said. "If you're carrying my child, I'd be very grateful to you if you'd see it through, have the baby. I mean that. In fact, if you're not up to raising a child, I'll take over. But I see this as a woman's choice first. You're in the driver's seat. You have to want to."

"Would I be such a terrible choice for a wife?" she asked pitifully.

He had a clear memory that started the night he met her a year ago, in a bar, when she was out with a bunch of young women, all in their late twenties. She'd had way too much to drink and was flirting like a wild woman. She was cute, hysterically funny, she made him laugh. He took her home because she was in no shape to drive, but didn't touch her. She shouldn't have gotten in a car with him, inebriated, he a stranger, but she never hesitated—she was a party girl, and she took chances. She was physically appealing and had a great sense of humor, however, so he called her. Truthfully, he called her because she didn't seem the kind of girl to be looking for a relationship—she was all about fun. He took her out to dinner and, sober, she let him know she wanted sex. Right away. He let her know he was more than willing to oblige. They had the talk—he claimed a recent relationship that had gone badly, which wasn't a total lie. He'd been carrying a torch for Vanessa for years and wasn't nearly over it. Terri was recently divorced and, likewise, didn't want to get into a rebound situation. So they made love and it was good. They'd had a repeat performance of that event a couple of times.

Where he'd really screwed up was coming home from Virgin River and calling her. Being with her while Vanni was married and his best friend very much alive—that was one thing. He was just a man; sometimes it was nice to have a woman in his life. Calling Terri after Matt's death when the only woman in the world he wanted to be with was Vanni—that was a critical mistake. It was his body calling her body, and for that he was going to pay, and pay dearly.

That was about six weeks ago. He told her when he called her that he was in rough shape, needed someone to talk to. He explained about Matt, about Matt's wife and the baby. He felt as if his heart had been ripped out and handed to him. He asked if he could take her out to dinner, somewhere quiet, have a drink and something to eat, just talk. It had been months since he had spoken to her, and he was prepared for her to say she had moved on, was with someone now. He was just looking for a little companionship; he didn't want to complicate her life.

But she had been happy to hear from him. She had a little more than talk in mind. No question, it had soothed him quite a lot. Having something, someone soft to fall into certainly relieved some tension. He hadn't thought about her since, and he assumed she hadn't thought about him. The relationship was beyond casual.

"I think you'll make someone a wonderful wife, when you find the right man," he said. "I'm not the guy, but I'll do whatever I have to do, Terri. I won't run, I won't hide. And God, Terri, I'm sorry. I sure didn't mean for this to happen."

* * *

Joe Benson had been a little worried about his friend Paul. He'd been back in Grants Pass a while now, but they hadn't connected. They'd seen each other on a couple of job sites in the past few weeks and talked about getting together for a beer, but Paul had been evasive, distracted, morose and probably depressed. Small wonder—his best friend from childhood had been killed several months ago and he'd stayed on with the family. Joe suspected a pressure cooker. So he did what a good friend does—he pushed. It was time for Paul to let it out, so he could move on.

He went to a small, dark, quiet bar and waited for Paul to meet him. Joe had picked the place—somewhere a man could talk about the stuff that was eating his gut. He looked at his watch several times, wondering if Paul was going to be a no-show. Joe had a beer and was thinking about either trying the cell phone or just leaving when Paul finally lumbered in, head down, looking the way he'd looked for too long now. The man was hurting all over.

"Beer," he said to the bartender before he even said hello. "Heineken."

"So," Joe said, picking up his almost empty beer, "you're in lousy shape."

Paul was quiet for a moment, waiting for his beer. When it came he took a long drink before he said, "Lousy."

"Listen, I thought maybe if we had a beer together, talked about it…"

"Believe me, you don't want to talk about this, Joe. Sticky. Messy."

"Business okay?" Joe asked, nibbling around the edges of this situation. Joe had been designing houses for Haggerty Construction for a long time now—Paul, his brothers and father. It was a good little company that did quality construction. While Matt might've been Paul's best friend since they were kids, Joe had been closest to him since Desert Storm when they joined the same marine reserve unit. They'd worked together for at least ten years and had gone back to Iraq together.

"Business is fine," Paul said. "Probably better than ever. That's not the problem."

Joe clamped a strong hand on Paul's shoulder. "You're not yourself lately, bud. You're having trouble moving on after Matt…. He wouldn't want this, you know."

"I know…"

"Maybe it's more than Matt," Joe said. "I get the feeling something's really eating you."

"Yeah?" he asked with a somber laugh. "Jesus, you're psychic." He took another long drink of his beer.

"Any chance you could just go ahead and get it out where we can look at it? Because if you're gonna drink that fast, you'll leave me in your dust pretty quick."

Paul shook his head. "I fucked things up pretty bad, Joe. I got myself in a mess I'm not gonna get out of." Then he laughed and said, "I couldn't have screwed things up any worse if I'd planned it."

Joe stared at him a long moment. Then he banged his glass on the bar and when the bartender came over he said, "Gimme another one of these, huh?" While he was waiting for a new brew, he turned to Paul and asked, "You have any idea how confusing you are right now?"

"Yeah. You should find more stable people to drink with."

"Well, until I do…"

It was a moment before Paul said, "I got someone pregnant."

"No," Joe said, stunned. "No, you're too smart for that."

Paul laughed. "I guess I'm not. Maybe I should sue Trojan, huh?"

"Oh, Jesus," Joe said. "Oh, God. Someone special? I hope?"

"Nice girl," he said with a shrug. "But it wasn't… Aw, man. It was… We aren't… Shit. It was just one of those things. You know? I've known her about a year, but I've only been out with her a few times. We really didn't have anything going on except…"

"Oh, Jesus," Joe said again.

Paul turned toward Joe. "I was in Virgin River since last fall. I didn't talk to her once during that time—that's how casual. Nothing. I came back here all the time to check on the company, my dad and brothers, but I never even called her. She didn't call me. But…"

"But…?"

"But I came home with my gut in a knot after Matt and I called her. On instinct, probably. And guess what happened?"

"Oh, damn," Joe said. "What are you gonna do?"

"What are my choices?" Paul asked, hanging his head. "I'll take care of her, of my kid. What else do you do?" He shook his head sadly. "I want it," he said. "I know—it's stupid. I should probably try something, like buying her off or something. Get her to make it go away—but if I have a kid coming, I want a part of that. I'm nuts, right?"

Joe smiled patiently. "I don't know. Maybe you're not nuts about that—but what about the mother? Is she someone you're going to be able to work with on that?"

"No telling," he said. "She said she wants to get married. I can't do that. That would really fuck her up, worse than she already is. I can't fake that—not something like that. I'd be the worst husband. You don't marry someone that fast."

Joe laughed. "Some of our boys have," he said.

"I don't love her," Paul said with conviction.

"Okay. Different circumstances. Our boys who married fast—they were hell-bent. You are not, which says you don't think it's the right thing to do."

"It's just that I slept with her when I loved someone else. Why the hell did I do that? What kind of sorry bastard does that? What was I thinking?"

Okay, here was where Joe was completely lost. Paul loved someone? It wasn't as though men got together and talked about women they had crushes on—they just didn't. They rarely said how they felt, period. But he'd known Paul a long time and there'd been very few women. He was the quiet one; he kept back. Even when they were in country together, at war, with a lot of tension to unload, Paul never hustled the women.

The bartender delivered Paul another beer, and he took a deep drink.

"The woman you love..." Joe repeated.

"I'm such a screwup...."

"The woman you love?"

"It's wrong, that's all. I had no business..."

"Paul. The woman you *love?*"

"Yeah. I've been a really horseshit best friend for years. Vanni. I just couldn't help it. I didn't want it to be that way, but—"

Joe drank a big gulp. He was prepared to help Paul through just about anything, but he hadn't seen this coming. And why hadn't he? Probably because he'd have done for Paul what Paul did for Matt—stay with the widow through everything. "Whoa," he finally said. "Ho shit."

"Ho shit," Paul echoed.

"Vanni?"

Paul nodded grimly. "You wanna try to imagine how guilty I feel about that? I tried like hell to talk myself out of it. Sometimes I got damn close. I stayed away, you know? Because I could talk to Matt just fine, but if I saw her… Aw, God." He put his head in his hand. "Think I could've messed things up any worse?"

Joe shook his head, but he was thinking—yeah. You could've been the dead guy. "You sure this baby is yours?" Joe asked. "Maybe it's not yours."

"I thought about that," he said. "Then I decided that was probably wishful thinking on my part. Wouldn't she have gone to the other guy with the news if it was someone else's? I even thought—maybe she had even less of a relationship with the other guy, but that seems impossible. And what she said was, there hadn't been a guy in a long time, which is why she got lazy on the pills. And what did I have? Some poor old condom in the wallet that thought it was never gonna get out of that package. I probably wore a damn hole it in just getting in and out of the truck. Nah, it's mine."

"But you're gonna find out for sure before you set up the college fund, right?"

"Yeah. Sure. Right now, though, I don't want to push on her too hard. She's a wreck, a crying, miserable wreck. If she gets the idea I'm not going to step up—who knows what she might do. I'm just going with the assumption it's mine, since it most likely is. We'll sort out the details later. At least a little later."

"What are you gonna do about Vanni?"

"Hell, what can I do? She's in a lot of pain right now. You think I could help that pain go away by telling her I've wanted her since the first second I saw her, but I went ahead and got some other woman I barely know knocked up?"

Joe smiled in spite of himself. "We might have to work on your delivery a little bit there, bud. Paul, keep your head here—it's not like you cheated on Vanni. Huh?"

"Why do I feel like I did?"

"You got your feelings all mixed up in guilt and regret, that's all. You have to think of all the possibilities, man. You might bare your soul to Vanni and she might just say, polite as she can, nice try, buster. Have you thought of that?"

He slowly turned his eyes toward Joe. "Oh, yeah," he said. "I'm pretty sure that's what'll happen. I still have to do it, though. I have to come clean, but… I thought it was too soon after Matt. You gotta believe me, I never wanted anything bad to happen to Matt."

Joe gripped Paul's biceps. "Of course you didn't. Still—this could all be behind you pretty quick. It wouldn't make the other situation much easier, really. You still got a woman you hardly know having a baby. That's gonna be complicated. But this business with Vanni? Who knows, Paul? Maybe she loves you like a brother, huh? You owe it to yourself to know where you stand before you borrow all this trouble."

"Yeah," he said, hanging his head. "She'll try to let me down easy as she can…."

"Then again, you never know," Joe said with a shrug. "Maybe it'll go your way for once. In which case, right after she says, 'I love you, too,' you're gonna have to say, 'I'm going to be a father pretty soon.' Whew." Joe gave a short, unhappy laugh. "That's gonna bite. I think, my friend, your ass is grass. Either way."

Paul leveled his gaze at Joe. Then he said, "We're gonna need a lot more beer."

MIRA®